NP

"Who are you and what have you done with Miguel Ramirez?" she asked jokingly.

Miguel reached out and caressed her cheek with the back of his hand. A gentle touch. He brought his hand down the side of her neck and held it there. Her pulse throbbed against his fingertips.

"I suspect that I do not know you any better than you do me, *señorita*." He turned and walked away.

Why was it she had such conflicting emotions where this man was concerned? What was it about Miguel that affected her so strongly?

But no matter how attracted she was to Miguel, she was not going to give in to her baser instincts. She had managed to stay in charge of every relationship in her life, and there was no way in hell she would allow this South American Romeo to seduce her.

Even if she wanted to be seduced.

Dear Reader,

Greetings! This is the first month that Silhouette Intimate Moments switches from six to four books, and we are delighted to bring you a strong selection of page-turning stories. Of course, the best way to beat the heat is to pick up July's adrenaline-rush reads. As you curse your failing air conditioner and wish you could take that exotic trip with [insert handsome action superstar here], relieve the stress by delving into the emotional ride where passengers fall in love during life's most extraordinary circumstances.

USA TODAY bestselling author Beverly Barton delights readers with a new romance from her popular miniseries, THE PROTECTORS. In *Ramirez's Woman* (#1375), a female bodyguard poses as a sexy politician's fiancée in order to foil a perilous threat on the campaign trail. Reader favorite Carla Cassidy returns with another WILD WEST BODYGUARDS story, *Defending the Rancher's Daughter* (#1376), in which a rancher hires her long-ago crush to protect her from harm. Can she keep herself from falling in love again?

Suzanne McMinn will bring out the beast in you with *The Beast Within* (#1377), the first in her PAX miniseries, in which a tantalizing hero shows his primal nature…and his estranged wife is charged with taming him! Harlequin Historical veteran Mary Burton debuts in the line with *In Dark Waters* (#1378), a creepy and provocative story about two divers who share a sizzling attraction as they investigate a grisly murder mystery.

These four stellar authors will fire up your summer and keep you looking for the adventure in your world. Be sure to return for next month's exciting lineup!

Happy reading!

Patience Smith
Associate Senior Editor
Silhouette Intimate Moments

Please address questions and book requests to:
Silhouette Reader Service
U.S.: 3010 Walden Ave., P.O. Box 1325, Buffalo, NY 14269
Canadian: P.O. Box 609, Fort Erie, Ont. L2A 5X3

BEVERLY
BARTON
THE PROTECTORS

Ramirez's Woman

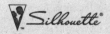
INTIMATE MOMENTS™
Published by Silhouette Books
America's Publisher of Contemporary Romance

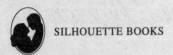 SILHOUETTE BOOKS

ISBN 0-373-27445-9

RAMIREZ'S WOMAN

Copyright © 2005 by Beverly Beaver

Books by Beverly Barton

Silhouette Intimate Moments

This Side of Heaven #453
Paladin's Woman #515
Lover and Deceiver #557
The Outcast #614
*Defending His Own #670
*Guarding Jeannie #688
*Blackwood's Woman #707
*Roarke's Wife #807
*A Man Like Morgan Kane #819
*Gabriel Hawk's Lady #830
Emily and the Stranger #860
Lone Wolf's Lady #877
*Keeping Annie Safe #937
*Murdock's Last Stand #979
*Egan Cassidy's Kid #1015
Her Secret Weapon #1034
*Navajo's Woman #1063
*Whitelaw's Wedding #1075
*Jack's Christmas Mission #1113
*The Princess's Bodyguard #1177
*Downright Dangerous #1273
*Ramirez's Woman #1375

Silhouette Desire

Yankee Lover #580
Lucky in Love #628
Out of Danger #662
Sugar Hill #687
Talk of the Town #711
The Wanderer #766
Cameron #796
The Mother of My Child #831
Nothing But Trouble #881
The Tender Trap #1047
A Child of Her Own #1077
†His Secret Child #1203
†His Woman, His Child #1209
†Having His Baby #1216
*Keeping Baby Safe #1574
*Laying His Claim #1598

*The Protectors
†3 Babies for 3 Brothers

Silhouette Books

36 Hours
Nine Months

The Fortunes of Texas
In the Arms of a Hero

3,2,1...Married!
"Getting Personal"

Lone Star Country Club:
  The Debutantes
"Jenna's Wild Ride"

Lone Star Country Club:
"The Rebel's Return"

Family Secrets
Check Mate

Grace Under Fire

On Her Guard

Sweet Caroline's Keeper

BEVERLY BARTON

wrote her first book at the age of nine. After marriage to her own "hero" and the births of her daughter and son, Beverly chose to be a full-time homemaker, aka wife, mother, friend and volunteer. This author of over thirty-five books is a member of Romance Writers of America and helped found the Heart of Dixie chapter. She has won numerous awards and has made the Waldenbooks and *USA TODAY* bestseller lists.

For my brilliant editor and dear friend,
Leslie Wainger

Prologue

Look at him, the smug, arrogant bastard. And that's what Miguel Ramirez is—a bastard. The son of a whore. What makes him think he's good enough to run for the highest office in the land? The leader of Mocorito has always been a member of the ruling class, an aristocrat, with the blood of royals running through his veins. Yes, it was true that Ramirez's father was the descendant of the last Mocoritian king, but Ramirez had been born out of wedlock, his mother a poor peasant girl who had grown up in the ghetto of the nation's capital, Nava. And Ramirez himself had lived in that same squalor until he was nearly grown. The stench of his plebeian upbringing could not be sanitized by his suave good looks, his beguiling charm or his American education at Harvard.

When Ramirez had qualified to run for office, the opposition had laughed, believing he had no chance of winning. But as the weeks and months went by and it became evident that the Nationalist Party candidate had become the unsung hero of the populace, the opposing party stopped laughing and began plotting. They had dug into Ramirez's past and found not even an inkling of a scandal. And in today's political climate, the fact that he'd been born poor and to an unwed mother only made him all the more appealing because he had overcome the handicaps of his childhood. The man had become a lawyer, who, for the past eight years, had worked tirelessly for the downtrodden and needy citizens of his country, endearing himself to them.

El Presidente, Hector Padilla, had been told that there was only one way to deal with Miguel Cesar Ramirez. Eliminate the son of a bitch. And do it soon. But make sure the assassin could never be traced back to the Federalist Party.

Miguel believed he had been born for this—to be a political force for good in Mocorito. It was past time to oust the corrupt Federalist Party and give power back to the people. His people. His mother's people. The majority vote was his. All the recent polls showed him winning by a landslide if the election were held today. He could think of nothing that would alter the outcome. In less than two months, he, Miguel Cesar Ramirez, the man of the people, would be elected president of Mocorito. The dream of a lifetime was on the verge of coming true.

As he approached the podium, flanked by his staunchest supporters and good friends, Roberto Aznar and Emilio Lopez, the cheering crowd went wild, shouting his name again and again— Presidente Ramirez, Presidente Ramirez.

Smiling, holding up his hands as if to embrace his public as he stood before them in the central downtown square in the heart of Nava, Miguel basked in the pleasure of being loved by his people. His relationship with the people was symbiotic. He loved them, fought for them, gave them his best. And in return, they would bestow upon him the great honor of allowing him to serve them as their leader.

After a good five minutes of trying to quiet the crowd so that he could speak, Miguel finally managed to calm them enough to begin his speech. Not words written by another, not false sentiments and fake promises. But words from his heart. A love letter to his supporters.

"Good people of Nava, now is the time for change," he told them.

The shouts and applause filled the square, drowning out Miguel's next words. But he didn't care. If this speech took him two hours instead of twenty minutes, what difference did it make? There was no place on earth he'd rather be than where he was this very minute.

Suddenly, Miguel heard an odd sound, then the earsplitting screams of frightened people. A spray of bullets ripped across the podium's wooden floor. Emilio knocked Miguel down and fell on top of him, protecting Miguel with his own body.

"Stay down," Emilio told him.

"Has anyone been hit?" Miguel asked.

"I do not know," Emilio replied.

Within minutes, silence prevailed on this warm Autumn afternoon. Eerie, unnatural quiet. Miguel shoved Emilio up and off him, then glanced around and noted the thinning crowd as people fled. On the podium behind him, two of his supporters lay covered with blood. Major Rodolfo and Jose Gomez.

Roberto rushed forward and helped Miguel to his feet. "Are you all right?"

Miguel shook his head. "I am fine, but how are Rodolfo and Jose? How could this have happened?"

"It was an attempt on your life," Emilio said. "We must take you away from here to safety. We can wait in the car until the police arrive."

"Not until we help Rodolfo and—"

"Only our blessed Father in Heaven can help them now," Roberto said. "They are both dead."

Crossing himself, Miguel whispered a hasty, heartfelt prayer.

"We must go. Now!" Emilio grabbed Miguel's arm.

Knowing at this point that his best course of action was to take cover and wait for the police, he allowed his friends to guard him as they crossed the square to reach the big black limousine waiting for them.

Carlos hopped out and opened the back door. "Are you all right, Señor Ramirez?" the chauffeur asked, true concern evident in his voice and his facial expressions.

Miguel patted him on the back. "I am fine, Carlos."

Once inside the limo, Emilio said, "The Federalists were behind this assassination attempt. I would stake my life on it. There is no other explanation."

"We cannot make accusations without proof," Roberto cautioned. "If it was the Federalists, then we will find the proof and tell the people. But it could have been a disgruntled citizen, someone out to kill a politician."

Shaken and angry, Miguel agreed with his two best friends. "Emilio is right. I believe the Federalists sent someone to kill me because they fear that Hector Padilla cannot win reelection. But, you, too, are right, Roberto. We cannot make accusations without proof."

"From now on, you must have a bodyguard with you at all times," Emilio said. "I tried to tell you from the very beginning that you would not be safe without protection."

"How can I parade around with a bodyguard at my side when my opponent has never resorted to using armed men to protect him?" Miguel balked at the thought of showing any weakness. "Padilla has made a point of telling the people that under his leadership, the president has no need for bodyguards as El Presidente of old had, back in the days when the government leadership changed at the drop of a hat and dictators and presidents alike were murdered on a regular basis."

"Miguel is right. He can show no sign of weakness. The Federalists would use it against him," Roberto said. "We must find another way to protect him, one that does not require a bodyguard."

"By not taking heed, you will not only put Miguel's life at risk, but jeopardize our party's chance to take power. We will lose the opportunity for a representative of the people to govern this country." Emilio glowered at Roberto.

"Do not argue, my friends," Miguel said. "I believe I know a solution to our problem."

Both men turned to Miguel, their expressions questioning.

"I was lucky today, but I may not be so lucky a second time. Two good men were killed because they were with me. I cannot show weakness by hiring an armed bodyguard, some burly man who will remind the people of the past. But if a beautiful young woman were in my company, day and night, no one would suspect her of being my protector. They would simply say how fortunate Miguel is to have such a lovely companion. If necessary, we can even pass her off as my fiancée, so as not to upset the female voters."

"Are you suggesting we hire a female bodyguard?" Roberto asked.

"That is a brilliant idea," Emilio said.

"There are no female bodyguards in Mocorito." Roberto threw up his hands in exasperation.

"But I am quite certain that there are female bodyguards in America," Miguel told them. "We will simply contact Will Pierce and ask him to arrange for one to be brought here as soon as possible."

"The CIA cannot send one of their agents here," Roberto said. "The Americans must appear to have no interest in this election. If they provide you with a—"

"I am sure Will can arrange something through an independent agency." Miguel narrowed his gaze thoughtfully. "I will suggest he find me a tall, elegant blonde. Everyone knows that I have a weakness for blondes."

Chapter 1

J. J. Blair zipped in and out of Atlanta traffic on her glacier-white Harley, loving the feel of riding the big, roaring brute. For a woman who was five-two and weighed a hundred and seven pounds soaking wet, the FXD/FXDI Super Glide Custom was big, even though it was actually one of the smaller motorcycles that Harley Davidson built. However, it fit her and her needs to perfection. She never felt more herself, more free and in control than when astride her customized hog. It had taken her three years to put aside enough money to pay cash for this sweet baby—a cool fifteen thousand, once she added all the extras. Two months ago, after purchasing her dream machine, she'd sold her old reliable FXR, the bike she'd bought used six years ago when she'd run away from her old life in Mobile, Alabama.

Having worked off her last case for the Dundee Private Security and Investigation Agency only four days ago, she had thought she might have a full week to kick back and relax. But Daisy Holbrook, the office manager, had phoned her late yesterday evening to inform her that their boss, Sawyer McNamara, needed her to show up for a meeting first thing in the morning.

All Daisy had said was, "The job is in Mocorito, so I figure since you and Dom speak Spanish fluently, you two will be assigned to this case."

"Know any details?" J.J. had asked.

"Nope."

J.J. did speak Spanish fluently, as well as French and some Italian. She also knew a little German, Japanese and Russian, but not enough to do more than order a meal or ask where the restroom was. Her father, Rudd Blair, had been a career soldier, so, as a kid, she'd lived all over, at least until her parents had divorced when she was eleven. Her teachers had been amazed at how adept she'd been at picking up foreign languages. But her mother Lenora had said fiddlesticks, her people, the Ashfords of Mobile, were all brilliant and Jennifer Joy was half Ashford, wasn't she?

As J.J. drove into the underground garage of the building that housed the Dundee Agency, which leased the entire sixth floor, she tried to remember what she knew about Mocorito.

Mocorito was a small island nation off the coast of South America, the population a mixture of races, but the strong Spanish influence of the earliest settlers dominated the country. Okay, so she remembered that much from either high school social studies or from having read something more recently. She wasn't sure which. One thing for sure—her father had never been stationed there.

After removing her shiny purple helmet and shaking loose her black curls, she unzipped her purple leather jacket and headed for the bank of elevators.

Hadn't she heard something on the ten o'clock news last night about Mocorito? She'd been in the kitchen making herself a cup of hot cocoa while the news was on and had returned to the living room just in time to catch the last snippets of the story. The presidential election was coming up in a few weeks and somebody had taken a potshot at one of the candidates. Yeah, that's what it was. Some guy named Romero or Rodriguez. No, no. Ramirez. That was it.

As the elevator zoomed upward, J.J. groaned. Surely that incident didn't have anything to do with this new Dundee assignment. After all, why would a South American presidential candidate hire a security firm based in the U.S.?

When the elevator stopped on the sixth floor, J.J. exited straight into the heart of the Dundee Agency, where she had been employed for the past three years. After leaving Mobile over six years ago, she'd traveled around the country on her FXR for a couple of years, picking up odd jobs here and there and trying to figure out who she was and what she wanted to do when she grew up. Then four years ago she'd wound up in Atlanta. Back in the South. But not the South in which her mother had been reared as one of the privileged Ashfords of Mobile, with hot and cold running servants, membership in all the exclusive clubs and an air of snobbery acquired over generations. No, Atlanta was part of the new South, having shed the past like a snake shedding dead skin.

She had worked for nearly a year at a local martial arts studio, where she'd finally acquired her black belt. Although she'd enjoyed that job, it hadn't been challenging enough for her. When she'd met an Amazonian redhead in a coffee shop near her apartment and discovered that the lady—Lucie Evans—worked for a private security and investigation agency based in Atlanta, she'd made inquiries about employment. Lucie had set up an interview for her the very next week, and, as luck would have it, one of their agents had just resigned.

J.J. had taken to the world of private security like a duck to water. Being trained in the martial arts and having served in the army as a second lieutenant after graduation from college had helped her zip through the six-week training course that Dundee required. Being one of only three women agents at Dundee, she had expected some ribbing, maybe even harassment from the men, but what she'd gotten was acceptance and camaraderie. Even the CEO, Sawyer McNamara, had told her that her looks were deceiving, that she had shown everyone during her training sessions that she was more than qualified for the job despite being a petite bombshell. Sawyer's comment had come shortly after she'd equaled his impressive shooting on the firing range. Her father had taught her how to use a gun when she was twelve and over the years, she had practiced relentlessly to perfect her skills.

Daisy Holbrook, the office manager, also known as Ms. Efficiency, glanced up from her desk located in a glass cubicle in the center hub of the office complex and smiled at J.J.

"Morning," Daisy said. "Love the purple jacket. Is it new?"

J.J. did a feminine twirl. "I splurged on this and a pair of boots to match." She lifted her jean-clad leg high enough for Daisy, who leaned over her desk, to see the supple leather boots.

"Don't you look good enough to eat," a deep masculine voice commented. "Like a delicious purple grape."

Laughing, both J.J. and Daisy turned to face Domingo Shea, Dundee's Latin lover. Some women might take his remark as a sexist comment, but J.J. knew Dom well enough to take what he'd said as the compliment he'd meant it to be. Dom and she were friends, comrades-in-arms and drinking buddies who often played cards with several other agents on a fairly regular basis.

"Well, good morning to you, too, Mr. Tall, Dark and Politically Incorrect." J.J. grinned at the drop-dead-gorgeous Texas heartthrob. Dom was one of those men who took your breath away because he was so good-looking. Jet-black hair that he'd been wearing a bit long and shaggy lately only added to his macho appeal. And when he gazed at a woman with those sharp black eyes, more often than not she melted into a puddle at his feet. Then there was that body. God almighty, what a bod. Six-three, muscular and lean.

"Are you here for the meeting this morning?" Dom asked.

J.J. nodded.

"Vic's coming in, too, for the same meeting," Daisy told them. "It seems he knows people in Mocorito from back in his spook days."

J.J. glanced at the clock on the wall behind Daisy's desk. "We're a little early. Is Sawyer here yet?"

"He's in his office with the door closed," Dom said. "He's holed up in there with Lucie. Some little disagreement concerning her expense account on her last assignment."

J.J. groaned. "There's no such thing as a little disagreement between Lucie and Sawyer."

"No, with those two, it's always all-out warfare." Dom glanced down the hall toward the CEO's office, which was behind the glass-enclosed office of his private secretary. "Who's the guy sitting there in Ms. Davidson's office? Somebody waiting for Sawyer?"

"His name is Will Pierce. I figure he's alphabet soup," Daisy said. "FBI, CIA, DEA. Take your pick."

"Six of one, half a dozen of the other." Dom, a former navy SEAL, knew as well as J.J. and Daisy that a good percentage of the Dundee staff, past and present, had come from various government agencies.

"A new agent?" J.J. looked at Daisy.

Ms. Efficiency shook her head. "We're fully staffed at present and not looking to hire, unless Mr. Dundee decides he wants to expand the business."

"Any chance of that happening?" Dom asked.

"How would I know?" Daisy smiled coquettishly, deepening the cheek dimples in her heart-shaped face.

Dom leaned his six-three frame over the office manager's desk. "Because, Daisy, my darling, you know everything there is to know around here. Don't you realize we're all aware of that fact that you're the one who really runs the Dundee Agency and not Sawyer."

Daisy giggled. "That silver tongue of yours must come from a combination of Latin charm and Irish blarney."

Before Dom got a chance for a response, Sawyer's office door flew open and Lucie Evans stormed out, tromped through Ms. Davidson's office and came barreling down the hall, hell-fire in her smoky brown eyes.

"That man infuriates me!" Lucie paused at Daisy's cubicle.

"Like that's a news flash," Dom said under his breath.

"What's he done now?" Daisy asked sympathetically.

Lucie took a deep breath, then let it out with a loud, exasperated whoosh. "Nothing he hasn't done before and nothing he won't do again. He's questioning a twenty-dollar charge on my expense account. It's ridiculous and I told him so. I'm sick and tired of this crap. I have half a mind to quit."

Dom laughed. "Now, Lucie, you and I both know that you are not going to quit, because that's exactly what Sawyer wants you to do and you'd walk over hot coals to keep from letting him have his way, now wouldn't you?"

Lucie huffed. "Yes, you're right. I wouldn't give him the satisfaction of quitting."

"Besides, you enjoy making his life miserable far too much to quit and leave the man in peace," Daisy added.

Lucie smiled, glanced at her friends, and then laughed.

Vic Noble joined the others. "Did I just miss a good joke?" he asked.

Lucie leaned over and kissed Vic on the cheek. "Why can't Sawyer be a sweetheart like you?"

Vic chuckled quietly. "You two been at it again, huh?"

"Considering you're ex-CIA, you wouldn't happen to know a discreet assassin I could hire to eliminate a certain pain in the ass, would you?"

"You don't want Sawyer dead," Vic told her. "You'd miss tormenting the man far too much."

A roar of good-natured laughter rose up inside and around Daisy's cubicle.

The laughter died the minute a deep, authoritarian voice called loudly from down the hall. "Dom. J.J. Vic." Standing outside his current secretary's office—the boss went through secretaries on the average of two a year—Sawyer McNamara motioned for them with a commanding flick of his big hand. Dressed to the nines like a model out of *GQ,* he looked like a wealthy business-man. But those who knew him well understood that beneath that handsome, stylish facade beat the heart of a deadly warrior.

"The master calls," Lucie said. "You'd better run or he'll threaten to send y'all to obedience school, along with me."

Everyone chuckled, but quickly left Lucie with Daisy and headed down the hall toward the boss's office. Once the three of them were inside, Sawyer closed the door and made introductions

"Will, these are the three agents I've chosen for the job," Sawyer told their visitor. "Vic Noble is a former CIA contract agent." Vic nodded. "Dom Shea is a former navy SEAL." Dom smiled. "And this is J.J. Blair. She's an expert marksman and is proficient in the martial arts. Dom and J.J. both speak Spanish like natives."

Mr. Pierce studied the threesome for a full minute, then nod-ded. "I'm Will Pierce, with the CIA." His gaze met with Vic's for a split second. "You may or may not know that yesterday af-ternoon, someone tried to assassinate Miguel Cesar Ramirez, the Nationalist Party candidate for president of Mocorito. Unoffi-cially, the United States government wants to see Ramirez elected. He's a new breed of Mocoritian. A man of the people, but educated in the U.S. He graduated from Harvard Law School and has numerous American friends."

"Our interest in this election wouldn't have anything to do with the fact that Mocorito is in possession of more oil than any other country in the western hemisphere, would it?" Vic asked.

Will pinned Vic with his pensive glare. "I don't think I need to answer that question, do I?"

"Señor Ramirez needs a full-time bodyguard," Sawyer said. "That's where the Dundee Agency comes in."

J.J. narrowed her gaze as she focused on her boss. "Why doesn't he already have bodyguards?"

"Neither the presiding president nor his opponent have bodyguards," Pierce explained. "In the past, before Mocorito was a democracy, the leader—either a president or a dictator or at one time the king—was always surrounded by a contingent of armed guards. President Padilla refuses to have bodyguards in order to show that he has nothing to fear from his people because they love him so much. Ramirez can hardly surround himself with guards and take the chance that he'll be perceived as either weak or afraid."

"Why send us? Why not U.S. undercover agents?" J.J. asked.

"We can't send in any of our people," Pierce said. "If it ever came out that we were backing Ramirez…well, let's just say, we don't want that to happen. And Ramirez has refused a regular bodyguard. The only way he'll agree to having twenty-four-seven protection is if the bodyguard is female and is willing to pose as his lady friend."

J.J.'s mouth gaped open. "Are you saying that I'm supposed to pose as this guy's latest paramour? Are we talking putting on a show for the public only or are we talking about being lovey-dovey in private, too?"

Will Pierce frowned. All eyes turned to Sawyer.

"Only Señor Ramirez, Mr. Pierce and Ramirez's two closest confidantes will know the truth," Sawyer said. "As far as everyone else is concerned—and that includes family, friends, supporters and any servants working in the house—you will be Ramirez's girlfriend."

"His lover, you mean?" J.J. glared at Sawyer.

"If you aren't comfortable in that role, then Señor Ramirez might be willing to present you to everyone as his fiancée," Pierce said.

"Oh, that makes me feel a whole heap of a lot better." J.J. bristled at the thought of having to fight off some Latin Romeo with whom she'd be forced to share a bedroom for the next few weeks.

Dom chuckled. "You can take care of yourself and we all know it. Just lay down some ground rules with this Ramirez guy first thing. If he steps over the line, show him a few of your best moves. You can kick his butt. You've proved you're capable of downing a guy twice your size."

"The election is in four-and-a-half weeks," Pierce said. "Ramirez is the front-runner. We can't allow anything to go wrong."

"While I'm playing kissy-kissy with the future el presidente, where will Dom and Vic be?"

"Vic will be working undercover to help find out who tried to assassinate Ramirez." Pierce glanced at Dom. "Mr. Shea will pose as a distant American relative who has come to Mocorito to cheer on his cousin in his bid for the presidency."

"Dom will be close by if you need him," Sawyer told her. "He'll be living in the same house and his job will be to find out if there's anyone inside Ramirez's organization who can't be trusted." He pinned her with his imposing glare. "J.J., your sole duty will be to protect Miguel Ramirez. Do whatever you have to do to keep him alive and do it without seeming to do it. You understand?"

She nodded. "Cling to Ramirez's arm, bat my eyelashes at him, giggle and smile and act all feminine, but if anyone tries to harm him, stop them without making it obvious that I'm actually a trained bodyguard who just saved the future president's life."

"You'll fly to Caracas by Dundee jet, then go first class into Nava, the capital city," Sawyer explained. "Arrangements have already been made for J.J. and Dom to fly together. Vic will go in separately. Dom, you and Vic go home, pack your bags and meet back here by noon." He turned to J.J. "You go shopping. Buy whatever you need to look totally feminine. Daytime wear, a couple of evening gowns, sportswear and…" Sawyer cleared his throat. "Some negligees, underwear…"

"Say no more." J.J. held up her hand in a stop gesture. "I get the idea."

"When y'all come back into the office, I'll brief you, as a group, on what your roles will be. J.J., you and Dom will use your own names. Our government will do whatever is necessary to make sure any inquiries about one or all of you are handled through proper channels."

Understanding that they'd just been dismissed, Vic, Dom and J.J. headed for the door. Being the last of the threesome to exit, J.J. paused before leaving and asked, "What's my budget for this wardrobe I'm supposed to buy during the next few hours?"

She had asked Sawyer, but it was Will Pierce who answered. "Spend whatever you think is necessary, Ms. Blair. And get whatever you feel you'll need to adequately do your job."

Miguel's home in Nava had once belonged to his father's cousin, Count Porfirio Fernandez, an extremely wealthy old man who had died unmarried and childless. Cesar Fernandez had inherited his uncle's home, various properties throughout Mocorito and his millions. In turn, he had deeded the house to his illegitimate son and set up a trust fund for the child he hadn't known existed until the boy was thirteen. Cesar had never acknowledged Miguel as his own flesh and blood, not legally or in any public way. He had taken care of him financially and sent him to the best schools, educating him in America, as generations of Fernandez men had been educated. But Miguel and his father had met only twice. The first time had been a brief visit at his father's office in downtown Nava when Miguel was eighteen and leaving for Harvard. It was an unemotional exchange, with little said except an admonishment from his father to do well in his studies. Then, three years ago, when Cesar lay on his deathbed, Miguel had been called to the old man's home. It was only then, on the day his father died, that Cesar's legitimate son and daughter had learned of their half-brother's existence. And it was only then that Cesar had mentioned Miguel's mother.

"Luz Ramirez was a very pretty girl, if I remember correctly,"

Cesar had said. "You have her golden-brown eyes, but the rest of you is pure Fernandez."

That was the closest his father had come to acknowledging him.

By anyone's standards, Miguel was wealthy, but although he lived in this beautiful old home and used his trust fund for the upkeep and to pay the servants required to maintain the house and grounds, he had left the bulk of his fortune untouched. Occasionally he used the money to help others, whenever he saw a desperate need. Since returning to Mocorito after law school, he had worked tirelessly for the poor and downtrodden in his country, providing the general public with legal assistance, something few citizens could afford under Hector Padilla's reign.

Often he felt guilty for living so well, surrounded by luxury, here in this magnificent old home, but, God help him, since moving in eight years ago, he had grown to love every square foot of the palatial two-story mansion. This was a home meant to be shared with a wife and filled with the laughter of many children. He intended to marry someday, had hoped that by now he would have met the perfect woman, a lady who would not only love him, but love his dream for Mocorito's future.

Perhaps the lady with whom he planned to dine tonight would turn out to be that person. Emilio's wife, Dolores, was hosting a small, intimate dinner party for six, here in Miguel's home. After yesterday's assassination attempt, Dolores had suggested canceling the dinner, but Miguel had insisted that they proceed as planned. So, Emilio, Dolores and Roberto, as well as Miguel's old and dear friend, Dr. Juan Esteban, and the lovely Zita Fuentes were due to arrive at any moment.

He had met Zita at a political rally several weeks ago, where she had pledged her support to his campaign. Since Zita was a wealthy widow, her support meant more than lip service. She had made a sizable donation that had helped pay for the television ads running day and night now that the election was a little over a month away. Zita was the type of woman who would make a traditional first lady: cultured, demure and subservient to her husband's wishes. Having been married very young to a millionaire industrialist, she had been trained to be the perfect wife for a professional.

He couldn't say that it had been love at first sight for him, but he had been quite attracted to the lady. Black-eyed and auburnhaired, the tall, slender Zita possessed an appealing air of elegance and sophistication. However, now that the U.S. government had arranged to send him a female bodyguard who would pose as his girlfriend, he could hardly begin courting Zita Fuentes. But after the election was over, and his fake relationship with the Dundee agent had ended, he would initiate his plan to woo the alluring widow. He only hoped that making his affair with another woman so public wouldn't ruin his chances with Zita.

"Miguel," a sweet, feminine voice called his name from the open French doors leading from the house to the patio where Miguel stood enjoying the serenity of the enclosed garden.

He smiled and turned to greet a very pregnant Dolores Lopez, his second cousin, who was as dear to him as any sister could be. "You look lovely tonight."

She tsked-tsked and shook her head. "You are wonderful to lie to me. I know I look more and more like a hippopotamus every day."

Emilio, only a few inches taller than his five-six wife, came up behind her and slipped his arm around her waist. He patted her protruding belly. "But you are my little hippopotamus and the prettiest mother-to-be in the world."

She turned and kissed her husband on the cheek, then focused on Miguel. "We are the first to arrive, are we not? I would not want to neglect my duties as your hostess. But you really should have a wife, Miguel. When you are elected president, you will need a first lady."

"I believe Miguel can handle his own love life," Emilio said, always eager to defend the man who had been his best friend since the two were boys.

"I'm not so sure of that." Dolores walked over and kissed Miguel on both cheeks. "He is thirty-five and still unmarried."

Miguel slipped his arm around his cousin's shoulders and hugged her to his side. "I promise you that as soon as this election is over, I will get down to the serious business of finding myself a wife."

"A wife for you and a first lady for Mocorito," a gruff male voice called from behind them.

All three acknowledged Miguel's good friend, Roberto Aznar, who joined them on the patio. Roberto, a staunch Nationalist, was Miguel's campaign fund-raiser, and Emilio was the campaign manager, overseeing every detail of their quest to win the election.

"I will leave you men to talk politics," Dolores said. "I need to speak to Ramona to make sure dinner will be ready at precisely seven-thirty." As she headed toward the open French doors, she asked Miguel, "Did the florist deliver the arrangements I ordered?"

"Yes, yes," Miguel replied. "The flowers are perfect, the dinner table is perfect and we all know that Ramona's meal will also be perfect."

"But of course," Dolores said. "However, I simply must see to everything myself."

Once Dolores disappeared inside the house, Emilio spoke quietly, as if he were afraid his wife would overhear. "I do not like keeping secrets from Dolores. This business of an American bodyguard posing as your lady friend is something we should tell my wife. Otherwise, she'll worry herself sick that you're involved with some American floozy."

"The fewer people who know, the better," Roberto said. "I am very fond of Dolores, but you know as well as I do that she cannot keep a secret. If we tell her, we might as well tell the world and that would defeat the purpose of having a female bodyguard in the first place."

Miguel clamped his hand down on Emilio's shoulder. "In this case, Roberto is right. As much as I love Dolores, I can't trust her with this information. It would be bad enough if the public were to discover I had a bodyguard, but think how the voters would react to learn that I have a woman guarding me."

"I know, I know," Miguel replied. "But once this woman from the Dundee Agency shows up, Dolores will make it her business to become acquainted with her. She guards your back like a fierce mama tiger."

Dom and J.J. took a taxi from the airport to Miguel Ramirez's home in the oldest and one of the most prestigious neighborhoods of Nava. Huge brick and stucco mansions lay behind iron gates, every impressive structure and sprawling lawn well- maintained. Only the very rich and powerful could afford to live here.

"I thought this Ramirez guy came from humble beginnings," J.J. whispered to Dom, speaking quietly on the off chance the cabdriver understood English. "These are rich folks' homes."

"He inherited the place from a relative," Dom said. "Didn't you read the bio on Ramirez that Daisy gave you?"

"I didn't have time to do more than skim it before we left. It took me four hours of intensive shopping to find a suitable wardrobe for this assignment." She adjusted the neckline on the simple beige crepe-knit dress she'd worn on the plane. "I must have missed the part about him living in a palace."

The cabby turned off the street onto a brick driveway that led to a breathtaking two-story, white stucco house, with a red-tiled roof and a veranda that appeared to span the circumference of the mansion.

Speaking in Spanish, the cabby said, "Is Señor Ramirez expecting you? If not, you will not be able to get in to see him without passing inspection."

"Miguel is my cousin," Dom replied. "I live in Miami and when he was visiting there this past spring, he invited me to come for a visit."

"A cousin, you say." The cabby's mouth opened in a wide,

friendly smile as he parked the car and turned around to look at Dom and then at J.J. "This lovely lady, she is your wife?"

"No, she's a friend of mine and of Miguel's," Dom said. "Her family has entrusted me with her care while we are visiting here."

The cabby looked J.J. over thoroughly, then nodded. "It is good that her father did not allow her to travel alone. Too many young women are acting like men these days, ruining their reputations and making them unsuitable for marriage."

J.J. had to bite her tongue to keep from making a comment, but when her eyes widened and she clenched her teeth, Dom grinned, knowing full well that she was more than a little irritated.

After they got out of the cab, Dom helped the driver take their suitcases to the veranda, then he tipped the guy generously. "We'll just leave our luggage here for now," Dom said. "Thanks."

As the cabby drove away, Dom rang the doorbell. "Get ready for the performance of your life."

"My playing a lovesick fool will require an Academy-award-winning performance."

A heavyset, middle-aged woman opened the door. Without any expression on her slightly wrinkled, makeup-free face, she sized up the two guests.

"I am Domingo Shea," he said in Spanish. "I am Señor Ramirez's cousin from Miami. And this—" he indicated with a sweep of his hand "—is Señorita Jennifer Blair."

"You are expected?" the woman asked.

"Yes, I believe he's expecting us tomorrow," Dom told her. "But we were able to get away earlier than anticipated. I do hope our early arrival will not be an inconvenience."

"Please, come inside and I will announce you."

Dom and J.J. waited in the massive, marble-floored foyer. Overhead a huge chandelier shimmered with what appeared to be a hundred tiny lights, all reflecting off the crystal gems. A wide, spiral, marble staircase led from the foyer to the second level, the wrought-iron banisters circling the open landing.

"This is some place," Dom said. "I can't imagine any presidential mansion being more impressive."

"Actually, it reminds me a little of my Grandmother Ashford's place in Mobile."

"Poor little rich girl."

"My mother is rich. My stepfather is rich. Me, I'm just an ordinary woman who works for a living."

Moments turned to minutes as they waited. And waited. And waited. After a good ten minutes had passed, a tall attractive man, with thick salt-and-pepper hair and a thin, dark moustache, appeared and greeted them. J.J. guessed his age to be somewhere around forty. Mentally reviewing the photos she'd been shown of the people closest to Ramirez, she realized that this was Roberto Aznar.

"You have arrived a day early." Aznar seemed genuinely agitated.

"I hope that won't be a problem."

"No. No problem. I'm sure the servants can prepare your rooms tonight. I'll ask Ramona to see that your bags are taken upstairs and if you'd like to freshen up—"

"We'd like to see Miguel," Dom said.

"Yes, well…you see, he has guests. He's giving a small dinner party for—"

"Wonderful." J.J. sighed. "I'm starving. You know how airline food is. Like cardboard, even in first class. Please, be a dear and lead us to the dining room." J.J. slipped her arm through Roberto's, much to his astonishment. "Besides, I know Miguel will be thrilled to see us. I'm sure he's missed me as much as I've missed him."

Dom followed as Roberto led J.J. down the hall and into the dining room. The table sat twenty, but this evening the guests were placed at the far end of the table, the two men and two women flanking the head of the table where Miguel Ramirez presided.

When Roberto entered, bringing J.J. with him and Dom coming in behind them, Ramirez rose from his chair.

Impressive, J.J. thought. The man's photographs didn't do him justice. He was one-hundred-percent male, from his wide shoulders to his lean hips and long legs. He was handsome without being pretty. His bronze skin was a shade darker than Dom's, but he had the same blue-black hair, only his was cut conservatively short and neatly styled. But it was his unique golden-brown eyes that captured J.J.'s attention. Large, expressive eyes, the color of dusty topaz.

"Your cousin Dom has arrived a day early," Roberto said. "And look who he has brought with him."

Ramirez hesitated for a moment as he studied J.J. Then he smiled, scooted back his chair and walked hurriedly around the table and straight to her. He opened his arms in an expression of welcome, then reached down and grasped both of her hands in his.

"*Querida,* it is so good to see you again." He kissed first one hand and then the other. "Please, come in and let me introduce you to everyone."

They stood there in the dining room, just beyond the threshold and stared at each other, his gaze locked on her face. J.J.'s heart skipped a beat. Uh-oh, that wasn't a good sign. As a general rule, most men didn't have this effect on her, but when one did, that meant she was in trouble. She had hoped the man she would be protecting wouldn't set off a frenzy of crazed butterflies in her belly. So much for hoping. The little buggers were doing a Saint Vitus dance in her stomach right now.

He led J.J. farther into the room, then paused while the others stared at her.

A very pregnant, black-haired woman glanced from J.J. to Miguel. "Who are these people?"

Dom spoke up first. "I'm Miguel's cousin, Domingo Shea, from Miami."

"And this is Jennifer." Miguel's voice embraced her name. "She is—"

"I am Miguel's fiancée," J.J. said, deciding on the spur of the moment that she did not intend to spend the next month being treated like a mistress. Then she turned and looked Miguel right in the eyes, daring him to contradict her. "That is, if your proposal is still good and you still want me." She batted her eyelashes.

His eyes widened in surprise, but, barely missing a beat, he replied. "Of course, I still want you, *querida*. More than ever."

Chapter 2

The lady was not what he'd been expecting. No six-foot Viking goddess. No cool, sophisticated Grace Kelly blonde. Not even a hard-as-nails, pro-wrestler-type female with a killer look in her eyes. No, Jennifer Blair was none of those things. What she was was a petite, raven-haired beauty with an hourglass figure and the most striking blue-violet eyes Miguel had ever seen. And the way she'd taken charge of the moment—accepting a fictitious marriage proposal in front of an audience—told him she expected to run the show. Call him old-fashioned, call him a macho pig, but he preferred his women to defer to him in all things. And that included his female bodyguard. Miguel chuckled to himself as he held the lady's small, delicate hands. She didn't look as if she could swat a fly, let alone protect a man more than twice her size.

"*Querida,* let me introduce you to everyone." Miguel slipped his arm around her tiny waist and led her farther into the room. Without glancing back, he said, "Come along, Dom."

Dolores glowered at J.J., so much so that he felt his cousin's hostility as if it were a viable thing. "You asked this woman to marry you and you have told no one here about her? I find that very strange."

Emilio cleared his throat, then said hastily. "Miguel told me about Miss Blair, but he swore me to secrecy. Otherwise, you know I would have told you."

"Dolores, don't be upset with Emilio," Miguel said, falling hurriedly into the act that he would have to perpetuate for the next few weeks. "I met Jennifer on my trip to Miami. She is a friend of Dom's and he introduced us. We had a whirlwind romance and I—" The words caught in his throat. Lying about loving a woman was something he'd never done. "We fell in love and I asked her to marry me. But we agreed that she would wait to give me an answer, that we would put some time and distance between us to make sure what we felt was…real love."

Skewering J.J. with her cynical gaze, Dolores came toward her. Dolores knew Miguel the way a sister knows her brother, so convincing her that he was in love with this American woman would not be easy.

"You have decided that you love Miguel and wish to be his wife?" Dolores asked.

"Yes, that's right," J.J. replied, keeping her phony smile in place.

Emilio wrapped his arm around his wife's shoulders and hugged her to him. "Then congratulations are in order, are they not? We should ask Ramona to bring in champagne….er… uh…and sparkling cider for you, my sweet."

"I did not know we had a cousin in Miami." Naturally, the ever-skeptical Dolores was not convinced that J.J. and Dom were genuine. His cousin's feminine instincts had warned her that something wasn't quite right about the situation, that something was rotten in Nava tonight.

"He is my cousin, not yours." When Miguel tightened his hold around J.J.'s waist, he realized that his actions had told her that he was tense, that already the lies were bothering him. "He is from the other side of the family. The son of one of Papá Tomas's cousins."

"Hmm…" Dolores glanced from Dom to J.J. "Have you had dinner?"

A collective sigh permeated the room. Miguel loosened his tenacious hold about J.J.'s waist. Dolores's cordiality did not mean she had accepted these strangers on face value, but it did mean she was giving them the benefit of the doubt and would allow them to prove themselves to her.

"As a matter of fact, we haven't." Dom went around the room, shaking hands and making nice. When he paused by the chair where the elegant redhead sat, the woman stopped glaring daggers at J.J. and smiled at Dom.

"And who is this enchanting creature?" Dom asked.

Not waiting for a proper introduction, she spoke for herself, "I am Zita Fuentes and am I delighted to make your acquaintance, Señor Shea." She cut Miguel to the quick with a withering glare.

"If you all will entertain Dom, I need a moment alone with Jennifer." Not giving anyone a chance to halt him by word or action, Miguel grasped J.J.'s arm and all but dragged her out of the dining room.

Once outside in the hall, she jerked free and stopped dead still. "Do not ever pull that Me-Tarzan-You-Jane routine with me again."

Totally exasperated with this woman, Miguel groaned. "Lower your voice. Sound carries in this old house, especially in the hallways."

She looked him square in the eye and said softly, "Then let's go somewhere more private. We should set up the ground rules for this charade immediately. That way, we'll both know where we stand and what to expect from the other person."

"Agreed. Come with me."

He did not touch her again; instead he allowed her to fall into step beside him as he led her away from the dining room. A few minutes later, he opened the massive double doors to the mahogany-paneled library with bookcases on three sides that reached to the top of the fourteen-foot ceiling.

"Would you care to sit, Ms. Blair?" He indicated one of the two leather chairs flanking the fireplace, in which a warm blaze emitted delicious heat on this unseasonably cool October evening. Here in Mocorito the temperatures seldom dropped below the high sixties.

"I'll stand." She tilted her chin defiantly.

Wonderful, Miguel thought. He was dealing with a hot-headed little feminist. How was it possible that a woman could look like a beautiful young Elizabeth Taylor and be a ball-bashing women's libber? He had encountered numerous women such as this during the years he had spent in the United States, but none had been as lovely as Ms. Blair. And none had been assigned to him as his bodyguard; nor had they played the part of his fiancée for several weeks.

"Suit yourself," Miguel told her.

"I usually do."

Miguel huffed.

"First thing you should know is that there will be no sex between us while we're playing lovers." She crossed her arms over her ample chest, as if it to make a point.

Point duly noted. And her large, full breasts were duly noted, also. "Of course," he replied. "No sex."

"In public, I will play the part of a dutiful, obedient fiancée, a woman totally besotted with you. But in private, I will be myself. Understand?"

"Yes, I understand. And I will do the same. In public, I will be your adoring future husband."

"In matters of your security, my word is law," she told him. "You will make that clear to Emilio Lopez and Roberto Aznar. Neither they nor you will question my authority in that area."

"I assumed Mr. Shea would—"

"Dom is here to do an internal investigation and to act as my backup. I am completely in charge of you."

Miguel groaned silently as the image of this lovely creature dominating him in a very intimate way flashed through his mind, sending arousal signals to his lower anatomy. Willing his traitorous body under control, he nodded, then said, "I am not accustomed to taking orders from a woman."

"Well, 'el presidente,' you'd better get used to taking orders from this woman." She tapped herself in the middle of her chest. "Because until you take the oath of office and we unearth the people behind the plot to kill you, I'm going to be your worst nightmare."

Bristling at her derogatory use of the title, he glowered at her. "Meaning?"

She smiled. "Meaning you're going to obey me, not the other way around. When I say jump, you ask, how high?"

Enough of this nonsense, he told himself. Who did this arrogant, cocksure woman think she was? Miguel Cesar Ramirez had spent his life proving to himself and the world around him that he was a man of integrity and self-assurance, a leader and not a follower. He was on the verge of being elected the president of Mocorito, a country where the majority of women knew their place.

"You overstep your authority, Ms. Blair. You have not been assigned to this job to issue me orders. You are here to watch over me, to ensure my safety, and even to take a bullet for me, if necessary."

She didn't so much as flinch nor did she blush with embarrassment as most females would do. "I haven't been here thirty minutes and already we seem to be at odds over the ground rules. And I had so hoped that your being educated in the United States would have prepared you to deal with a woman as an equal. I will play the subservient female in public, but in private, I am in command. Take it or leave it, Señor Ramirez."

He surveyed her from the top of her head to the tips of her toes. "Your ego is bigger than you are."

"Don't let my size fool you. You know the old saying, don't you?" She grinned mockingly.

He lifted an inquisitive eyebrow.

"Dynamite comes in small packages," she said.

"In your case, I do not doubt it for a moment." And he did not doubt that under the right circumstances, his little American bodyguard would be as hot as a firecracker in bed. In his bed. He would truly enjoy setting her off and seeing the sparks fly.

"Then we understand each other? I'm the boss."

"If you need to think of yourself in those terms, then by all means, do so," he told her.

"Are we at an impasse?"

"If by that you mean it is apparent that neither of us is willing to back down from our position, then yes, Señorita Blair, we are definitely at an impasse."

She heaved a deep sigh, apparently as aggravated with him as he was with her. "We're in a no-win situation. I suppose you realize that. We're stuck with each other, whether we like it or not. There is no way another female agent can come in and pose as your fiancée now."

"Ah, yes, my fiancée. Who gave you permission to announce yourself as my fiancée?"

"I was told that you were willing to pass me off as your fiancée, if the circumstances warranted it." She shrugged. "I felt it was necessary. There's no way I'm going to pretend to be your mistress for weeks on end. Not here in this male-dominated country where mistresses are second-class citizens."

He could not deny the truth of her statement. Mistresses *were* treated as second-class citizens, a fact he knew only too well. His sweet, caring mother had been treated like dirt beneath the feet of the ladies and gentlemen of Mocorito because she had borne her lover's child out of wedlock.

"I had assumed that being an American woman, you would not mind being thought of as my mistress, but apparently I was wrong."

"You were dead wrong."

He studied her closely, forcing himself to break away from those hypnotic violet eyes. She wore a simple dress of some non-wrinkling fabric in a shade of cream, a complimentary shade to her pale olive complexion. The garment was not too tight, but it draped her body like a well-fitting glove. Until this moment he had not truly taken in her appearance, other than to note that she was beautiful, in a sexy, earthy way. Her short black hair curled about her face in soft waves, enticing a man to run his fingers through the silky locks. Her lips were full and painted hot pink, bringing to mind a set of other moist feminine lips. His body reacted in a natural way, warning him that arousal was imminent.

He glanced away, took a deep breath and then turned his back on her. He could not allow himself to continue reacting to her in such a carnal way. "Unless my life is in danger, in public you will be the demure, adoring fiancée. Any disagreements we will keep private, between the two of us. Agreed?"

"I suppose I can live with those terms," she told him, her lips twitching in a barely restrained smile.

"Agreed?" he demanded harshly.

"Agreed, agreed."

He glowered at her. "I will tell my guests that you were tired and wished to have dinner in your room tonight. They will understand."

She laughed.

Damn the woman.

"I take it that I'm being dismissed and sent off to the attic for being a bad girl?"

"Your room is far from an attic. It is the master suite. Ramona will bring you a dinner tray and unpack your suitcases and attend to any of your needs. If you require a personal maid while you are here, I will provide you with one."

"You're giving me the master suite? How kind of you to give up your personal quarters—"

"I give up nothing," he told her. "As my fiancée, you will share my suite and my bed. Since you are an American and assumed not to be a virgin, it will be expected."

"Hold up just a minute there, 'el presidente.' Sharing your suite is okay. As your bodyguard, I will need to be close to you, but—"

"Feel free to sleep on the floor, if you wish, as long as none of the servants are aware that you are doing so."

Tilting her chin so that she could look him directly in the eyes, she said, "Believe me, sleeping on the floor will be preferable to sharing your bed."

A scrapper to the bitter end, Miguel thought. Such passion. "You, Señorita Blair, are in a minority. Most of the women I've known would much prefer to share my bed."

"You'll find that I'm not like most women."

"I have already discovered that fact."

She gave him a sharp nod. "Very well. I'll go quietly upstairs to *our* room for the evening, but beginning tomorrow morning, I'll be stuck to your side like glue, twenty-four-seven."

He bowed graciously, then smiled at her. "I look forward to every moment. Now, if you will excuse me, I'll send Ramona to see you to *our* room, then she'll bring your dinner up on a tray. And I'll see that Paco takes care of your and Mr. Shea's luggage."

"Perhaps you should call us Dom and Jennifer, even in private," she told him. "It will help you become accustomed to our names. After all, you wouldn't want to slip up and call your cousin Mr. Shea or your beloved fiancée, Ms. Blair."

"Point taken…Jennifer. Or would you prefer that I call you *querida?*"

"You choose, depending on your mood."

If he called her what his present mood dictated, his grandmother would come down from heaven and wash his mouth out with soap, as she had done when he was a child and had dared to use foul language in her presence.

* * *

With Señorita Blair—Jennifer—ensconced in his suite upstairs and his "cousin" Dom regaling his friends with a completely fictitious story of how Miguel had contacted him on his most recent trip to Miami, Miguel breathed a sigh of relief as he rejoined the others in the dining room.

"You've missed dessert," Dolores told him, then eyed him inquiringly. "Or perhaps you consider time alone with your future wife sweeter than any of Ramona's delicious pastries?"

"Well put, little sister," Miguel said, but his gaze connected with Zita's. Her expression told him that she was displeased, that she had come here tonight expecting this to be the first evening of many they would share. He could hardly tell her that he, too, had wanted the same. But those plans had been altered by circumstances beyond his control. First and foremost, his loyalty and dedication belonged to the people of Mocorito. Any personal happiness had to come second.

He turned to Roberto. "My dear friend, will you please see Señora Fuentes home? I'm afraid the sudden arrival of my darling Jennifer and Cousin Domingo must, of necessity, bring our evening to an early close."

"Of course, Miguel, I would be delighted to escort the *señora* home." Roberto walked over and held out his hand to Zita, who smiled graciously and rose to her feet.

"I shall say good night, also," Dr. Esteban said. "I have early rounds at St. Augustine's in the morning and will be rising before dawn."

"Juan, thank you for coming tonight." Miguel shook hands with his old friend, a man who shared his hopes and dreams for a true democracy in Mocorito.

"You must bring your lovely fiancée to dine with Aunt Josephina and me one evening soon, before the two of you are flooded with invitations," Juan said. "Everyone in Nava will be eager to meet Señorita Blair."

"And naturally, I would be honored to receive an invitation to your engagement party," Zita told him as Roberto led her past Miguel.

"Of course. How very gracious of you, my dear Zita." Miguel was not sure she would ever forgive him for this farce, even if he explained everything to her when the danger had passed and he had been elected president. It was possible that this evening's events had destroyed any possible future he might have had with the charming young widow.

"Since all of you are making it an early evening, I think I'll do the same," Dom said. "If you will have someone show me to my room, I'll call it a night."

"I have sent Paco for your and Jennifer's bags," Miguel said. "Once he has delivered Jennifer's luggage, I'll have him show you upstairs."

"In the meantime, why don't you walk Emilio and me to the door?" Dolores said to her cousin.

Miguel would have preferred to avoid being drilled by Dolores. But better to get it over with tonight and hope he could persuade her of his sincerity. His little cousin knew him too well and even if he swore to her on his mother's grave, she would still have some doubts. Whenever she was around, he would have to be doubly careful because she would watch him with Jennifer Blair as a hawk watches a chicken.

They had no sooner exited the dining room than Dolores checked to make sure Roberto and Zita were not within earshot, then she began the inquisition.

"She does not look pregnant, your fiancée," Dolores said. "So why are you marrying this woman you barely know? An American woman! Is she Catholic? Is she willing to give up her United States citizenship? Do you truly love her or is it just great sex that has you acting like a fool?"

Emilio mumbled under his breath, evoking God to take pity

on them—he and Miguel. "Dolores, *querida,* have faith in Miguel. Everything he does, he does for the right reasons."

Halting before reaching the foyer, she snapped her head around and glared at her husband. "Exactly what does that mean?"

Miguel put his arm around her shoulders. "It means that I am engaged to be married to a woman who will be sharing my life these next few weeks as she stands at my side and helps me win the presidency. Jennifer has come to me to help me, not harm me in any way. She understands the duties she must perform as my fiancée and she will not fail me. I trust her with my life."

Dolores studied Miguel contemplatively. "Do you have any objection to my spending time with her? To our becoming better acquainted?"

"None whatsoever," Miguel replied. "As long as you treat her with the respect she deserves as my future wife."

"Do you love her?"

"Would I ever ask a woman to marry me if I did not love her?"

Dolores sighed, then reached up and caressed his cheek. "Then I pray that she loves you as much as you do her."

Emilio emitted a nervous chuckle. "As far as you are concerned, no woman would ever be good enough for Miguel."

"Perhaps that is true," she agreed.

"Come, come. We must go and get you to bed, little mother. You need your rest." Emilio hovered over his wife, petting and soothing her as best he could.

Miguel stood on the veranda and watched his guests leave. First Roberto and Zita, then Juan Esteban and finally Emilio and Dolores. The evening had not gone as he had hoped due to the unexpected arrival of his American guests.

"Lovely evening," Dom Shea came up beside Miguel.

"It was."

"Sorry that we stormed in on you without warning, but our orders were to get here as quickly as possible."

"Will Pierce's idea, no doubt."

Dom glanced all around, then asked in English, "Do your servants speak English?"

"No, they do not," Miguel replied.

"Then I suggest that whenever we need to talk concerning private matters here in your home, that you, J.J. and I speak English."

"J.J.?"

"Her name is Jennifer," Dom replied. "But no one calls her that."

Miguel nodded. "Was she the only female agent available?"

Dom chuckled. "She's a handful, isn't she? But she's good at her job. You'll be in safe hands with her." Dom took a deep breath of fresh evening air. "To answer your question, no she wasn't the only female Dundee agent available, but she was the best-qualified for this assignment. As you must have noticed, she speaks fluent Spanish."

"Yes, her command of the language is excellent."

"You should know from the years you spent in the U.S. that American women are not like Mocoritian women. And J.J. is a breed apart. You look at her and you see sultry sex kitten, but I suspect you've already learned that in her case looks can really be deceiving."

"That, Mr. Shea, er, Dom, is the understatement of the century."

"May I give you some advice on how to handle J.J.?"

Miguel turned and looked at Domingo. The two of them being of almost equal height, they stood eye-to-eye. "I would appreciate any advice you can give me."

"Don't try to boss her around. She hates that. Let her think something is her idea, not yours. Make suggestions, but ask her opinion. Allow her to believe that she is totally in charge."

Miguel smiled. "You know her well, do you? There is a personal relationship between the two of you?"

"I've worked with J.J. for three years. I like and respect her. We're friends. Nothing more, nothing less. But I should warn you that if you do anything to hurt her, you'll have at least half a dozen of Dundee's best men coming after you."

"I certainly do not want that."

Miguel and Dom stood on the veranda for several more minutes, not speaking, then Dom broke the silence. "We need to discuss something you probably prefer not to talk about at all."

"And that would be?"

"The loyalty of your friends, closest supporters and household employees. My job is to make sure there are no traitors in your camp."

"I trust my friends and employees completely, as I do the supporters I have known for many years."

"But you don't have any objections to my digging around in their lives, do you? I will do it as discreetly as possible."

"Is that really necessary?"

"Someone tried to shoot you yesterday, Señor Ramirez," Dom said. "And behind the shooter is the person who hired him. That person wants to see you dead."

"We are relatively certain that the Federalist Party was behind the assassination attempt, which means Hector Padilla was part of the plot."

"That may be true, but I doubt President Padilla actually hired the rifleman who fired at you. We need to find the person or persons who paid the assassin. Often, behind something like this, you'll find a small group of people, not just one person."

"You will discover that none of my friends, supporters or employees are involved," Miguel said with total assurance. "But I give you permission to do the job Will Pierce hired you to do."

"Hmm…"

"What?"

"Another bit of advice."

"Yes?"

"When you speak to J.J., try not to use those exact words."

"What words?"

"Don't ever say to her that you give her your permission to do something. That would be like waving a red flag in front of a bull."

Miguel snorted. "Other than the fact she speaks Spanish fluently, what possible reason could your superior have thought she was the ideal person to pose as my girlfriend?"

"Your fiancée, not your girlfriend."

"Yes, she chose to become my fiancée instantly, without consulting me. That is a case in point of why she is unsuitable."

"She really ticked you off, didn't she?"

"Let us just say that I would prefer facing a mountain lion without a weapon than having to deal with your J.J."

"She's not my J.J. She's your J.J., Señor Ramirez, at least for the next few weeks."

"*¡Que Dios me ayude!*" Miguel said aloud, then repeated the prayer to himself. God help me!

Chapter 3

Miguel's bedroom suite comprised three rooms—bedroom, sitting room and bath—and a massive walk-in-closet that had probably, at one time, been a small nursery. A huge round iron chandelier hung in the middle of the ten-foot-high ceiling, crossed with weathered wooden beams. The stucco walls possessed a soft gold patina, as did the cast-stone fireplace, which was flanked by sets of double French doors. A plush coral velvet sofa hugged one wall. Round tables and nail-head-trimmed chairs in taupe leather served as bookends for the marble-topped decorative-iron coffee table in front of the sofa. Across the room, two rich gold arm chairs sat like fat mushrooms growing out of the antique Persian rug.

Luxurious was the first word that came to mind.

Paco had deposited J.J.'s bags in the closet and told her that Ramona would see to the unpacking in the morning. That had been at least twenty minutes ago and it had taken her every second of that time to explore the rooms she would be sharing with

Miguel for the next few weeks. It wasn't that she hadn't known luxury before—she had when she'd lived with her mother and Raymond, her stepfather, in their twenty-room mansion in Mobile. But this was no antebellum mansion, although she suspected it was as old, if not older than many of the homes built pre War Between the States.

The French doors led to a large balcony that overlooked the courtyard gardens. J.J. had stood out there for several minutes, breathing in the cool night air and thinking about how she would handle her first night with the future president of Mocorito. If she weren't terribly attracted to him on a purely physical level, it might be easier to share these intimate quarters without her mind wandering from the job at hand to considering what it would be like to actually be engaged to this man.

She would never—not in a million years—marry a man like Miguel Cesar Ramirez, a male chauvinist from the old school of male superiority. But the very thing that she disliked about him the most was what also attracted her to him. That powerful male essence that declared to one and all that he was king of the hill, master of all he surveyed. Her father had been that kind of man. *Was* that kind of man. Rudd Blair was a career soldier, having moved up the ranks over the years. The last she'd heard, he was a general and his son, eighteen-year-old Rudd, Jr., had just graduated from military school. She had spent her entire life trying to earn the privilege of being what her half-brother became the moment he was born—the apple of their father's eye. Hell, she'd even joined the army after college graduation in the hopes that her becoming a soldier would please her father as much as it pissed off her genteel, Southern-belle mother. But it hadn't mattered to Daddy Dearest that she had graduated top in her class or that she'd excelled in her duties as a second lieutenant. As far as Rudd was concerned, J.J. was nothing more than a female offspring who should get married and do her best to produce some grandsons for him.

Okay, so it was unfair to compare Miguel to her father, despite the fact that they were probably cut from the same prejudiced cloth. She figured that over the next few weeks, she would learn to dislike Miguel intensely for reasons that had nothing to do with her past history with her father.

A soft rapping at the door drew J.J.'s eyes in that direction. "*¿Sí?*" she asked.

"I have your dinner, *señorita,*" a woman's voice called from the other side of the door.

Ramona, no doubt. "Please, come in." J.J. rushed across the room to open the door.

Carrying a small silver tray covered with a white linen cloth, Ramona entered the room, walked over and placed the tray on the coffee table and turned to J.J. "If you require anything else, *señorita*—"

"No, thank you. Not tonight."

Ramona nodded, then turned and left the sitting room. The woman had been neither friendly nor unfriendly. J.J. wasn't certain how she should interact with the servants in Miguel's house. The servants who worked for her mother were treated well, but were thought of as socially inferior, and one never associated with them on a personal level. However, her mother was especially fond of her old nanny; Aunt Bess, as everyone in the Ashford family referred to the woman, was now eighty-six and living in an assisted-living facility paid for by Lenore Ashford Whitney.

J.J. hated barriers of any kind—social, economic, race or religion. And sex. Her mother had been a snob, her father sexist. She prided herself on being neither. That was one reason she could not allow herself to judge Miguel without getting to know him better. He deserved to be judged on his merits and flaws alone and not on some preconceived idea J.J. had of him.

Wondering what Ramona had brought for her to eat, J.J. removed the white linen cloth from the silver tray. Cheese, bread, grapes, wine and some sort of cake that looked sinfully rich. She grabbed the grapes and nibbled on them as she strolled into the bedroom. This room intrigued her, and for more than one reason. She had no intention of this area becoming a battleground tonight or in the nights ahead.

What makes me think he's going to try something? she asked herself.

The answer came immediately. He's a man, isn't he?

But I don't think he likes me any more than I like him.

Maybe not, but that unnerving charge of awareness you felt wasn't a one-sided thing. That sensation of I-want-to-rip-your-clothes-off-and-have-you-here-and-now tore through his gut just like it did yours.

She'd seen that look in his eyes. Had he seen it in hers? If so, he would make his first move tonight.

The bedroom was as large as the sitting room, but where the latter had been decorated in warm, earthy shades, the decor in this room reflected peace, tranquility and age-old charm. Everything in the room, from bed linens to lamp shades, reflected the simple elegance and color scheme of the ivory stucco walls. Color came from the rich glow of the dark wooden floors, accent pieces, and dark wooden bedside tables. The king-size bed was modern in size and structure, but an intricately carved wooden arch made a dramatic antique headboard.

The bed was large enough that she could actually lie beside Miguel and never touch him. Yeah, sure, like she was going to take the chance that he wouldn't touch her.

Scanning the twenty-by-twenty room, J.J. sought and found an alternative place for her to sleep. A large, comfy chaise lounge, covered in ivory damask, sprawled languidly in front of the floor-to-ceiling windows. All she needed to make the chaise her bed was a pillow and a blanket. Both items would be easy to discard come morning, to keep the servants unaware that she had not shared a bed with Miguel.

Finishing off the grapes, J.J. returned to the sitting room and hurriedly ate part of the cheese and bread, then lifted the glass of wine and carried it with her as she headed for the bathroom. Would she have time for a leisurely soak in the massive marble tub before Miguel came upstairs for the night? Nope. Better not risk it. A quick shower would have to suffice.

She entered the walk-in closet, set her glass on top of a highboy to her left, then bent over and opened one of her suitcases. Without giving much thought as to which peignoir set to wear, she yanked up a lavender silk gown and matching robe from the large bag. She hurriedly turned around and grabbed her wineglass on the way back into the bedroom. When she entered the bathroom and hung the gown and robe over the vanity chair, she sighed as the light hit the almost iridescent silk. At home she slept in pajamas in the winter and an oversize T-shirt in the summer. Since it was rare that a man ever saw her in her sleepwear, she didn't own anything really sexy, certainly nothing like the items she had purchased with her corporate charge card.

Stop it, right this minute, she warned herself. She could not—would not—allow herself to wonder what Miguel would think or how he would react when he saw her in the ultrafeminine lavender peignoir set. Besides, if she timed things just right, she'd be asleep on the chaise by the time he came up for the night and she could either rise early and be out of the bedroom before he got up or she could sleep late and let him be the first to leave.

He had been expecting a telephone call about Miguel's secret bodyguard, but not tonight. His contact—the spy with Ramirez's camp—had told him the Dundee agent would arrive tomorrow.

"His American bodyguards arrived early. They came tonight instead of in the morning as we'd been expecting."

"Did you say two bodyguards? I thought there would be only the woman." He swirled the liquor in the crystal tumbler, sniffed the aroma and took a sip.

"Yes, there are two," said the quiet voice at the other end of the line. "One male and one female. They are telling everyone that the man is Miguel's cousin from Miami and the woman is Miguel's fiancée."

"Fiancée? I thought she was to pose as his mistress." He did not like it when plans changed—especially when the change was not in his favor.

"That was the original plan, but this American woman accepted his proposal there in front of everyone present tonight."

"Then our plan to use the woman against him will have to be altered." He set aside his glass, placing it atop a stone coaster on his desk. "A mistress can easily be discredited. A fiancée is a different matter. If the voters believe he plans to marry this woman, they will view her in a different light."

"If we cannot use the woman against him, we must find another way. I do not want Miguel killed, only frightened enough to withdraw from the presidential race."

Personally, he would prefer Ramirez dead and buried, but if they killed him, the people would see him as a martyr and possibly revolt. That was the last thing he and his party wanted. Besides, this traitor who had proved so useful to him was not the only Federalist who did not want to resort to murdering Ramirez. Some of them had no stomach for fighting dirty, for doing whatever it took to win. And some of those weak men already thought of him as a bloodthirsty tyrant.

"We tried scaring Miguel with the assassination attempt, but he simply hired a bodyguard, using his contact with that American CIA agent to hire her. If only we had some type of proof that Miguel has sold out to the Americans—"

"We have discussed this before, as you well know. If we could prove this to be a fact, it could well work against us instead of for us. A vast majority of the people here in Mocorito see the U.S. as an ally, a friend who will help us."

"Then perhaps we could reveal that the woman and man living in Miguel's home are actually American bodyguards, that he has lied to the people. That could make them turn against him."

"Putting out such a rumor will be easy enough, but proving it is a different matter. Unless you can prove your claims, trying to discredit Ramirez could harm us instead of him. The people adore him, unfortunately. They see him as their hero."

A very unpleasant thought suddenly crossed his mind. Once he had learned that the Dundee Private Security and Investigation Agency would be involved, he had made it his business to find out everything he could about them. The private bodyguard for Miguel did not worry him. But the fact that another agent had come with her did concern him. What if there were others? What if they were mounting an investigation? "Are the two American bodyguards who arrived tonight, the only two?"

"What?"

"Are there others? Perhaps working undercover?"

"If there are, I don't know of them."

"Find out."

"But how?"

"You will think of a way."

Dolores traipsed through the house in her bare feet, stopping outside the door to her husband's study when she heard him speaking in a low, quiet voice. She knocked on the closed door, then entered. Emilio jerked around and stared at her, his eyes wide, his hand clutching the telephone receiver.

"Who are you talking to this late at night?" she asked.

He covered the mouthpiece with his hand and replied, "Roberto. We are discussing how to handle the announcement of Miguel's engagement." He removed his hand and said into the telephone, "We will discuss this matter further in the morning." He hung up the phone and held open his arms for Dolores.

She went to him, allowing him to envelop her in his gentle, loving embrace. There had never been another man for her. Only

Emilio. Since they were children together—she, Emilio and Miguel—she had loved Emilio and had always known that someday she would become his wife. Their road to happiness had taken many years and numerous detours, but in the end, she had been blessed with all she desired. She had been Emilio's wife for two years and now she was carrying his child. His son.

"You must be tired, *querida.*" Emilio rubbed her back with wide, circular motions.

"You should rest more and not do so much work on Miguel's campaign. And now that he has a fiancée, you must allow her to take over the duties as his hostess."

"What do you know about this woman, this Señorita Blair?"

Emilio shrugged. "Only that Miguel met her on his last trip to Miami and asked her to marry him."

"It is not like Miguel to keep such important news from me."

"Perhaps he wanted to wait to see if she would accept his proposal."

"Hmm…perhaps."

Emilio turned her around and urged her into movement. "Come to bed with me."

She smiled at her husband. "And we will make love?"

"I would like nothing more, but if you are too tired—"

She stopped him with a kiss, one that quickly became passionate. His strong, smooth hands moved over her shoulders and across her heavy breasts. When he flicked her tight nipples with his thumbs, she moaned deep in her throat.

"Did I hurt you, my love?"

"No, no, you didn't hurt me."

Hand-in-hand, desire burning inside them, they rushed to their bedroom and closed the door. Within minutes, Dolores no longer thought about Miguel and his mysterious American fiancée or about Emilio's late-night phone call from Roberto.

Josephina Esteban Santiago did not sleep well. Her arthritic hips often woke her in the night and once awake, her overactive brain would not allow her to fall peacefully back to sleep. Since she often woke several times during the night, she usually went to bed early and stayed in bed late. The financial support of a loving nephew afforded her certain luxuries in her old age. Not that she was impoverished. Her late husband had left her comfortable, but she had used a great deal of her money to send Juan to medical school. She was so proud of him, her brother's only child, a boy she and her late husband Xavier had taken into their home shortly after his parents were killed in a car crash when he was nine.

As Josephina crept along the semidark hallway toward the kitchen, she thought she heard voices coming from the parlor. Surely not at this late hour. It was nearly midnight. But she paused and listened. Yes, that was Juan's voice. She would recognize it anywhere. Not meaning to eavesdrop, she turned and continued toward the kitchen, but before she reached her destination, Juan called out to her.

"Is that you, Aunt Josephina?"

"Yes, dear. I am sorry to have bothered you. I am going to the kitchen to prepare some warm milk. That often helps me sleep."

"I'll come with you and we will drink warm milk together," he told her as he came out of the parlor.

"You're up rather late, aren't you, dear?" She patted his cheek when he drew near enough for her to touch him. "Did Miguel's dinner party last this long?"

"No, it actually ended a bit early," Juan told her, then leaned down to kiss her cheek. "You heard me speaking on the telephone, didn't you?"

"Yes, I heard you speaking to someone, but I couldn't hear what you were saying."

"I was on the phone with St. Augustine's. I wanted to check on a patient whose condition greatly concerns me."

"You are such a good man. Such a conscientious doctor."

"You thought I was on the telephone with her, didn't you?" A frown marred Juan's handsome face. Handsome to her, although perhaps not to everyone. His wide, flat nose and high cheekbones revealed his mother's Indian heritage, while his height had been inherited from the Esteban family, who could trace their roots all the way back to Spain. What her nephew lacked in good looks, he made up for in brains and talent.

"It is none of my business to whom you speak," Josephina told him. "But you know how I feel about her. She is a woman betrothed to another man, yet she seeks you out time and again. If anyone discovers that—"

He grasped her hands in his and held tightly. "We are friends, Aunt Josephina. Only friends. She is very unhappy and needs to talk to someone she can trust. I am her doctor."

"And she tells you she does not want to marry this man because she does not love him. What nonsense. In my day, we married for better reasons than love."

"There is no better reason," Juan said, a wistful tone to his voice.

"You may be only friends with her, but you love her, do you not?"

"Come along and let me prepare us both some warm milk."

Josephina allowed him to change the subject momentarily as he led her into the kitchen and aided her in sitting at the table.

"If she does not marry this man, her family will disown her, especially if they discover she has feelings for you and learn that you are one of Miguel's dearest friends." Josephina cradled her stiff, aching hands in her lap. Arthritis was such a curse. "Have you told Miguel that you are friends with his sister?"

"His half-sister," Juan corrected. "And no, I have not mentioned my friendship with Seina to Miguel. There is no love lost between Miguel and Cesar Fernandez's family. Seina knows that Miguel is my friend. She has no animosity toward Miguel, not the way her brother and mother do."

"Be careful, my dear boy, that Seina Fernandez does not use you in any way."

"What are you implying?"

"As you say, there is no love lost between Miguel and his late

father's family. It is no secret that the Fernandez family support
the reelection of Hector Padilla. If they could use you against Miguel, they would."

"I would never allow that to happen."

"I hope not. Miguel is a good friend and he is the people's
hope for the future of Mocorito."

Roberto Aznar hung up the telephone and turned off the light.
The lady waited for him. He would be a fool to leave her, not
after such a warm invitation to stay the night, to share her bed.
Perhaps she had made the offer only because she was angry with
Miguel, but he was not a man who would turn down a beautiful
woman just because she wished he were another man. The loving would be just as good for him regardless of who Zita Fuentes
pretended was between her spread thighs. It wasn't as if he would
be betraying Miguel. After all, Zita and Miguel had not had even
one date and now that Miguel had a phony fiancée ensconced in
his home, in his bedroom, it was highly unlikely that Zita would
forgive him, even if the truth about the American woman came
to light. Besides, after the election, when he was assigned a
choice government position, he would be on a more equal foot-
ing, at least socially, with women such as Señora Fuentes. Who
knew, without Miguel as a rival for Zita's affections, she might
consider him as potential husband material. What a delectable
thought—having access to the lady's millions, as well as having
her in his bed every night.

"*Querido,* why are you keeping me waiting?" Zita called
from the head of the stairs. "I thought you had to make only one
phone call."

Taking the steps two at a time, he rushed upstairs and into the
welcoming arms of the luscious and naked widow.

Miguel stayed up past midnight, deliberately giving Señorita
Blair enough time to eat, bathe and go to sleep. He did not want
another confrontation with her tonight.

Standing outside the door to his bedroom suite, he hesitated, wondering if, when he went inside, he would find her asleep in his bed. Would she be curled up in the middle of the down mattress topper, sleeping like a little black kitten, purring softly as she breathed in and out, her breasts rising and falling with each heartbeat?

He could not continue doing this to himself. Yes, she was a highly desirable woman and yes, they would be together day and night, possibly for weeks. But an affair was out of the question.

Why was it out of the question?

She was a woman; he was a man. Neither of them was married or otherwise attached. Why shouldn't they consider an affair?

Miguel opened the door quietly and eased into the semidark room. Only the moonlight floating through the double set of French doors on either side of the fireplace illuminated the sitting room. Scanning the area, halfway expecting to find her asleep on the sofa, he moved toward the bedroom when he did not see her.

The bedroom was slightly darker, but enough light came through the floor-to-ceiling windows for him to make his way into the room without tripping over anything. Within minutes his eyes had adjusted to the dark and he noted that his bed had been untouched, except for a missing pillow. As he made his way across the room, heading for the closet, he paused and searched for her. She lay on the chaise lounge, a cotton blanket covering her from the waist down, leaving her bare shoulders and neck visible.

Was she asleep? Should he call her name? Or should he do the wise thing and ignore her? But how did a red-blooded man ignore the fact that a scantily clad woman was in his bedroom, sleeping only a few feet away from him?

Miguel entered the closet, flipped on the overhead light, then closed the door halfway. After finding his robe, he searched through the highboy for a pair of pajamas. He owned several, but seldom wore them, preferring to sleep in the raw.

Chuckling silently to himself, he wondered what Señorita Blair would think if she woke in the morning to find him lying naked in his bed? Being an American woman who had probably been with many men, he doubted she would be the least bit shocked.

Just how many men had there been in Jennifer's life? Two or three? A dozen? Two dozen? She looked young, no more than her late twenties, but American girls became sexually active in their teens, so it was possible that she'd had numerous lovers.

Why should he care how many lovers his make-believe fiancée had had? It wasn't as if he was actually going to marry this woman, or that she would be the mother of his children.

After rifling through every drawer in the highboy, he finally found two pairs of pajamas, one set silk and one cotton. He chose the black silk, which had been a gift from a lady friend a number of years ago. He'd never worn them. Hurriedly, he removed his shoes and socks, then slipped out of his slacks and dress shirt. He laid them out for Ramona, who would take care of the items in the morning. Wearing only his black cotton briefs, he hung the robe and pajamas over his arm and walked back through the bedroom and into the bath, forcing himself not to glance toward the chaise.

If he were spending the night making love to his phony fiancée, he would take the time to shave. He possessed one of those heavy black beards that required him to shave twice a day if he didn't want to go to bed with thick, prickly stubble, which women apparently hated. But tonight, he would be sleeping alone, as he did more often than not. Although he had known his fair share of women since reaching manhood, he had never been a Don Juan, and he had not indulged in what the Americans referred to as a one-night stand since his college days at Harvard.

Wearing the black silk pajamas and carrying the robe, he made his way back into the bedroom and went straight to his bed. While turning down the covers, he hazarded a quick glance toward the chaise. She had turned over, her back to him, and the cotton blanket lay on the floor beside her.

Don't go over there, he cautioned himself. If she becomes chilly, she'll wake, find the blanket and pull it up and over herself again.

But before he had finished the thought, he was halfway across the room. As he approached the chaise, he slowed his movements. Standing over her, he glanced down and wished he hadn't. She had turned in her sleep and her lavender silk gown had ridden up and twisted around her, revealing her calves and lower thighs. The material stretched tightly across her hips and derriere. Nicely rounded hips and full, tight derriere. A perfect upside-down-heart-shaped butt.

Miguel swallowed.

Her short, curly hair shimmered a rich ebony against the white pillow beneath her head. Her lavender gown was cut low in the back, almost to her waist, giving him a view of her smooth, satiny skin. His fingers itched to reach out and touch her.

Whatever you do, do not touch her.

Leaning over, he picked up the cotton blanket, spread it out and laid it over her from bare feet to slender neck. She stirred and mumbled the moment the blanket came into contact with her skin. Her eyelashes fluttered.

He held his breath, praying she wouldn't wake and find him standing over her. When she curled up in the blanket and sighed contentedly, he backed away from her, then practically ran to his bed. After crawling in and drawing the covers up over his chest, he lay there and stared up at the ceiling.

In the distance he heard St. Angela's church bell announce one o'clock. It was already early morning and he had an incredibly busy day ahead. Instead of lying here with an erection thinking of Jennifer Blair, he should be sleeping. He would need his rest for the hectic schedule facing him, not only tomorrow, but in the weeks to come.

After tossing and turning for what seemed like forever, he sat up in bed, unbuttoned his pajama top and removed it. Lying back down, he settled against the cool, soft sheets. He liked the feel of his naked skin against the luxurious cotton. But despite being more comfortable half-naked, he remained awake, longing for sleep that wouldn't come. Sometime after he heard the church bells strike twice, Miguel finally dozed off to sleep, his last thought of the woman lying only a few feet from him.

She woke before dawn and needed to go to the bathroom, but she didn't want to traipse across the bedroom and risk waking Miguel. She lay there until she couldn't wait a minute longer, then she tossed back the cotton blanket, slipped off the chaise and stood up on her bare feet. Tiptoeing across the room, she cast a quick glance at the large body lying sprawled in the middle of the king-size bed.

Ignore him. Pretend he isn't there.

She rushed to the bathroom, closed the door as quietly as possible, then, without turning on a light, she felt her way to the commode. Afterward, she washed and dried her hands in the dark, feeling for the soap and the towel and finding them without knocking anything over and causing a disturbance.

As she made her way back across the room, she found herself walking toward the bed instead of the chaise. She stood at the side of the bed and looked at Miguel, his body clearly visible in the moonlight. He lay flat on his back, his arms sprawled out on either side of his body and one leg bent at the knee. His chest was muscular and sprinkled with curly black hair that tapered into a thin line and disappeared into his pajama bottoms. Those black-satin bottoms rode low on his hips, low enough to reveal his navel. His long arms were large and well-muscled. He possessed the body of a man in his prime.

J.J. sucked in a deep breath, then released it slowly. Everything feminine within her reacted to all that was masculine in him.

This wouldn't do. No, sirree. She never—ever—got involved with a client, no matter what. But she had never been instantly attracted to a client—no, make that any man—the way she was to Miguel Ramirez. It didn't make sense to her. He was far from the first gorgeous man she'd ever met. And he wasn't the first whose blatant machismo reminded her of her father, whom she had adored as a young girl. Whatever it was about this man that attracted her so, she had to deal with it now and move past it.

Suddenly, Miguel rolled over onto his side and whispered one word as his big hand caressed the empty space beside him.

"Querida…"

She all but ran back to the chaise, snuggled into a ball and wrapped herself in the cotton blanket. Okay, so maybe she'd wait until later today to face her fears and find a way to vanquish them.

Chapter 4

J.J. woke with a start. Sunlight flooded the room, telling her that it was well past dawn and that she had overslept. Without thinking, she tossed back the cotton blanket and slid to the edge of the chaise lounge as she sat up and stretched.

"Good morning," Miguel said.

J.J. froze. Oh, God. In her early-morning haze, she had forgotten all about him.

Daring a glance in the direction of his deep voice, which came from the sitting room, she saw him standing in the doorway. Fully clothed in a lightweight charcoal-gray pinstriped suit, pale gray shirt and burgundy tie, he looked like a successful businessman—or a political candidate dressed for success. And here she was, his bodyguard, wearing a flimsy fluff of lavender silk that clung to every curve and bared way too much flesh. Reaching behind her in as nonchalant a way as possible, she felt around on the back of the chaise for her matching robe. It wasn't there. Damn, it was probably lying on the floor.

"What time is it?" she asked.

"Seven-fifteen," he replied as he walked into the bedroom.

No, don't, she wanted to shout. Go away. Don't come any closer. But instead she squared her shoulders and offered him a half-hearted smile.

"Give me fifteen minutes and I'll be ready to go."

He came closer and closer. Her heart caught in her throat. Although she wasn't naked, she felt as vulnerable as if she were. She had shared a bedroom with a client before, but she'd always slept in more appropriate attire—usually baggy sweat pants and T-shirt. And she'd never had a client who struck every female chord within her.

When Miguel walked past her, she let out a deep breath, but that relieved sigh was short-lived. From the corner of her eye, she saw him bend over and reach down for something, then suddenly he came up behind her and draped her sheer silk robe over her shoulders. When his big hands grazed her naked shoulders, she gasped.

He ran his hands across her shoulders, slowly, sensuously. She shuddered.

"While you dress and prepare yourself for the day, I'll put away the blanket and return the pillow to my bed," he told her as he gave her upper arms a gentle squeeze. "We cannot have Ramona or the other girls thinking we have had a lover's quarrel on your first night here, can we?"

J.J. swallowed. "No, we certainly do not want that."

She pulled away from him and hurried to the closet. Before closing the door, she peeked back into the bedroom. Miguel folded the blanket and placed it in the intricately carved walnut cabinet on the far side of the room, then he picked up the pillow and tossed it onto his bed.

Stop wasting time staring at the man, she told herself. If he knew he had her rattled, she'd lose the upper hand with him. And that was something she couldn't allow to happen. Let a man like

Miguel—like her father and all macho chauvinists—know they had any kind of hold over you and they would use it against you. She'd learned that the only way to deal with such a man was to show him that not only did he not intimidate her, but that his blatant masculinity had no effect on her whatsoever. Let the airheaded, silly women who needed a big, strong man to lean on feed those men's huge egos.

After closing the door, J.J. sorted through her choice of clothes. Damn, she had no idea what was on today's agenda and since she was not officially acting as Miguel's bodyguard, she could hardly wear her standard outfit of slacks, button-down shirt and jacket. Oh, no, on this assignment, she had to dress as if she were the candidate's fiancée and she'd have to carry her weapon—which Miguel was supposed to furnish—in a handbag. How inconvenient was that? The extra time it would take her to open the bag and get her hands on the gun could mean the difference between life and death for her or for Miguel.

What insanity! That a man's ego might cost him his life didn't make sense to her. That had been one of the things she'd never understood about her father. And no matter how much she had adored him—idolized him, really—she'd been forced to face a hard truth. Rudd Blair was one of those men to whom the birth of a female child was a disappointment.

J.J. cracked the door and peered out into the bedroom. Her gaze settled on Miguel's wide shoulders. Forcing herself not to do a quick survey, she cleared her throat and called to him.

"What is on today's agenda? How should I dress?"

Keeping his back to her, he replied, "We will attend a sort of pep rally this morning at the Nationalist headquarters, then I have a television interview at noon, followed by lunch with a group of supporters at the country club. Domingo will go with us for the rally, but then he will return here. This afternoon, I will be followed by a news crew as I tour St. Augustine's pediatric ward. We will end the day with a dinner held in my honor at the home of one of my most famous and influential supporters, Anton Casimiro. Of course we will return here to change before going to dinner."

"*The* Anton Casimiro, the famous opera tenor from Argentina?"

"Yes, that Anton Casimiro."

"I had no idea he was living in Mocorito."

"He keeps a penthouse in downtown Nava," Miguel told her. "Anton's mother was born here in Nava and he has cousins in the city."

"Oh." Switching gears, returning to her original concerns about how to dress for the day, she asked, "Then will a simple suit be appropriate for today?"

"Yes, I should think that would be quite appropriate."

J.J. closed the door and rummaged through her clothes, each outfit covered with a protective plastic bag. She had packed shoes and purses in another suitcase and jewelry in a smaller overnight case. The clothes she had chosen for this assignment reflected her mother Lenore's tastes. Simple elegance. Understated, yet fashionable.

With all the necessary paraphernalia in hand, she trekked back into the bedroom and felt a great sense of relief when she found the room empty. The door to the sitting area was closed, so she assumed Miguel had done the gentlemanly thing and given her some privacy.

She'd taken a shower last night, so a quick sponge bath this morning should suffice. And being blessed with curly hair, which she kept cut fairly short, all she needed to do was brush the curls into place. Although she often didn't wear any makeup, today she would. Lipstick. Blush. A bit of eye shadow. Just enough, but not too much. Makeup should always look natural, or so her mother had told her numerous times.

Before she stripped, she made sure the door was locked, then she bathed, brushed her teeth and put on her underwear. She hated pantyhose with a passion, so when forced to wear a dress or suit, she preferred wearing a garter belt and stockings. Yesterday she'd worn pantyhose on the flight from Atlanta to Caracas on the Dundee jet and from Caracas to Nava on a commercial flight. After peeling them off and tossing them away, she'd been doubly glad that she'd packed a couple of garter belts and a dozen pair of stockings in various shades to wear for the rest of the time she was in Mocorito.

Although she'd heard that men loved to see women in garter belts and stockings, she had never chosen to perform in that particular attire for any man. She wore them to please herself, not to satisfy some drooling male who treated women as nothing more than sex objects.

Out of the blue, an unwanted image flashed through her mind. Miguel in his pajama bottoms sitting in his bed, his back propped against the elaborately carved headboard, watching her as she removed her clothes, down to her bra, panties, garter belt and stockings. A foreboding shudder rippled up her spine. It would be a cold day in hell before she'd strip for any man, and that included Miguel Ramirez!

"Dr. Esteban, I am not sure what to do." Juan's nurse, Carmen, caught him between patients. "Señorita Fernandez insists on seeing you. She is waiting in your private office."

"When did she arrive?"

"About five minutes ago, Carmen replied. "I told her you were very busy this morning and in the middle of doing rounds here at the hospital, but she said she would wait however long it takes."

Juan patted Carmen's back. "I will see her now. It must be important or she would not have come here to the hospital so early this morning."

As they walked together down the corridor toward the elevator, Carmen caught him by the arm to slow his pace. He paused and looked at her questioningly. Carmen had been with him since he finished his residency here at St. Augustine's and became a member of the staff. She was round and plump, with gray hair and expressive hazel-brown eyes that often revealed the emotions stirring in her compassionate heart.

"It is not my place to advise you in personal matters, but…" Carmen lowered her voice as they entered the elevator. Once the doors closed and they were alone, she continued. "Señorita Fernandez belongs to a very powerful family and if her brother were to find out that—"

"I don't need you to warn me," Juan said. "Aunt Josephina spoke to me only last night about the dangers of becoming involved with Seina."

"Did you listen to your aunt? No, you did not. If you had taken heed to her warning, you would have told me to explain to the *señorita* that you could not see her today."

The elevator doors opened on the ground floor where Juan's office was located. He held the door for Carmen, then together they walked down the corridor. When they neared his private office, he paused and turned to her.

"Go to the cafeteria and bring back some coffee for us…in about fifteen minutes," Juan told her.

"It is not wise for you to be alone with her."

"Please, do as I ask."

Huffing indignantly, she glowered at him. "I will return in fifteen minutes. And I will not knock on the door." She didn't look back as she walked away hurriedly.

Juan heaved a deep sigh as he grasped the doorknob. No one needed to tell him the foolishness of being in love with Seina Fernandez. He knew that there could be no future for them. Even if she were not engaged to another man, one chosen by her family, Seina and he could never marry. Not unless she broke all ties to her family and gave up her inheritance. He was not a poor man, but he could never give her the kind of lifestyle into which she had been born.

Garnering his courage, praying for the strength to do what was right for Seina, he opened the door and entered his private office. The moment she saw him, she sprung from her chair and rushed toward him. Despite his best efforts to remain aloof, he found himself opening his arms to her and holding her with gentle strength as she wrapped her arms around his waist and laid her head on his shoulder.

"Mother has made plans for my engagement party," Seina said. "In three weeks. She and Lorenzo's mother have set the date for our wedding. It will be six months from the night our families officially announce our engagement."

"You knew this day would come." Juan tightened his hold on her.

She lifted her head and stared pleadingly at him with her huge black eyes. "We must find a way to be together. I do not love Lorenzo. I love you. I want to be your wife. Please, Juan, please, do not tell me that marrying another man is what is best for me. You cannot want me to be Lorenzo's wife."

Juan grasped her shoulders and held her away from him. "I die inside thinking of him touching you, kissing you, making love to you."

"Oh, Juan…"

He shook her gently. "But I will not allow you to lose everything to be with me. In time you would come to hate me."

"I would never—"

He shook her again, then released her. They stood there staring at each other. Tears gathered in Seina's eyes. Juan swallowed the emotions threatening to choke him.

"I should never have allowed this to happen. That first time, when you came to see me as a patient and we felt an instant attraction, I should have sent you to another doctor that very day."

"But you didn't because you felt as I did. You knew we were meant to be together."

He shook his head. "We are not together and we never can be."

"You want me. I know you do." Tension etched frown lines in her lovely face.

"I would never dishonor you." Juan looked at the floor, knowing he dared not look at her. She was temptation personified.

"Then you are willing to send me to another man still a virgin, knowing he will take from me what I long to give you."

Juan's stomach muscles clenched into knots. "You must not say such things."

"I say only what is in my heart. If…if I cannot be with you, my life is not worth living."

He snapped his head up and looked directly into her eyes. Tears streamed down her cheeks. *"Querida…"*

"I shall kill myself."

"No, Seina, you must not say such a thing. You must not even think it."

Suddenly the door opened and, unannounced, Carmen walked in carrying two cups. "I apologize for interrupting you, Dr. Esteban, but I knew you would want your coffee before returning upstairs to finish your rounds."

Juan glared at his nurse. "Please, place the coffee on my desk. Señorita Fernandez and I have not completed our—"

"No, no, I do not want to keep you from caring for your patients," Seina said.

"Thank you for being so understanding, *señorita*." Carmen placed the coffee on the desk. "If you would like, I can see you out. Do you have a car waiting or did you drive yourself?"

With her gaze downcast, Seina replied shyly, "I do not drive. A friend brought me. She is waiting for me in the parking lot."

"Seina…Señorita Fernandez…" Juan looked at her longingly. He knew it was best for both of them if she left, if they never saw each other again. But a man in love seldom chose what was in his best interests. "We will speak again."

"When?" she asked hopefully.

"Soon."

* * *

Gala Hernandez waited in the parking lot of St. Augustine's Hospital for her dearest friend. When Seina had telephoned her early this morning and pleaded with her to drive her here to see Dr. Esteban, she had done everything she could to dissuade Seina. Not only was her friend's secret relationship with the doctor dangerous for Seina, but it also put Gala in a no-win situation. She had made some foolish mistakes several years ago and had it not been for Diego, Seina's older brother, intervening on her behalf with the police, she would now be serving time in prison for drug use. Diego had not only protected her, he had sent her through a rehabilitation program and kept the whole thing in strictest confidence. And not once since then had Diego ever asked anything of her—until a few weeks ago.

"I know that Seina is slipping around seeing Juan Esteban," Diego had told Gala. "I will, of course, put a stop to that relationship, when the time is right. But for now, it may be of use to me. To us."

"I don't understand. I thought that if you found out, you'd be furious."

"I am displeased, but I trust you to keep me informed of what is happening with my sister and Dr. Esteban. If you think she is on the verge of sleeping with this man—"

"Seina is still a virgin. I swear she is."

"Good. I know that you two share everything. She tells you what she is feeling, what she is doing. You know more about her than either I or our mother, and that is why I want you to report to me every time she sees Esteban. I want to know every word she says about him. I want to know what they talk about, who they discuss."

"You think they discuss Miguel Ramirez?"

"It is possible. Especially if you were to encourage Seina to ask Esteban about his good friend. Encourage her to learn more about her half-brother. She is curious about him, and she has said that she believes we should get to know him. I'm afraid my little sister has a soft heart. Use your powers of persuasion to gain whatever information you can."

Unlike his younger sister, Diego Fernandez did not have a soft heart. Handsome, charming and powerful, he could be a good friend. Unless you opposed him. Then he was ruthless. He hated his half-brother and would do anything to keep him from winning the presidency. She didn't know for sure, but she suspected that he was somehow involved in the recent assassination attempt on Miguel Ramirez's life.

The morning sun grew warmer by the minute. Even with the top down on her small sports car, Gala had begun to perspire. Seina had promised her she would be gone only a brief time, but she'd already been inside the hospital for nearly thirty minutes.

As she kept watch on the side entrance to the hospital, Gala's cell phone rang. She knew before answering who the caller was.

"Hello."

"Is she still with Dr. Esteban?" Diego asked.

"Yes."

"I want a report the moment you take her home."

"Very well."

"And I have an assignment for you."

"What sort of assignment?" Gala asked, her stomach tightening with apprehension. She could not refuse Diego. Her life was in his hands. He could, even now, see that she went to prison. If that happened, not only would her life be ruined, but her parents would be brokenhearted and disgraced.

"There is a luncheon at the Nava country club this afternoon in honor of Miguel Ramirez. I want you to attend. I've arranged for your name to be on the guest list."

"But everyone knows that Seina and I are close friends."

"Yes, I know. You will, however, publicly disagree with our family's politics. And you can even imply that my sister secretly supports her half-brother, although she cannot publicly commit to him."

"What purpose will this—"

"You are a beautiful woman, Gala. Ingratiate yourself to whatever man you can within the Ramirez camp, perhaps even Ramirez himself. I want you trailing the Nationalist candidate. Become a camp follower. Keep your eyes and ears open. I am especially interested in any information about Ramirez's new fiancée, Señorita Blair."

"You ask too much, Diego. It is bad enough that you have made me betray my best friend, but now you want me to work as a spy for the Federalists."

"Of course, you have a choice."

Gala swallowed the fear lodged in her throat. "I will do as you ask."

"Good. You have made the right choice. I am good to my friends, as you already know."

"I have to go now. I see Seina," she lied.

"Ask her about her visit with Esteban, then take her home. If she gives you any interesting information, call me. Otherwise, show up at the country club at one-thirty, then I will contact you this evening."

Miguel shook hands with everyone on staff at the television station directly following his fifteen-minute interview on the noon news. Afterward, with his fake fiancée at his side, he spoke at length to the huge audience crammed into the small auditorium at the station. He noticed the way she not only kept watch over him, but continuously surveyed the area around them. Everyone seemed as interested in meeting Jennifer as they were in him. But who could blame them? The woman even intrigued him.

The television station was owned by a member of the Nationalist Party who provided Miguel with a weekly interview as well as numerous free one-minute ads that ran often during each twenty-four-hour period. When the reporter doing the interview had asked about Miguel's fiancée, he had been given little choice but to bring her on camera and introduce her to the people of Mocorito. His lovely Jennifer had surprised him. The ease with which she appeared on camera, a warm smile in place and her hand clasping his the whole time, told him that she had done this type of thing before today. She was what the Americans referred to as "a natural."

When asked how she felt about her future husband being a candidate for president, she had replied without missing a beat, "I am very proud of Miguel and support him without reservation. I will do everything within my power to help him become el presidente because I know in my heart how much he loves Mocorito and all the people of this wonderful country."

"Thank you, J.J. I am a fortunate man to have found such a loving and caring helpmate," he had said as he'd gazed lovingly at her.

He had deliberately referred to her as J.J., the nickname that Domingo Shea had told him everyone close to her used. For half a second, she'd reacted, her eyebrows lifting ever so slightly, but then she had simply smiled and continued looking at him as if he were the sun and moon and stars to her.

If he had not known better, he would have believed every sweet word out of her mouth. The lady had been quite convincing, all that he could have asked for in a fiancée. Not only had she shown her support by word and deed, she had presented herself as a fashionable yet conservatively dressed lady. The simple purple suit she wore was accented with pearl earrings and necklace. Her shoes and handbag were a rich, dark purple leather. Everything about her whispered aristocratic sophistication. Understated and elegant.

After the interview ended, he told her in a quiet voice, yet loud enough for everyone around them to hear, "You were perfect."

"Thank you, Miguel."

She gazed at him with those incredible blue-violet eyes and he found himself unable to resist the urge to kiss her. Only at the last minute, with Roberto clearing his throat behind them, did Miguel manage to restrain himself and simply brush her cheek with a tiny peck.

"Miguel, my friend," Mario Lamas, the TV station's owner clamped his hand down on Miguel's shoulder. "The phones have been ringing off the hook. Your lady is a huge success. The people love her." Mario turned to Jennifer, took her hand and kissed it. "You, my dear Señorita Blair, are a definite asset in this election. You must accompany Miguel everywhere from now until election day."

"I plan to do just that, isn't that right, *querido?*" Jennifer slipped her hand into Miguel's. A subtle yet effective sign of affection.

"Absolutely." Miguel confirmed her statement.

"I don't mean to rush you," Roberto said, "but if we are to arrive at the country club at one-thirty, we must leave now."

"Yes, yes, go, go," Mario told them, waving his hands expressively. "And next week, you and your lady will come back here for another interview. Each week until the night before the election, you will speak to the people for an hour. Yes?"

"Yes. Thank you, Mario."

Miguel shook Mario's hand before slipping his arm around Jennifer's waist and, following Roberto, escorting her outside to the waiting limousine. Roberto waited until they were safely ensconced in the back of the limo before he slid inside with them and closed the door.

Knowing what was next on Miguel's schedule, Carlos shifted into Drive and headed the car away from the downtown television station and onto the main thoroughfare that would take them a few miles out of the city limits to Ebano, a suburb of Nava, where many of the up-and-coming middle-class and upper-middle-class citizens lived. Dolores and Emilio had purchased a home in Ebano only six months ago and Juan Esteban lived there with his aunt in one of the older sections of the area that had been updated in recent years.

Once inside the limousine, Miguel had expected Jennifer to move as far away from him as possible. But she didn't. She remained at his side, although several inches separated them.

"You put on quite a performance, Señorita Blair," Roberto said, an odd tone to his voice.

Miguel glowered at him.

"You object, Roberto?" she asked, using his first name, as she would have done had she truly been Miguel's fiancée. "I would think you would approve of the fine acting job I did. We don't want the people to suspect that I'm not only a fraud, but that I am Miguel's bodyguard."

"I apologize if it appeared I was criticizing," Roberto said.

"It sounded that way to me, too," Miguel told him.

"Then I apologize to both of you. I meant it as a compliment, although I admit I was surprised that an American woman, especially one trained as a bodyguard, could so effectively present herself as a lady of breeding."

Jennifer's laughter stopped Miguel from chastising his friend. Undoubtedly she found Roberto's comment amusing.

"You can thank my mother for that aspect of my personality. You see Lenore Ashford Whitney is a lady of breeding and nothing would please her more than to know I am capable of presenting myself as a carbon copy of her when the situation calls for it."

Miguel studied her closely. Those seductive blue-lavender eyes. That mane of shiny black curls. The pouty pink lips. The oval-shaped face, the tiny nose and the translucent, creamy complexion. If he allowed himself the luxury, he could easily fall under her spell. And if other matters were not far more important in his life, he would set about seducing the beautiful Jennifer.

Suddenly, without any warning, a loud bang reverberated through the limousine. The car bounced, then skidded off the

road, onto the shoulder and crashed into the ditch. The wreck
happened so quickly that there was no time to think, only to react.
As the limo came to a jarring halt, Miguel reached out and
grabbed a tumbling J.J. seconds before his left shoulder slammed
painfully against the crushed back door.

Chapter 5

"Phase one has begun," he told his comrade. "I just received a phone call telling me that Miguel Ramirez's limousine has wrecked. It seems a tire blew out and the vehicle is now in a ditch."

Hector Padilla smiled broadly, the corners of his thick black mustache lifting. "Perhaps if Miguel is not afraid for himself, he will soon realize that those near and dear to him are in danger. Since we have no proof his fiancée is a fraud, we can't use that against him. Not yet. And now that she has appeared on television with him, the people seemed to be quite taken with her."

"If Miguel truly cares more for others than himself, then convincing him that the lives of others are in danger because of him could be more effective than trying again to eliminate him."

"With the American bodyguards on duty around the clock, it will be more difficult to strike Miguel himself, so your plan to show him how vulnerable others are was quite brilliant."

"Thank you, Hector. You know there is no one in Mocorito who wishes to see you reelected more than I do."

Hector laughed. "Despite our being friends, I am no fool. What you want, more than anything else, is to see Miguel Ramirez defeated."

"The man does not deserve to be president. He is an upstart. The bastard son of a whore, a man with delusions of grandeur."

Placing his hand on his good friend's shoulder, Hector asked, "And when is the next incident set to occur?"

"There will be a minor incident at the luncheon, if Ramirez makes it to the country club. I have arranged for an unpleasant surprise for his guests. But tonight, at Anton Casimiro's party, we have something more significant planned."

J.J. found herself on top of Miguel after the crash. Everything had happened so quickly that it took her a couple of seconds to get her bearings. The first thing that struck her was her awkward position—her body intimately pressed against Miguel's and his arms securely holding her, one hand cupping her hip.

"What the hell happened?" Miguel spoke first.

"I believe a tire blew out, Señor Ramirez," Carlos said.

"Is everyone all right?" Roberto asked. "Miguel? Señorita Blair?"

"I am unharmed," Miguel replied. He ran his hands over J.J. with gentle familiarity, as if the two were actually a couple. "How are you, Jennifer?"

Looking him square in the eyes, she lifted herself up and off him. Then when she had firmly planted her behind in the seat beside him, she responded. "None the worse for wear."

"I think perhaps we should call a wrecker," Miguel said.

"Good idea." J.J. scooted across the seat and opened the door. "Everyone stay put. I'm going to check the tires, see if one of them did blow out and try to determine the cause."

"Do you suspect foul play?" Roberto asked.

"I assume this limousine is kept in excellent condition," J.J. said. "That being the case, the odds that a tire just blew out are slim to none. I'll bet money that someone using a long-range, high-powered rifle shot the tire."

"If that is the case, then why aim at the tire and not at me?" Miguel asked.

"These windows are tinted." J.J. swirled an index finger around, indicating the darkened windows. "Firing into the vehicle could have resulted in a death, but not necessarily your death."

J.J. hopped out of the car and onto the rocky, uneven ground. Immediately the heels of her shoes dug into the soft, sandy soil. Damn! On any other assignment, she'd be wearing a pair of sensible shoes, but here she was dressed to the nines and forced to climb out of the ditch in two-and-a-half-inch heels. After briefly inspecting all four tires and taking a closer look at the one flat tire, she surmised that her theory about a rifle shot blowing the tire had been correct.

But something didn't add up here. Carlos had been driving the speed limit, which wasn't much more than a slow crawl in afternoon traffic. Why would anyone shoot out a tire and cause a minor accident that was unlikely to result in any major damage to the occupants of the limo? If Miguel was the target, why not shoot at him while he was entering or exiting the television station? Unless "they" knew he was being protected by a bodyguard, who might have taken the bullet in his place. How was it possible that Miguel's enemies knew she was his bodyguard and not his fiancée? She had been told that only Miguel and his two closest associates knew the truth. Roberto was here with them, but that didn't rule him out as a suspect, did it? And Emilio was family. However, family had been known to betray family.

Of course, her theory that Miguel's enemies knew who she really was and why she was posing as Miguel's fiancée was only that—a theory.

As J.J. mulled over the possible scenarios and scanned the area, trying to figure out from which direction the bullet had come, she suddenly noticed that dozens of cars had stopped on the highway and people were heading in their direction. She cursed under her breath.

A rapid barrage of questions flew in her direction. Insistent, concerned questions that demanded answers.

"Is Señor Ramirez all right?"

"Is there anything I can do to help?"

"Has an ambulance been called?"

Before J.J. could respond, Miguel did exactly what she'd told him not to do. He emerged from the limousine, climbed out of the ditch and came straight to her. Putting his arm around her waist, he faced the crowd of concerned citizens.

"We are all well," Miguel told them in his most charming, yet authoritarian voice. "J.J. and I appreciate your concern. Our limousine had a flat tire and my driver was unable to stop the car from going into the ditch. We have called a wrecker, so everything is under control. I am afraid we are causing a traffic jam, so I want all of you to return to your cars and clear the roadway."

One by one, the people returned to their vehicles, all except an elderly man who approached Miguel. J.J. moved to stand between them, but Miguel held her to his side. She glowered at him and whispered, "Let me do my job."

"I know this man." Miguel held out his hand to the silver-haired gentleman. "Uncle Tito, how good to see you. What brought you into the city today?"

"I am returning from a doctor's visit," Tito replied. "Señor Miguel. You are not harmed? You and your lady?"

Miguel shook hands with the old man. "We are fine." He tightened his hold on J.J.'s waist. "Jennifer, I would like to introduce you to an old family friend, Tito Lopez. He is Emilio's great-uncle. Uncle Tito, this is my fiancée, Señorita Jennifer Blair."

Tito's wrinkled face brightened. He nodded and smiled at her cordially. "It is my great pleasure to meet Miguel's lady." He looked to Miguel. "You are on your way to the club for a luncheon, are you not? Our little mother, Dolores, is hosting the event today. It is all she has talked about for weeks now. You cannot disappoint her. Please, allow me to drive you and the *señorita* to Ebano."

"Thank you, Uncle Tito. We would be honored to have you drive us."

J.J. grabbed Miguel's arm and whispered, "I don't think this is a good idea."

"Nonsense," he replied in a hushed voice so that only she could hear. "I trust Uncle Tito implicitly."

Groaning, J.J. accepted defeat, knowing that without creating an unpleasant scene—which would probably accomplish nothing—she had little choice but to go along with what Miguel wanted.

By the time they arrived at the Ebano Country Club, only ten minutes late, everyone there had heard about the accident, which was the story Miguel had told Roberto to issue to the media. Dolores met them at the entrance, tears glistening in her large, dark eyes. She waddled toward them the minute they exited Uncle Tito's old car.

"Tell me that you are unharmed." Dolores threw her arms around Miguel and hugged him as closely as her round belly would allow.

"I am fine." He held her away from him, far enough to kiss her first on one cheek and then the other. "Jennifer and I are both unharmed. It was only a flat tire. I left Roberto with Carlos to wait for the wrecker."

"Only a flat tire?" Dolores looked at J.J. "Is he telling me the truth?"

Miguel put his arms around Dolores's shoulders and then J.J.'s. "Come along, ladies. We have kept our guests waiting long enough."

Dolores did not protest, but she glanced in J.J.'s direction, the look in her eyes telling J.J. that the two of them would talk later.

When they entered the main dining room of the Ebano Country Club, the hundred-plus women assembled rose to their feet and applauded. J.J. found herself immediately swept up in the moment, becoming a part of the enthusiasm, reluctantly seeing Miguel through his admirers' eyes. Their adoration was real, almost worshipful. How could this many women admire and support a man unless he had numerous redeeming qualities? Had she misjudged him? Or had he simply enchanted his female followers with his good looks and charm? Surely this many women weren't all susceptible to such superficial qualities. But then again the Mocoritian women were different from American women. They were more old-fashioned, more accustomed to men ruling the roost, so to speak.

The group consisted of women of various ages, ranging from the early twenties to elderly ladies with white hair. But, to a woman, they looked at Miguel as if he could walk on water. No wonder he possessed such an air of confidence, even cockiness. This kind of adoration could easily go to a man's head.

When they reached the raised podium where Miguel's table had been placed, J.J. noted there were five chairs and five place settings. Two women were already seated at the table. One she instantly recognized—Zita Fuentes, the auburn-haired beauty who had been at Miguel's home when J.J. and Dom arrived last night. The lovely widow watched J.J., not Miguel, her dark eyes studying J.J. as if she were a specimen under a microscope.

Sizing up the competition? Was Señora Fuentes more than a friend and political supporter? Did she see J.J. as a rival?

Reaching down to grasp J.J.'s hand, Miguel paused and spoke to Señora Fuentes. Nothing more than a cordial hello and thank you for being here today. J.J. sensed an odd tension between the two and knew she had guessed correctly. If there wasn't something intimate between these two, then one or both of them wished there was.

Miguel led J.J. to the other side of the table where an elderly woman, rather regal in appearance, sat. When they drew nearer, a warm smile appeared instantly on her weathered face.

"Dear Aunt Josephina." Miguel leaned down and kissed the woman on the cheek.

She grasped his hand and looked directly at J.J. "And this must be your fiancée. Introduce us, dear boy."

"Aunt Josephina, may I introduce my betrothed, Señorita Jennifer Blair." He lifted J.J.'s hand to his lips and kissed it. "*Querida,* this is my friend, Juan Esteban's aunt, Señora Josephina Esteban y de la Romero viuda Santiago."

"I am delighted to meet you." Josephina inspected J.J. closely. "You have done well, Miguel. She is lovely." The good doctor's aunt concentrated her sharp gaze on J.J.'s face. "I assume you are madly in love with our Miguel, as we all are. He is irresistible, is he not?"

"Yes, Señora Santiago, I am madly in love with him and I found him irresistible the moment we first met."

Nodding approval, Aunt Josephina laughed. "You are a brave woman to marry such a beloved man. You know you will have to share him with his people for the rest of your lives."

"I'm not jealous of Miguel's love for his people." J.J. said what she thought this old woman would want to hear. "Knowing how deeply he cares for his country, for his people, only makes me love him all the more."

"Ah-ha! Now, I know why you have chosen this rare gem to be the first lady of Mocorito." Aunt Josephina reached out and grasped J.J.'s hand. "Take good care of him, dear child. He is the hope for the future of this country. Give him many fine sons."

J.J. had to struggle to keep her smile in place. This dear old lady had no idea that her last comment had struck a nerve in J.J., reminding her that men like Miguel—and men like her own father—wanted sons. Appreciated sons. Loved sons.

Miguel wrapped his arm around J.J.'s shoulders again. "Every man wants a son, Aunt Josephina, but I want a daughter, also."

"Of course you would want a daughter, wouldn't you?" Josephina smiled. "Jennifer, my dear, if you give him a daughter, beware. A little girl will wrap this one around her little finger."

J.J. felt as if a huge boulder had been lifted from her chest and she was able to breathe freely again. She had never expected Miguel to express any desire for a daughter or that this old woman who seemed to know him so well would believe Miguel could be beguiled by a little girl of his own.

"Sit down, sit down." Dolores motioned to them. "I will introduce you and then you must introduce Jennifer as you did on the newscast earlier today."

The next hour seemed surreal to J.J. from the second round of unrestrained applause for Miguel, to his glowing introduction of her as his fiancée. Because he appeared to be besotted with her, his loyal supporters accepted her wholeheartedly. She couldn't help wondering how their breakup, after the election, would affect his popularity with his constituents. The best thing for him to do would be to lay all the blame at her feet, to accuse her of not being the woman he'd thought she was, of running off and leaving him when he needed her most. If he did that, he'd probably have women coming out of the woodwork eager and willing to offer him comfort.

Although everyone had been exceptionally nice to her, J.J. felt uneasy. With her stomach muscles tied in knots and her mind swirling with unexplained apprehension, she nibbled at her delicious lunch. Call it a sixth sense or just gut instinct, but she had the strangest feeling that something was wrong—or soon would be. But nothing seemed out of place. She did her best not to be obvious as she surveyed the dining room, the women in attendance and the numerous waiters and waitresses. This entire event was a security agent's nightmare. But without a staff of agents and a client willing to accept his vulnerability, there was little she could do except stick to Miguel like glue.

As she picked at her dessert, some elaborate chocolate concoction, and listened while Miguel made small talk with the others at their table, a sick feeling hit her in the pit of her belly. Like an animal whose hackles had risen, she sensed danger.

Then it happened.

Someone screamed.

J.J.'s first thought was to protect Miguel.

She shot out of her chair and prepared to hurl herself at him and knock him out of his chair and onto the floor. However, he grabbed her and pulled her down into his lap, as if he intended to protect her, not the other way around.

"Wait." He spoke only that one word.

Another scream echoed from the back of the room. And then another.

"Snakes!" several women cried out.

"There are snakes crawling around on the floor," Dolores cried. "Look. See them. There."

"My God!" Josephina gasped. "Are they poisonous snakes? Does anyone know?"

"There must be at least a dozen of them," Zita Fuentes said. "Someone must do something immediately."

Before she could stop him, Miguel came up out of his chair and planted J.J. on the floor, then barreled off the podium and into the audience. Standing quickly, J.J. jumped off the podium right behind him, landing haphazardly on her high heels. She almost smacked into his back when he stopped abruptly to study one of the slithering creatures near his feet.

With women screaming, some climbing on their chairs, a few already on top of the tables and others trying to escape through the nearest exits, which seemed blocked by even more snakes, Miguel picked up one of the reptiles.

Smiling as he held the cold-blooded creature in his hand, Miguel called out in a loud, clear voice. "They are not poisonous. Please stay calm. These are hognose snakes. They're harmless."

"They're not poisonous?" J.J. eased out from behind him and, avoiding the snake he still held, came to his side.

He shook his head. "Completely harmless, but they seemed to have served their purpose." He glanced around at the panicked women. "Someone released these snakes to make a point."

"To show you how vulnerable you are, how easily they can get to you," J.J. said. "The same reason they shot out the tire earlier today. Scare tactics."

The country club's manager and male members of the staff rushed into the dining room. When they saw the snakes slithering around on the floor, several men balked, but when Miguel assured them the reptiles were harmless, they set about capturing the creatures. Miguel handed over his captive to the manager.

In her peripheral vision, J.J. caught a glimpse of a tall, slender brunette in a striking hot-pink dress as she bent down and grasped one of the snakes and handed it to a waiter. Only after the fact did J.J. realize that Miguel had seen the incident, and now the attractive woman was smiling at him as she walked toward him.

"A fearless woman," Miguel said to her as she approached them.

"Señor Ramirez…" She held out her slender, well-manicured hand to Miguel. "What a shame that someone had to play such a dreadful prank and ruin the luncheon for everyone."

Miguel kissed the woman's hand. She batted her long eyelashes at him and smiled coyly.

"A day is never ruined when I make the acquaintance of such a lovely and brave lady. I am afraid you have me at a disadvantage," Miguel said. "You know who I am, but I do not know who you are."

"I am Gala Hernandez."

"It is my pleasure, *señorita*. It is *señorita*, is it not?"

She giggled. The silly woman actually giggled. J.J. glared at her.

"I'm Jennifer Blair, Miguel's fiancée." J.J. stuck out her hand.

Gala glanced at J.J.'s hand, but quickly returned her attention to Miguel. "I must tell you, before someone else does, that I have ties to the enemy camp."

Miguel lifted an inquisitive eyebrow.

J.J. tensed.

"Your sister…your half-sister, Seina, is my oldest and dearest friend."

Getting close enough to brush her shoulder against Miguel's, she lowered her voice to a whisper, making it difficult for J.J. to hear what she was saying. So J.J. pressed up against Miguel's other side.

"Your sister secretly supports your bid for the presidency," Gala told him. "She does not dare speak publicly on your behalf. I am certain you can understand. So, she has sent me in her place."

Miguel eyed the woman suspiciously. Good for him, J.J. thought. At least he's not buying her story hook, line and sinker. For all they knew, Gala Hernandez could be a spy for the enemy camp.

"Please tell Seina that I appreciate her support and when I am president, I hope that she will be able to publicly acknowledge me as her brother."

"I am sure that is her heartfelt wish," Gala said.

"Miguel, *querido…*" J.J. tugged on his arm. "I do not mean to take you away from a new convert, but you really should make a statement to the ladies who are still here, then we need to contact Roberto and Carlos to make arrangements for a car to pick us up. We're due at St. Augustine's in less than an hour."

"Oh, please, allow me to drive you back to Nava," Gala said. "It would be my honor."

J.J. groaned internally. Bad idea, she wanted to shout, but kept quiet. Surely, Miguel would decline the woman's offer.

"How very kind of you, Señorita Hernandez. Thank you. But I am sure my driver has arranged for another car and will soon arrive to pick us up."

J.J. breathed a sigh of relief and looked at Miguel with new respect.

* * *

A crew of news people had followed Jennifer and him as Juan introduced them to the children at St. Augustine's. His lovely fake fiancée had shown genuine compassion and caring for the residents of the pediatric ward and somehow he had not been the least surprised to find that the lady had quite a way with children. The little ones had responded to her warm smile and gentle touch.

After returning home, both of them weary from the events of the long day, J.J. had gone upstairs to his bedroom suite and was now soaking in his marble bathtub. But he was not alone. Per J.J.'s instructions, Domingo Shea stayed at his side.

"Whenever I can't be with you, Dom will be. After all, he is supposed to be your cousin and there's no reason for anyone to be suspicious when he's often with you."

Miguel had called in Emilio and Roberto to discuss the two possibly unrelated incidents that had plagued him today. A rifleman shooting out one of the limousine tires and someone releasing a dozen hognose snakes at the Ebano Country Club luncheon. Neither had been life-threatening, although each had been momentarily unnerving.

"What information do you have for us about the limousine?" Miguel asked Roberto. "You kept the incident confidential, as I asked."

"We took the car to a trusted auto shop," Roberto replied. "The tire has been replaced and some of our people are running a check on the bullet. Señorita Blair was correct about the tire being shot by a rifle."

"For what purpose?" Miguel glanced from one man to the other.

"To scare you?" Roberto suggested.

"To make a point," Dom said.

"And that point is what? That they could take a shot at me anytime they choose and there's nothing I can do about it. We already knew that."

"Dolores was very upset by what happened at the club," Emilio told them. "If shooting out the tire on the limo was to scare you, to make a point, what did they hope to accomplish by letting a dozen hognose snakes loose in the dining room during your luncheon?"

"Once again, to make a point," Dom said.

"And perhaps to make a laughingstock of you," Emilio added.

"No, there is more to it than their wanting to show me that they can reach out and touch me at their will. The assassination attempt already proved that is possible." Miguel feared the real reason was far more frightening, but he hesitated voicing his thoughts aloud.

"You can't have overlooked the obvious," Dom said as his gaze connected with Miguel's, the two men sharing a silent acknowledgment.

"And that would be?" Roberto asked.

"They already know that I am willing to put my life on the line, that they cannot frighten me into withdrawing my candidacy," Miguel said. "But what if, now, they want to see if I'm willing to risk the lives of others?"

"You can't mean that you think—" Emilio's eyes widened in shock.

"I think only that it is a possibility." Miguel grimaced. He prayed he was wrong. What if he had to choose between the presidency and the safety of the people he loved? What would he do if he was forced to make that kind of decision?

Chapter 6

J.J. had intended to soak in the tub for no more than ten minutes. But she had stayed twenty before reluctantly getting out, drying off and putting on her silk robe. Now, she had to choose the proper attire for tonight's dinner party. Miguel had told her that it was not a formal affair, that he wouldn't be wearing a tuxedo, only a suit and tie and suggested she wear something suitable for a cocktail party. As she stood inside the huge walk-in closet, flipping through her choices that hung alongside Miguel's numerous suits, she thought about today's events. While she'd been soaking in the tub, she had deliberately erased all thoughts from her mind, concentrating on total relaxation. If the blown tire and the fiasco with the snakes were any indication of how tonight's dinner party would play out, then she had to be prepared for just about anything. It appeared that Miguel's enemies were trying a new tactic.

Perhaps the first assassination attempt had been solely to frighten him into withdrawing from the race—which it hadn't—

and now they were showing him they could get to anyone at anytime, could easily harm his friends and family. That was the most reasonable explanation for what had happened today. But what if they also knew Miguel now had a bodyguard, posing as his fiancée? There would be no way they could prove such an accusation, even if they knew it for a fact. And if they knew the truth about J.J., that meant someone very close to Miguel had leaked the information. She felt certain that if she mentioned her suspicions to Miguel, he would defend Emilio and Roberto with every breath in him. Being a loyal man himself—and she instinctively felt this—Miguel would trust his two closest friends, would never question their allegiance to him. But she would and did question their loyalty. After all, it was her job, wasn't it, to distrust everyone associated with Miguel?

"Jennifer?" Miguel called to her from the bedroom.

Her heart lurched halfway out of her chest. Damn, she had to stop reacting like an idiot every time he got near her.

"I'm in the dressing room, choosing something to wear to tonight's dinner party."

"Before you choose, come out here, please. I have something for you, something that may help you make a final decision about your attire for Anton's party."

Taking a deep, get-hold-of-yourself-girl breath, J.J. tightened the belt on her robe, opened the dressing-room door and walked into the bedroom. Miguel had removed his jacket and tie and undone the first three buttons of his shirt, thus revealing a peek of the dark curling hair on his chest. She was so engrossed in his handsome face, his charming smile and his to-die-for body that at first she didn't notice the jeweler's case he held in his hand.

"What's that?" she asked.

"A gift from Nava Jewelers," he replied. "An engagement gift for you."

"You—you bought me a gift?" She froze half a room away from him, unable to make her feet move any farther.

"It would be expected," he told her.

"When did you have time to—"

"I telephoned them this morning and placed a specific order." He held out the large jeweler's case."

Move feet, damn you, move! Taking slow, deliberate steps, she made her way across the room and when she neared him, she held out her hands and accepted the gift. When she opened the case, she noted that there were three smaller cases nestled inside, one obviously a ring box. Her heart did a nervous pitter-patter. Several years ago, she had sworn to herself that if she ever did find a man she wanted to marry, she would tell him that if he wore a wedding band, she would, but that she did not want a fancy engagement ring. She'd been engaged once, had worn her fiancé's one-carat diamond solitary for several months before coming to her senses and breaking things off with the man her mother had chosen for her.

J.J. flipped open the lid on the ring box. Her mouth gaped as she gasped silently. Oh, my God! The center jewel was an oval-cut amethyst, at least four carats, and was surrounded by small half-carat diamonds. A ring that size should have been gaudy and ostentatious . But it wasn't. It was exquisite, like a ring belonging to a princess.

"Miguel, this is…"

"You don't like it?"

She glanced up at him. "No, I mean yes, of course, I like it. It's exquisite."

"It will be expected," he told her by way of an explanation.

"Yes, certainly. I understand."

"Here, let me help you." He reached out and removed the ring from its velvet bed. While she held the large case in her right hand, he took her left hand, held it up and slipped the ring on her third finger. "Ah, a perfect fit. And the perfect ring for you. If only there was a touch more blue in the gem, it would match your beautiful eyes."

Oh, please, don't say something like that to me. She might not be a silly, gullible woman, easily influenced by flattery, but she was discovering that she wasn't completely immune to Miguel's Latin charm.

"That's a good line," she told him. "Very convincing. It's something you must tell people when they aah and ooh over the ring."

"Yes, you are correct. If I repeat that line, everyone will be convinced that I adore you." He snapped open the lids on the other two boxes within the jeweler's case. "The necklace and earrings are an engagement present. Everyone will expect to see you wearing them tonight and for every special occasion from now until our wedding."

The earrings and necklace were diamonds. Breathtakingly beautiful diamonds, the settings simple and classic.

"I am told that diamonds, like pearls, go with anything a woman chooses to wear," he said.

"Yes, you're right. That's exactly what my mother always said. A woman can wear pearls or diamonds with a designer gown or with a pair of blue jeans."

"Later, when you are dressed for the evening—" His eyes raked over her silk robe, lingering on her pebble-hard nipples "—if you need my help with the catch on the necklace, let me know." His gaze locked with hers.

A tingling sensation spiraled out from her central core and radiated through her body. No wonder the man was such a successful politician. He possessed an overabundance of charisma.

"I…yes, thank you."

They stood there and stared at each other for what seemed like endless minutes. Finally Miguel broke the silence.

"Ramona has unpacked and put away your things satisfactorily?" he asked.

"Oh, yes. Yes, thank you."

"Will you require a maid to help you prepare for this evening?"

"Huh?"

He smiled, apparently amused with her puzzlement.

"An unnecessary question, I'm sure. I cannot imagine you would want someone to assist you in dressing."

"Oh, no. You're right about that." She chuckled softly. "Even my mother doesn't have a lady's maid."

"Most of the younger women in Mocorito do not use lady's maids, either, only the older ladies, such as my father's wife and her kind."

J.J. caught just a hint of resentment in his voice, a subtle trace of ridicule. "You're not old-fashioned about everything, are you?"

He eyed her questioningly. "You consider me old-fashioned?" He shook his head. "The people of Mocorito think of me as a very modern man, even a liberal to some degree."

"You—a liberal?" J.J. laughed out loud.

"And what do you find so amusing about that?"

"In America you would be considered an old-fashioned, conservative, male chauvinist. But surely you know that since you went to college at Harvard."

"But we are not in America, my dear J.J. We are in Mocorito and only in the past twenty years have women been allowed to vote. And only the younger generation of women have been allowed the freedom of choosing their husbands, although some, such as my half-sister, are trapped by the old traditions imposed on them by their parents and grandparents. One of the things I want to change, when I am president, is women's rights."

J.J.'s mouth fell open in astonishment. "You're kidding me?"

"I assure you that I am not."

She stared at him, searching his face for the truth. Why should he lie to her? "I thought you didn't approve of aggressive, pushy women? Aren't you the man who is passing me off as his fiancée because he doesn't want anyone to know that he has a female bodyguard? Aren't I suppose to be demure and ladylike at all times?"

"This is like asking me if I am a man. Yes, I prefer my women gentle and accommodating and I would like a wife who would allow me to, as you Americans say, wear the pants in the family. Men, like countries, do not change overnight. We change gradually. Mocorito will never be like America, but we can be a country where our women have equal rights. Who knows, perhaps one day my daughter or granddaughter will be president of Mocorito."

"Who are you and what have you done with Miguel Ramirez?" she asked jokingly.

Before she realized what he intended to do, he reached out and caressed her cheek with the back of his hand. A non-threatening gesture. A gentle touch, yet all the more seductive because of the gentleness. He brought his hand down the side of her neck and held it there. Her pulse throbbed against his fingertips.

"I suspect that I do not know you any better than you do me, *señorita*." He held her captive with his hypnotic gaze. "We have preconceived ideas of who the other is and in reality, we are strangers who do not know what is in each other's heart."

She couldn't speak, but managed to nod agreement with what he'd said.

Miguel removed his hand, but kept his gaze locked with hers. "If you have a little black dress in your wardrobe, wear that tonight…with the diamonds I gave you."

He turned and walked toward the bathroom.

"Miguel," she called after him.

He paused and glanced over his shoulder. "Yes?"

"You do realize that there is a good chance that something else could be planned for tonight, another incident in the same vein as the blown tire and the snakes at the luncheon."

"Yes, of course. But I am unafraid. I have a bodyguard to protect me."

With that said, he went into the bathroom and shut the door. Momentarily dazed, J.J. stood there, uncertain whether she should laugh or tell him to go to hell.

Why was it that she had such conflicting emotions where this man was concerned? One minute she found herself as suscepti-ble to his charm as any other woman and the next minute she wanted to kick his butt for being such a…a man! What was it about Miguel that affected her so strongly? It wasn't as if she hadn't known her share of swaggering males with egos the size of Texas. She'd been a soldier's daughter and had learned first-hand what being a he-man was all about, learned from the mas-ter himself—Rudd Blair. And from the age of twelve, when she'd blossomed into a bosomy girl who had inherited her moth-er's beauty, but none of her Southern-belle femininity, she'd been fighting off male advances. To her mother's dismay, J.J. had spent more time trying to earn her father's approval by acting like one of the guys than she had in learning the art of being a femme fatale.

No matter how attracted she was to Miguel, she was not going to give in to her baser instincts. She had managed to stay in charge of every relationship in her life—except the one with her father—and there was no way in hell she would allow this South American Romeo to seduce her.

Even if you want to be seduced? an inner voice asked.

After answering his cell phone, Dom Shea walked outside into the center courtyard of Miguel's home. The lush, tropical gar-den surrounded him as he sat on the stone bench several feet away from the house.

"Are you alone?" Vic Noble asked. "Can you talk?"

"I'm alone, but even if one of the servants overhears my end of the conversation, they won't know what I was saying. None of them speak English."

"Are you sure?"

"I asked Ramirez. He should know."

"He should, but… Does he know that his good friend, Dr. Juan Esteban, has been having secret rendezvous with his half-sister, Seina Fernandez?"

"Hmm… Interesting. If he knows, he hasn't mentioned it to me or to J.J."

"He should be told," Vic said. "It's possible that the half-sister is using Dr. Esteban to gain inside information. Or it's possible that the good doctor is a traitor."

"Have you checked out Emilio Lopez and Roberto Aznar? On the surface, each man seems to be devoted to Ramirez, but—"

"Lopez has been Ramirez's best friend since they were boys and now they're family. I've found out nothing, at least not yet, that would implicate either Lopez or Aznar. But my sources tell me that the Federalists know J.J. is Miguel's bodyguard."

"That means there is a traitor in Ramirez's camp," Dom replied. "Someone close."

"Find out if he or Lopez or Aznar has told anyone else about J.J.'s true identity. If they haven't, then either there's a leak on our end—meaning the CIA—or one of Ramirez's best friends has sold him out."

"What does Will Pierce think?"

"I haven't made contract with Pierce since we arrived in Mocorito. We're supposed to meet up tomorrow. But I already know what he'll say. He'll assure me that none of his people have leaked the info because our government sending Dundee agents into Mocorito was top-secret and on a strictly need-to-know basis."

"Have you come up with anything on the shooter? Any names? Any links to the Federalists?

"I have a few names and I'll be checking them out, one by one. But so far, that's it. My guess is any ties between the shooter and the Federalist Party are invisible. Proving a connection will more than likely be impossible."

"We had a couple of odd incidents today." Dom explained about the blown tire and the snakes.

"Kid stuff. Especially the snakes. That was more of a prank than anything else. What's your take on it?"

"I'm holding off judgment until after we see how tonight's dinner party at Anton Casimiro's penthouse goes. J.J. and I will be on alert, but not knowing for sure what sort of game our opponents are playing puts us at a disadvantage."

"Are you going to the party?"

"Yes, Ramirez invited me."

"Y'all won't know whether to expect a potentially dangerous attack or another prank of some sort."

"The only thing we can do is make sure Ramirez is safe."

"Yep, that's your job." Vic chuckled. "How's our J.J. handling playing the dutiful, subservient fiancée?"

"If I didn't know better, I'd swear she's taken to it like a duck to water."

"You're kidding!"

"Hey, Ramirez is good-looking, charming, rich and powerful. That's a combination that any woman would find hard to resist."

"J.J. isn't just any woman," Vic reminded him. "Her hobby seems to be cutting men down to size, even guys like Ramirez."

"I'd say in this case, the odds are fifty-fifty as to who will wind up cutting the other down to size."

J.J. surprised him. He had been certain when he'd asked her to wear a little black dress this evening, she would deliberately choose the exact opposite. If he'd bet on her actions, he would have lost.

She stood at the top of the stairs looking like a beautiful princess. His princess. No, not a princess, a first lady. El presidente's lady. He and Dom Shea watched her as she descended the stairs, her Dundee partner apparently as entranced by her as Miguel was.

Luscious red lipstick stained her full, pouty lips, making her creamy skin appear even lighter than it was. Her dress was black, a classic style, with a rounded neckline that showed just a hint of décolletage and a hem that stopped an inch below her knees and showed off her shapely calves encased in black silk stockings. The dress fit her as if it had been molded to her body, yet was not skintight. She had brushed her short, curly hair behind her ears to show off the diamond earrings. The delicate diamond necklace sparkled around her slender neck.

It was at that moment that Miguel knew he had never seen anything more beautiful in his entire life. Jennifer was truly beauty personified. He wanted her with a desperate passion.

And he would have her!

"Good evening." She glanced from Dom to Miguel, then as if sensing the desire raging inside him, she turned her gaze back on her fellow Dundee agent.

"What did you do, rob a jewelry store?" Dom stared at her diamonds.

She touched the shimmering necklace. "I'm wearing engagement gifts from my fiancée." She wiggled her ring finger in front of him.

Dom let out a long, low whistle. "Aren't you a lucky girl."

"I'm pretending to be."

Miguel cleared his throat. The easy camaraderie between Dom Shea and Jennifer bothered him. Admit the truth, he thought to himself. You are jealous of Dom. Of any man who is her friend.

Ignoring Miguel completely, J.J. asked Dom in English, "I assume you're carrying a weapon, right? The gun Miguel provided for me is in my handbag."

"You are both expecting something unpleasant to happen tonight?" Miguel asked, also in English.

"Possibly," Dom replied.

"Probably," J.J. added.

"I will be among friends and supporters. I doubt Anton will have invited anyone who would attempt—"

"You were surrounded by admirers at the Ebano Country Club today and yet somehow, someway, a dozen snakes were released in the dining room and created havoc," J.J. quickly reminded him.

"Then you expect another silly prank?" Miguel asked.

"We don't know what to expect," Dom said.

"Before we leave, let me remind you that if anything does happen, I'm your bodyguard," J.J. told him. "It's my job to protect you, not the other way around. Do you understand?"

"Yes, I understand. But as a man, it is simply my nature automatically to protect a woman."

"Don't think of me as a woman," she told him. "Think of me only as your protector."

"I will try, Señorita Blair, but it will not be easy."

When J.J. caught a glimpse, in her peripheral vision, of Dom grinning, she cast him a don't-you-dare-laugh glare.

"Shall we go?" J.J. slipped her arm through Miguel's.

Dom followed them outside to the limousine. Carlos stood by the open door, waiting for them. J.J. steeled her nerves as she slid into the limo. She didn't know which concerned her most—her irrational attraction to Miguel or not knowing what might happen at tonight's dinner party.

Anton Casimiro's penthouse apartment in downtown Nava was large and lavishly decorated with the best money could buy. Tonight, the crowd gathered here were all avid supporters of Miguel Ramirez, many devout Nationalists and others simply new converts to the party because of their admiration for the beguiling Ramirez.

How Diego had managed to acquire an invitation for her tonight, Gala did not know. And she dared not ask. She was here on an assignment, one Diego expected her to carry out without fail. All she knew was that she had an accomplice who would actually do the deed, but she carried the means of accomplishing that deed in her purse.

"You will carry this purse tonight." Diego had handed her the designer, one-of-a-kind, cobalt-blue leather handbag, etched with a floral design in burgundy thread. "You will leave your purse wherever the other ladies leave their bags. After that, you are free to enjoy yourself. Flirt with Ramirez. If you can draw him away from his fiancée, all the better. It would be amusing if you could place him in a compromising situation."

"That should not pose a problem. He was very attentive when I met him at the country club today."

"Be careful not to give yourself away." Diego had grasped her chin and clamped his fingers harshly into her cheeks. "Ramirez is no fool. If he smells a trap, he will run. Or he will turn on you."

She knew what she had to do. She had already left her purse with the other ladies' purses and was now free to search for amusement. If she could not seduce Miguel, then she would turn her attention to someone in his group of close confidantes. Emilio Lopez perhaps. With his wife fat as a cow at present, he should be easily seduced. If not, there was always Roberto Aznar. There was a smoldering sensuality about the man that intrigued her.

As she made her way through the crowd milling about drinking and nibbling on hors d' oeuvres, she heard someone shout, "He's here."

Standing on tiptoe for a better view of the foyer, Gala Hernandez frowned the moment she saw the way Miguel's fiancée clung to his arm, her gaze glued to him with rapt attention. Miguel looking at her adoringly. Jennifer Blair might be beautiful, but how talented was she in the bedroom? Gala did not know any man who could resist the promise of oral sex. As soon as she could get near enough to Miguel, she knew exactly what she would whisper in his ear.

Chapter 7

Having acquired a guest list for this evening's event, J.J. knew before she arrived that this would be a buffet-style dinner instead of the sit-down meal she had hoped it would be. A sit-down dinner usually limited the number to twenty or less, whereas with a buffet, the guest list could swell to fifty or more. From the wall-to-wall people she saw when they first entered Anton Casimiro's spacious penthouse apartment in the heart of Nava, J.J. surmised that there were already a good fifty people in the huge living room/dining room combined. There had been no way she and Dom could check out the apartment beforehand, which they would have done on any normal assignment. And with a crowd this size, they would have used at least two more agents disguised as guests to mix and mingle. Although a part of her mind was immersed in her role of playing Miguel's fiancée, the protector side of her personality told her to stay alert, to be vigilant and prepared for anything.

Dom came up behind her and spoke quietly into her ear. "You

stay with Miguel. I'll start mingling and look things over. My gut tells me that we're in for a surprise, and probably not a pleasant one, before the evening ends."

She nodded and smiled. And kept her hand securely in Miguel's. She had no intention of letting him out of her sight, not even for a minute. In a crowd this size, it would be easy to become separated. And that's all an assassin would need—one unguarded moment.

As they entered the lounge, heads turned. Hushed whispers blended with the chatter, laughter and tinkling of wineglasses. Dom eased away from them and made his way practically unobserved into the crowd. Suddenly a hefty, bearded man wearing a flamboyant orange silk shirt burst through the crowd and, with arms outstretched, came zooming toward them. Thankful that she knew what their host looked like, J.J. tried to relax when Anton Casimiro encompassed both Miguel and her in a bear hug. When he pulled back, laughing, his dark eyes twinkling with mischief, Anton sized J.J. up and then grabbed her hand. After kissing her hand, he held it and while looking right at her, spoke to Miguel.

"You lucky devil, you," Anton said. "Your fiancée is the most delectable creature I have ever seen." He kissed her hand again, then told her, "If he ever disappoints you in any way, come to me, lovely lady, and I will be very good to you."

Accepting Anton's flirting in the good-natured way she was sure he had intended it, J.J. responded in kind. "I will certainly keep your offer in mind, *señor.*" She cuddled closer to Miguel. "But I know, in my heart, that Miguel will never disappoint me. In any way." She winked at Anton.

The world-famous tenor laughed boisterously. "Come, come. Everyone is eager to see you. Both of you."

When Anton led them from the edge of the foyer and into the lounge, the other guests applauded and several called out his name in a resounding cheer.

"You must say a few words," Anton suggested.

Keeping his arm around J.J.'s waist, Miguel held up his other arm, signaling the guests to end their exuberant welcome. But only after he began speaking did the round of applause and cheering cease.

"Thank you, one and all, for being here tonight." He gazed lovingly at J.J. "Jennifer and I look forward to speaking personally to everyone. But this is a dinner party, not a political rally. Let's eat and drink and enjoy one another's company."

J.J. saw the woman halfway across the room, her gaze riveted to Miguel. Damn, how had she finagled an invitation? Her name wasn't on the guest list. Undoubtedly she had persuaded some man—any man—to bring her here tonight as his date. If J.J. thought that Gala Fernandez's interest in Miguel was only personal, she wouldn't be as concerned. But all her instincts and training told her that there was more to Señorita Fernandez's sudden appearances in Miguel's life than met the eye. Although she'd been giddy and flirtatious this afternoon at the country club, the lady had also seemed slightly nervous. And tonight, as Gala gazed at Miguel, J.J. thought she saw something more than desire in the woman's expression. But she wasn't certain if that barely concealed emotion was fear, anger or concern.

When a waiter approached with a tray of champagne flutes, J.J. accepted a glass, as did Miguel. But before either could take the first sip, several people cornered them and immediately gushed and gooed over Miguel. They were true fans, pledging their allegiance to the Nationalist Party and promising their full support for Miguel, not only with their votes, but with their checkbooks.

While Miguel made small talk with his admirers, J.J. stayed right at his side, commenting occasionally when she thought it appropriate, always keeping in mind that she was playing the part of the demure, steadfast helpmate. In fact, while Miguel charmed the guests, she was worrying about the wine, the food and the catering staff. Emilio and Roberto had assured Miguel that the guest list, the caterers and the musicians for Anton's party had been thoroughly checked out and, to-a-person, no one posed a threat. No one had any ties whatsoever to the Federalists Party.

No one except Gala Hernandez, who had not been on the guest list.

How easy it would be to poison Miguel's drink or his food. And even though Anton had promised that each musician and caterer would be inspected before entering his apartment, it might be possible for one of the hired help for tonight's shindig to manage to smuggle in a weapon.

What about the guests themselves? J.J. asked herself as she continued smiling graciously while Miguel shmoozed with his constituents. Gala probably wasn't the only person here who had finagled her way in, coming along as the date of an invited guest. However, considering that the woman wore a skintight red dress, J.J. doubted there was a concealed weapon on her.

Glancing over the throng of celebrators, J.J. searched for anyone who looked the least bit suspicious. As her gaze surveyed the room, she noticed Dom mixing and mingling, doing just what she was doing—hoping to spot potential trouble. Preventing a disaster of any kind would have been so much easier if the Dundee agency was in charge. Having to placate Miguel's ego and allow Emilio and Roberto to make decisions they were not trained to make undermined the Dundee agents' efficiency. Having to do things Miguel's way made their job ten times more difficult.

J.J. recognized only a few people. Roberto had escorted Señora Fuentes and the two seemed quite chummy where they stood in the corner, sipping champagne and gazing into each other's eyes. Across the room, seated on one of the three sofas, Josephina Santiago appeared deep in conversation with her nephew, Juan Esteban. Here and there, J.J. saw a vaguely familiar face, a few women she'd met at the country club earlier today and some people from campaign headquarters this morning. Emilio had phoned to tell them he and Dolores would not attend tonight since Dolores was still quite shaken by the snake prank at the club.

For a man who knew his life was in danger, Miguel appeared calm, cool and collected. Was he really not concerned about his own welfare or did he think he was invincible? Perhaps neither. He was a man with a mission that apparently meant more to him than anything else on earth. Even more than his own life?

When Gala Fernandez walked straight toward them, J.J. tensed. She tried to tell herself that the knot in her gut was there because she didn't trust Gala, that she feared the woman was dangerous. But when Gala smiled at Miguel and placed her hand on his arm, J.J. realized she was jealous. The idea hit her like a bolt from the blue. She did not want this woman—or any other woman—touching Miguel in a familiar way.

This is totally unacceptable, she warned herself. It was only natural to feel protective of a client, but what she felt went way beyond the norm. She felt not only protective, but possessive. The inner primitive female inside her was screaming, Hands off, bitch, he's my man.

"Good evening, Miguel." Gala all but purred as she ran her hand down his arm. "I am utterly delighted to see you twice in one day." She ran the tip of her tongue over her lips.

Oh, get real, J.J. thought. How obvious could a woman be? She'd practically propositioned Miguel—and with his fiancée clinging to his arm. And clinging was just what J.J. was doing. Realizing she was holding on a little too tightly, she loosened her grasp.

"Señorita Hernandez, you look lovely tonight." Miguel's arm around J.J.'s waist tautened, drawing her closer. "Almost as lovely as my beautiful Jennifer." As if it were the most natural action in the world, he leaned down and kissed J.J.'s temple.

Skyrockets went off in her belly, surprising her. No, actually shocking her. Good grief, she had to get a grip. What was wrong with her? Feeling jealousy over a man she barely knew. Going weak in the knees because he kissed her forehead.

Gala's smile vanished for a moment, but she recovered quickly and replaced the genuine smile with a phony one. "You are a very fortunate woman, Señorita Blair, to have such a devoted fiancé."

"I am the lucky one." Miguel lifted J.J.'s hand and held it over his heart.

"If you will excuse me, I see my date is looking for me." Gala quietly slipped away and hurried over to a short, stout man in his midforties, someone she had apparently taken advantage of in order for her to attend tonight's dinner party. Poor fool. He probably had no idea what a sucker he was.

"You laid it on a little thick, didn't you?" J.J. removed her hand from Miguel's.

"I beg your pardon?"

When those golden-brown eyes of his settled on her face, a troop of fluttering butterflies danced maddingly in her stomach.

"Does Gala Fernandez frighten you so much that you felt it necessary to fawn over me to warn her off?"

Miguel chuckled. "My dear Jennifer, the lovely and sexy Gala wants me very badly." J.J.'s mouth dropped open. "The only thing is I'm not sure whether she wants to make love to me or to kill me."

J.J. let out a relieved sigh. "Then you don't trust her anymore than I do, do you?"

"No, I do not trust her. She is trying much too hard to insinuate herself into my life. Of course, it is possible that she finds me so irresistible that—"

J.J. playfully poked Miguel in the ribs with her elbow.

"What?" he asked guilelessly. "You doubt that a woman could find me irresistible?"

"Oh, no, I don't doubt it for a moment. You can be charming and attentive and make a woman feel as if she's the only woman in the world. In a moment of utter weakness, she just might find you completely irresistible."

Leaning close—too close—his nose grazing her cheek, he whispered, "If only you were that woman, *querida*."

While her heart beat ninety-to-nothing and tingling warmth spread up her neck to flush her cheeks, J.J. struggled to think of just the right response. But she was saved by Roberto and Zita's appearance.

"Would you mind terribly if we left early?" Roberto asked.

"No, of course not," Miguel replied. "Is everything all right?"

Zita Fuentes slipped her arm around Roberto's waist. "Everything is perfectly fine. But I have a slight headache and Roberto has kindly offered to take me home."

Yeah, right, she had a headache. Surely Miguel didn't buy that old excuse. It was obvious that these two wanted to go somewhere to be alone. Although they weren't making a public spectacle of themselves, it was apparent they could barely keep their hands off each other.

"Wait here," Roberto said to his date. "I'll get your purse and wrap and then we'll leave."

J.J. wondered if she should say something to Zita, something to soothe the awkward moment. After all, Miguel had to realize that one of his best friends was going to take this woman home and make love to her. If Miguel had feelings for Zita or she for him, one or both of them must be slightly embarrassed and perhaps even upset.

"I was surprised that Señor Casimiro has a jazz ensemble here tonight." J.J. said the first thing that popped into her head. The cool jazz number the group was playing right now had caught her attention. The alto sax moaned the melody of "The Good Life" as the piano, bass and drums played softly in the background.

"Anton loves jazz," Miguel replied. "He plays the piano and sometimes sits in with the group. He has very eclectic tastes in almost everything, especially in music."

Suddenly Zita's gaze zeroed in on J.J.'s left hand. Her eyes widened, her mouth opened into a perfect oval of surprise. "Your ring is lovely." She looked at Miguel. "You chose it for her, of course."

"Of course." Miguel looked like a man who'd been caught doing something he shouldn't be doing.

"I don't know what is keeping Roberto." Zita glanced around the room, avoiding direct eye contact with either Miguel or J.J.

Poor woman, J.J. thought. She's in love with Miguel and it's breaking her heart seeing him engaged to someone else. But the question that plagued J.J. was—did Miguel love Zita? If he did, wouldn't he have shared the truth with her, that his engagement to J.J. was not real?

"It appears he has been waylaid by someone near the buffet table," Miguel said. "If you'd like, I can go rescue him."

When Miguel turned, intending to go toward the buffet table, J.J. clasped his arm, momentarily halting him. He gave her a puzzled glance, then sighed and nodded when he apparently remembered her cautioning him not to leave her side this evening.

"No, that won't be necessary," Zita said. "I will go and wait for him in the foyer, away from all this noise." She rubbed her right temple. "I am afraid my headache has become worse."

"I'm so sorry," Miguel said sincerely.

"Perhaps Señor Casimiro has some aspirin or—" J.J. offered.

"I'll be all right, thank you." Zita all but ran away from them.

J.J. glared at Miguel.

"Why are you looking at me as if I were an ax murderer?" Miguel asked.

"Just how involved are you with Señora Fuentes?"

"Lower your voice, please. We don't want anyone overhearing you. You sound very much like a jealous woman."

J.J. huffed. She was not jealous. She had simply asked a logical question. "It's obvious the lady is upset that you're engaged," J.J. said quietly. "I think I have a right to know—"

"Zita and I are not lovers," Miguel said. "We have not even dated."

"But?"

"But I had given some thought to courting her and I believe she found the idea quite agreeable."

"Are you in love with her?" Oh, God! She couldn't believe she'd asked him that.

Grasping her around the waist, he pulled her close and whispered, "Retract your claws, little she-cat. Your jealousy is showing."

J.J. gasped aloud, which made Miguel laugh. Several people near them turned to see what was going on.

Miguel shrugged and laughed again as he faced those inquisitive stares. "I am afraid I said something that caught my fiancée off guard and embarrassed her. You know how young ladies can be when we men are too blunt-spoken."

The devil! The charming, smooth-talking devil.

Forcing herself to smile at the onlookers, she didn't withdraw when Miguel led her toward the balcony, where several other couples were dancing or gazing up at the moon. She balked when they reached the double set of open French doors.

"You might consider the possibility that I'll be tempted to toss you over the balcony railing if we go out there," J.J. said for his ears only.

"I will take my chances. I very much want to hold you in my arms right now. Besides, if we don't dance at least one dance, everyone will wonder why not."

"I'm hungry," she said. "Why don't we eat first, then dance?"

As if she hadn't spoken, he led her out onto the balcony and pulled her into his arms. "First we dance. We can eat later."

"Of course, *querido*. Whatever you say. After all, you're my lord and master and I would never want to do anything to displease you," J.J. told him in English, a phony smile plastered on her face.

"Quite a few people in Mocorito speak English. We wouldn't

want anyone here tonight to realize you were speaking to me in such a sarcastic manner."

J.J. kept quiet as Miguel led her into the dance. She didn't protest when he pulled her so close that her breasts pressed against his chest. Being this close to him was hypnotic. Like all his other attributes, Miguel's dancing was flawless. As the music wove itself around them and their bodies moved slowly and rhythmically under the starry, tropical sky, it was all J.J. could do to keep her wits about her. This was like a scene from some old forties movie—an American heiress being wooed by a South American playboy. Only Miguel wasn't actually a playboy and although she would someday inherit several Ashford millions, she wasn't a true heiress, not in the traditional sense.

When one tune ended, another began almost immediately, which probably explained why Miguel didn't release her. The moment the music started again, a bluesy rendition of "You Don't Know What Love Is," he reached down and tilted her chin with his crooked index finger. Standing there in his arms, she looked up at him.

Be still my heart.

When had she ever been this foolish? Not even as a teenager had she fallen so hard and so fast for a guy.

"After this dance, we can go through the buffet line," he told her. "I would rather take you home early, but since I…we are the guests of honor, we can hardly be one of the first couples to leave, can we?"

She managed to nod her head, temporarily rendered mute by the surge of passion heating her from the inside out. She had to put a stop to her raging hormones and do it ASAP. This guy was good. Damn good. He knew just what to say and do to seduce a woman, to make her feel as if she was special. But she knew better. She meant nothing to Miguel. For goodness sake, she was his bodyguard. Letting herself fall under his spell could prove dangerous for both of them.

All he wants is for you to be his latest conquest. One more notch on his bedpost. Once he's had you—

What the hell was she thinking? No way was she going to give in to temptation.

"Why don't we cut this dance short?" J.J. suggested. "I really am starving and that boiled shrimp looked delicious."

He eased her out of his arms, but grabbed her hand when she started to walk away. She paused and fell into step beside him as they left the balcony.

"You may have my share of the shrimp and cocktail sauce," Miguel told her. "I do not like shrimp. I made myself sick on shrimp as a teenager and have avoided eating it ever since."

"I did that with popcorn when I was a kid and I was twenty before I could stand the smell of the stuff."

Miguel squeezed her hand as they entered the buffet line of half a dozen people. "You realize that we are sharing confidences, stories of our childhoods." He smiled. "It is what lovers do to become better acquainted."

"We are—" She'd been about to say, "we are not lovers," but he squeezed her hand really hard, warning her to be careful what she said. "We are becoming better acquainted every minute we're together."

Miguel lifted a plate and handed it to J.J., then picked up one for himself. The people ahead of them in line offered to let them prepare their plates first, but she and Miguel declined simultaneously.

Then, just as J.J. reached out to the platter of boiled shrimp, someone called out loudly, "Do not eat anything else! Five people have become very sick in the past few minutes."

J.J. froze to the spot for a half second, then she stood on tiptoe so that she could discern the identity of the speaker. Dr. Juan Esteban made his way through the shocked crowd, coming directly toward them. She scanned the room, searching for Dom. Standing head and shoulders above three-fourths of the men and women there, he was easy to spot. Her gaze locked with Dom's and a silent understanding passed between them. What if someone poisoned the food?

"I have called for an ambulance," Dr. Esteban told Miguel. "Five people have become deathly sick—vomiting and diarrhea—in the past few minutes. One of the ladies has fainted."

"Could it be food poisoning?" Miguel asked.

"That would be my first guess. Have you eaten anything? You or Señorita Blair?"

"No, we haven't eaten a bite." J.J. put her plate down on the buffet table, then grabbed Miguel's plate and put it atop hers.

"I must go with those who are sick to the hospital. There could be others," Juan said. "In case there are, I will send another ambulance to be on standby."

"What is wrong?" Anton Casimiro approached them, a concerned frown wrinkling his forehead and creasing his plump cheeks.

"We fear food poisoning," Miguel said. "Several people have become violently ill."

"That cannot be!" Anton's round face turned beet-red. "I have used these caterers before and never has anything like this happened."

"It isn't your fault," Miguel assured his friend.

"It is probably only one dish," Juan said. "Otherwise everyone who has eaten would be ill and everyone is not."

"All the food should be left right where it is," J.J. told them. "Each dish will have to be analyzed to find out which one was either spoiled or tampered with on purpose."

Anton's eyes widened in shock. "Are you suggesting someone deliberately poisoned a specific dish? Whatever would make you think such a thing, *señorita?*"

"Jennifer is a great fan of murder-mystery novels," Miguel hurried to explain.

"Murder?" Anton gasped.

Off in the distance the sound of sirens shrilled loud and clear.

"The ambulance should arrive any moment." Juan turned and rushed back into the bedroom to see about his patients.

"I believe it might be a good idea to explain to everyone what has happened," Dom Shea said as he came up beside Miguel. "If we could figure out which dish is the culprit, we could narrow down those who might yet become ill."

"I will make an announcement," Anton said. "This is my home, my party…"

While Anton spoke to his guests, Dom asked Miguel, "Do you have a favorite food?"

"What?"

"Did your host ask about a favorite food he could provide for you tonight?"

"No." Miguel shook his head.

"Would he or the caterers, or anyone for that matter, know you would be sure to eat one thing in particular tonight?"

"I can think of nothing. I enjoy a wide variety of food, but there is nothing on the buffet table tonight that is a particular favorite."

"But there is something that is not a favorite," J.J. said. "How many people know you hate shrimp and won't touch a bite of it?"

"What?" Miguel and Dom asked.

"If you were not the target—"

Dom cursed under his breath. "It makes sense, after the other two incidents today."

"What are you talking about? How does not poisoning me, but poisoning others make sense?" By the time the words were out of his mouth, realization dawned on Miguel. "Mother of God! They are striking out at my friends and supporters, at the very people I would do anything to protect."

"They're showing you how vulnerable your people are," Dom said.

"If you won't withdraw from the presidential race out of fear for your own life, then perhaps you will do it to protect others," J.J. told Miguel.

"Before we run with this theory and know for sure that's what's going on, we need to have the shrimp and the cocktail sauce tested," Dom said. "Tonight, if possible. I'll make a phone call and have someone come and pick up the remaining shrimp and sauce."

Miguel nodded. "I should go to the hospital and check on those who were stricken. If any one of them were to die… To put myself in danger is one thing, but to put others in danger…"

"This isn't your fault," J.J. told him. "Stop beating yourself up about it. And whatever you do, don't make any decisions about your candidacy tonight. If you think your supporters would want you to withdraw from the race to protect them, then you aren't thinking straight."

"You two go on to the hospital and find out how seriously ill the poison victims are," Dom said. "My guess is that the intent was not to kill anyone, only to make quite a few people sick. Enough to send a warning message."

J.J. hated the pained expression on Miguel's face. This was a man who cared for others, cared deeply. Right now, he was feeling guilty, taking the blame for what had happened upon himself. She couldn't let him do that. She wasn't sure why it was so important to her to support and encourage Miguel, but it was.

She slipped her arm through his. "I'll call down and have Carlos bring the car around, then we'll go straight to St. Augustine's. And once we find out that everyone is going to be all right, I'm taking you straight home." She turned to Dom. "You'll stay here and guard the food, especially the shrimp and sauce, until the proper person takes samples of everything."

"Yes, ma'am." Dom grinned.

"She is rather bossy, is she not?" Miguel said, then looked at J.J. appreciatively. "It is good for a man to have a fiancée who can take care of him when the situation calls for it. Feel free, *querida,* to continue issuing me orders tonight. I believe you know better than I do what is best for me."

Moisture glistened in J.J.'s eyes. Damn him! He'd done it again. Said just the right thing to touch her heart and make her want to wrap her arms around him.

Chapter 8

J.J. and Miguel waited at the hospital for news about the people who had taken ill at Anton's dinner party. When all was said and done there were fifteen altogether. Eight men and seven women. Within an hour after she and Miguel arrived at the hospital, both Emilio and Roberto appeared. Dom had telephoned Emilio and he in turn had contacted Roberto. The two men had approached Miguel with different opinions on what he should do and how he should handle the situation.

"You must make a statement to the press immediately," Roberto had said.

"No, no, that is the wrong thing to do," Emilio had told them. "Wait until Juan tells us what the situation is, if anyone has died or if everyone will survive."

"You must make it clear to the people of Mocorito tonight that you will not be intimidated, that nothing can convince you to remove yourself from the presidential race." Roberto had glowered at Emilio, as if daring Emilio to contradict him.

Without blinking an eye, Emilio had shot back, "He cannot do that. It would send the wrong message. What if the people believe Miguel is not concerned for the welfare of those closest to him, that he is willing to risk other people's lives?"

While the two had argued, J.J. had persuaded Miguel to walk to the chapel with her. She supposed that eventually Roberto and Emilio would realize Miguel wasn't still there listening to them squabble, but she really didn't care. All that mattered right now was helping Miguel, doing whatever she could to relieve the stress he felt and ease the guilt eating away at him.

Though the small hospital chapel was devoid of the niceties of a real church, the small statue of the Madonna on one side of the altar and the large painting of Jesus on the cross hanging behind the altar gave the sparsely decorated room a spiritual feel. She wasn't Catholic, but she had attended services several times with various Catholic friends. She had been raised a Protestant, her father Baptist, her mother Presbyterian. It had always seemed to her that there was something profoundly reverent about a church, no matter what the denomination.

She sat beside Miguel on the first bench in a single row of six wooden benches. After he had lit candles for Juan's patients, he had taken a seat and closed his eyes. J.J. knew he was praying and that fact touched her deeply. After quite some time, she reached over and clasped his hand. He opened his eyes and looked at her.

"What would you do?" he asked.

"What would I do if I were you? Is that what you are asking me?"

"Yes."

"I would wait. I would not make any hasty decisions. We don't have all the facts."

"And if the worst happens, if someone dies and we know for certain someone poisoned the shrimp or the sauce?" He took a deep breath, then released it slowly.

"If our worst fears are confirmed, then you must decide what you are most afraid of on a personal level—of innocent people being killed or of the Federalist Party maintaining power and slowing the progress of Mocorito, possibly even taking your country back in time instead of forward."

"The many or the few," he said sadly. "You do not mince words, do you, Jennifer?"

"One of my many faults," she admitted, then said in English, "I call 'em like I see 'em."

He frowned. "Do I have the right to sacrifice others for a cause I believe in with my whole heart?"

It was a difficult question. One to which she had no answer. What would she do, if she were in Miguel's shoes? What if a family member's life or the life of a friend hung in the balance, and she alone had the power to decide their fate?

"You can give the people the right to choose for themselves." She paused, then looked him right in the eye. "I would definitely wait until I had all the facts, then if what we suspect is true, I would take this information to the people it concerns the most. Put their fate in their own hands. Speak with your family, closest friends and most avid supporters first and ask them what they want you to do. Then, if and when circumstances warrant it, go directly to the people in a radio or television broadcast."

The corners of his lips lifted in a half-hearted smile. "You are a very wise woman for one so young."

"Thank you." Everything in her longed to comfort Miguel. It was all she could do to stop herself from wrapping her arms around him and telling him she would make everything all right for him.

When the closed chapel door opened, J.J. shifted in her seat so she could glance over her shoulder. She nudged Miguel. "It's Dr. Esteban."

Miguel shot to his feet, still clasping her hand and inadvertently dragging her up with him. "Please, tell me you have good news."

"I have good news," Juan said. "Several of the patients are severely dehydrated and they will all be sore from the retching, but it appears all fifteen will recover completely. Probably by tomorrow morning."

"Thank God." Miguel grabbed J.J. and hugged her fiercely.

She threw her arms around his neck and laughed when he lifted her off her feet.

"Take him home, Señorita Blair," Juan said. "See to it that he gets a good night's rest."

"Yes, thank you, doctor, I'll do just that."

Juan nodded. "I must return to my patients."

"I will call first thing tomorrow to check on everyone," Miguel said as he set J.J. back on her feet.

"Come on, let's follow doctor's orders." J.J. tugged on Miguel's hand.

Just as they exited the chapel and had walked no more than ten feet, Dom came around the corner.

"Emilio told me he thought I could find you two in the chapel," Dom said.

"Have you heard the good news?" J.J. asked.

"Yes, just before I showed up, Dr. Esteban had informed Emilio and Roberto that everyone was going to live."

"Do you have any news for us about the food?" Miguel asked.

Dom shook his head. "It will be tomorrow sometime before we know anything for sure. Will Pierce will call me as soon as his people know anything. They took samples of all the food at Casimiro's buffet table before the police arrived."

"Good. Good." Miguel clenched his jaw.

"You don't trust the police?" J.J. asked.

"Some of them, I do. But many of the higher-ranking officials here in Nava are loyal to Padilla. They are, how do you say it in America? On his payroll."

"Then one of your first official acts as president should be to clean house in the police department here in the capital city." J.J. glanced at Dom. "Are there any reporters downstairs?"

"Hordes," Dom replied. "That's why I had Carlos take the limo around to the back entrance to wait for us."

"Shouldn't I make some kind of statement tonight?" Miguel asked.

"Let Emilio or Roberto make it for you," J.J. said. "Have them say that you are well and greatly relieved that all those who got food poisoning at the dinner party are going to be all right. Leave it at that. For now."

Miguel put his arm around her shoulders. "You are quite adept at public relations, *querida*. You would make a most admirable first lady."

Dom lifted his eyebrows speculatively, the expression on his face clearly asking if there was something intimate going on between her and Miguel. She chose to pretend she hadn't noticed that inquiring look.

"What are you doing here?"

Diego was furious. She knew he would be, but she did not give a damn. Within a few minutes of learning that fifteen people had been poisoned at Anton Casimiro's dinner party, Gala had begun feeling guilty. Although she hadn't known that the vial hidden in her designer handbag had been filled with poison, she had suspected as much. What she hadn't suspected was that whoever had retrieved the vial from her purse had used it to doctor one of the food items at the buffet table. She had assumed it would be used in Miguel Ramirez's champagne. Not caring what political party ruled Mocorito, what did it matter to her if Diego and his friends eliminated the Nationalist Party's candidate? But poisoning fifteen people was something else. If they had died, it would have been mass murder.

"I came to tell you that I will not do any more of your dirty work." Gala glared at Diego. Even though she was still afraid of him and the power he held over her, the liquor she had consumed before coming to his home had infused her with false bravado.

"Lower your voice." He grabbed her arm and pulled her with him into the front parlor. After flipping on a lamp, he shoved her into the nearest chair and came down over her, bracing his hands on either armrest. "My mother and sister are upstairs asleep and several of the servants are still up and stirring in the back of the house."

"You should have told me that you planned to poison innocent people. I would never have helped you do such a despicable thing."

Diego laughed, then put his face up to hers. "No one died from the poison. Killing innocent people was not our goal. We simply wanted, once again, to show Miguel that he cannot protect his friends, family and supporters."

"And if convincing him that your people can harm those he cares about does not stop him, what will you do then?" she asked. "You should kill him. Hire another assassin. Don't harm innocent people."

"We do not want Ramirez dead," Diego told her. "Killing him would be a last resort. If he is killed, the people could turn him into a martyr and revolt. No, we cannot risk that. What we want is for Ramirez to withdraw from the presidential election."

"Why did you wait until only weeks before the election to—"

"Not until recently did we realize there was a chance he could win," Diego replied. He grabbed her by the shoulders and shook her. "Go home and sober up. And do not ever come back here telling me that you will no longer obey my orders. Have you forgotten that I could send you to prison, just like that?" He snapped his fingers.

"No, I have not forgotten." Tears sprang into her eyes.

He released his painful hold on her shoulders and yanked her to her feet. Their gazes connected for a brief moment and she thought she saw a hint of sympathy in his eyes. God, was she losing her mind? There was no sympathy, no compassion in Diego Fernandez. At least not for her.

He tickled her under her chin. She gasped.

"Be a good girl and do as you are told," Diego said. "I do not want to see you in prison. There are far better places for a beautiful woman such as you."

She shivered at his touch and hated herself for actually being aroused. There had been a time when she had thought herself in love with Diego. Years ago when she had been just a girl, she had admired her best friend's big brother from afar.

"If you please me, I will see that you become the mistress of someone very rich and powerful, perhaps one of Hector's ministers."

His words were like a slap in the face. What had she expected? Diego would never see her as she had once been—an innocent. A virgin, like Seina. No, he knew about her drug addiction years ago and about the men she had given herself to in order to support her habit.

"I am willing to do almost anything you ask," Gala said. "But please, Diego, don't make me a part of harming innocent people. Even I must draw the line somewhere."

He grabbed her arm and escorted her out into the foyer and through the front door. When they stood on the portico, he forced her to face him.

"Did you have any luck with enticing Ramirez? Perhaps you will be of more use to us if you can become his lover."

She started to tell Diego that there was no chance of Miguel Ramirez being unfaithful to his fiancée, that the man seemed hopelessly in love with the American woman.

"We spoke tonight at the party," Gala said. "And flirted a little." She had flirted; he had not. "A second meeting might prove more productive. A meeting where there are no snakes and no poison."

Diego laughed. "Go home, Gala, and tomorrow we will figure out a way for you to come in contact with Ramirez again."

A true friend would not have allowed her to drive herself

home. After all, she had had much too much to drink. She wasn't exactly falling-down drunk, but she was far from sober. However, Diego wasn't a true friend. He wasn't a friend at all. He was a master manipulator who had no qualms about using her.

Gala managed to open her car door and get inside, but it took her several tries to stick the key into the ignition switch. Finally, she got the car started, then pulled out of the driveway and into the street. Less than two blocks from the Fernandez mansion, she heard the screeching of brakes and horns honking. Her last coherent thought was, "Did I run through that stop sign?" Then suddenly she felt a jarring impact as another vehicle broadsided her.

Seina Fernandez hid in the dark, in a secluded nook at the back of the entrance hall. Trembling, her heart hammering inside her ears, she held her breath as Diego closed the front door and locked it. After he walked up the stairs, she crept out from her hiding place just enough to look up so that she could see if he had gone to his room. Then and only then did she release her breath.

Only a few minutes ago, she had come downstairs to ask Conchita to prepare her some warm milk because she had found it impossible to fall asleep tonight. After an argument with her mother over her upcoming engagement party, she had been heartsick and longed to go to Juan for comfort. But what excuse could she have given for leaving the house so late in the evening? Slipping away to see Juan was much easier during the day. Since neither her mother nor Diego suspected she was seeing another man, they did not keep close tabs on her during the daytime.

Her life was already plagued by problems she could not solve alone. And now? Dear God in heaven, what would she do now that she had heard what her brother had done? What he had forced poor Gala to do? She had never meant to eavesdrop, had had no idea to whom Diego was speaking so harshly when she passed by the front parlor.

Why, oh why, had she not gone on to the kitchen instead of stopping to listen, wondering who Diego's late-night visitor was? How could she deal with this information, with the knowledge that her brother was involved in the plot to destroy Miguel? She had known, since their father's death, that Diego despised their half-brother, but she had never dreamed he was capable of such despicable acts. This was not the Diego she knew and had loved all her life. Yes, he could be domineering and controlling, as their father had been, but never cruel, never dangerous.

How could Diego have involved her best friend Gala in his murderous plots? He was actually blackmailing Gala, using her past drug use against her. There had to be some way she could help her friend, some way she could stop Diego. If she went to him and talked to him? No, that would accomplish nothing. If Diego's hatred had taken him over the edge into obsession, talk would not be enough to convince him how very wrong he was.

And speaking to their mother would be useless. She adored Diego so much that she would support him in whatever he chose to do, even if he killed Miguel with his bare hands. Perhaps she could not blame her mother for hating her husband's illegitimate son. Perhaps she would feel the same if her husband had betrayed her. But try as she might, she could not hate Miguel. In truth, she admired him.

Should she go to Juan and tell him what she knew? He could then go to Miguel and warn him. But if she did that, would she not be betraying Diego? Would she not be choosing one brother over the other?

Dear God, what must I do? Please, help me make the right decision. I do not want to betray those I love, but how can I stand by and do nothing?

Miguel, J.J. and Dom arrived at Miguel's home in the early-morning hours. Ramona met them at the door, concern in her weary, dark eyes. Miguel did his best to reassure his house-

keeper that all was well, but knowing him as she did, she saw
through his false optimism. He wanted to believe that today's
three incidents were the beginning and the end of his enemy's
scare tactics, but he knew better. Hector Padilla and his corrupt
Federalist Party were running scared. Since all the independent
polls showed Miguel winning the election by a wide margin, the
opposition party had only one choice—either kill him or force
him to drop out of the race. If they killed him, the people might
turn him into a martyr and rebel against Padilla and his kind. The
more Miguel thought about it—and he had been thinking of little else these past few hours—the more he realized that the best
course of action for his enemies was to force him to withdraw
his candidacy.

"Good night," Dom said as he paused outside his bedroom
door. "Try to get some rest. Both of you."

"Good night." J.J. looked at Dom. "If you hear anything—"

"I will let you know the minute I get a call about the lab results."

J.J. nodded, then she grasped Miguel's hand and led him
down the hall to his bedroom suite on the other side of the house.
She opened the door and turned on several lamps while he
trudged to the liquor cabinet.

"Would you like a drink?" he asked.

"No, thanks, but you go ahead. I'm going to clean all this
makeup off my face, sponge off and put on my pajamas."

He nodded, then lifted a bottle of whiskey and poured himself half a glass. The liquor sailed down his throat, warming
his esophagus on the way down, then hit his belly like a hot
coal. He coughed a couple of times, then took another swig.
His head ached, his stomach churned and his conscience
nagged at him. How was it that a man with good intentions,
with his heart in the right place, could cause harm to others?
All Miguel had ever wanted was to make life better for the
people of his country. Having grown up in poverty, the bastard son of a woman thought of as a whore, seeing daily the

plight of people forgotten by their government, he had known, even as a child, that someday he would change things for the better.

After finishing off his drink and feeling the effects as a warming sensation that settled in his belly and took the edge off his nerves, Miguel sat down on the side of his bed and removed his shoes and socks. Just as he took off his jacket and tie, J.J. emerged from the bathroom. He took one look at her and became instantly aroused. She wore her lavender silk robe, loosely belted at the waist. As she walked across the room, she unintentionally revealed one calf and thigh and he caught a glimpse of the sexy black lace garter belt to which her black silk stockings were attached.

He swallowed hard.

The whiskey had helped a little. Sex would help a lot. Nothing relieved a man's tension better than sex. Fast, furious, hot and wild sex.

With J.J.

Miguel closed his eyes and tried to erase the picture of her branded in his mind. But instead, his imagination went to work. He could see her coming toward him, removing her robe and standing in front of him wearing only her stockings, garter belt, bikini panties and bra. When she began stripping, removing her bra first, Miguel opened his eyes and cursed softly.

J.J. was nowhere in sight. She had disappeared into the walk-in closet. Miguel sighed heavily, then stood, removed his shirt and added it to the haphazard pile of clothing he had tossed on the floor. What he needed was another drink.

Lifting his arms over his head, he stretched his taut muscles. He thought he heard a soft gasp and when he lowered his arms and glanced over his shoulder, he saw J.J., in a pair of ivory satin pajamas, standing several feet away, staring at him. She came toward him, her hands outstretched.

"What should I do with these?" she asked, holding out the diamond earrings and necklace she had worn to Anton's party.

"Put them wherever you want," he told her. "You'll be wearing them again in the days ahead." He glanced down at the engagement ring he'd given her. "Don't take that ring off. Keep it on day and night. It is a bad omen for a woman to remove her engagement ring before the wedding."

J.J. simply nodded. No arguments. No reminders that their engagement was not real and that there would never be a wedding. She turned quickly and went back into the closet. While she was gone, Miguel poured himself another drink. If he couldn't get laid, he'd get drunk. A stupid thing to do, maybe. But right now, for a few hours, he did not want to be a pillar of strength, the savior of Mocorito. All he wanted was to stop thinking, stop worrying, to cease to feel anything.

When she returned to the bedroom, J.J. paused several feet away from him and cleared her throat. With the second glass of whiskey in his hand, he turned to her.

"Is there something you want?" he asked.

"Isn't that your second drink?"

"Yes, it is."

"Do you think you should be drinking so much?"

"Yes, I think I should."

"Miguel…" She took several tentative steps in his direction. He held up a restraining hand. "No, do not."

"Do not what?"

"Do not come any closer."

At first she didn't say anything, just stood there and stared at him. Then she turned around and walked over to his bed. His heartbeat accelerated. She turned down the covers. His sex hardened painfully. She reached out and grabbed one of the feather pillows. His mind screamed. *Damn, damn, damn!*

"You should go to bed and try to sleep," she told him as she went to the armoire, opened it and removed a cotton blanket. "But if you would like to talk—"

"I believe we have already said all there is to say, have we not?" He brought the glass to his lips and downed a sizable amount of whiskey. He coughed, then blew out a hot breath.

"Miguel, please don't drink any more."

He grinned. "Do you have another remedy that will work better than liquor?"

She frowned. "On top of all your other problems, if you drink much more, you will wake up with a horrible headache."

"I already have a headache," he told her. "As a matter of fact, I have two headaches."

She stared at him, her frown deepening. "I think you've already had too much to drink."

Bossy American female! If she had no intention of giving him what he really needed, then to hell with her. He didn't need her. Didn't want her. Could do just fine without her.

Liar!

In an act of childish defiance, Miguel lifted the liquor bottle and filled the glass to the rim, then he saluted her with the glass and took another hefty swig.

She whirled around and marched over to the chaise lounge, placed the pillow at the top, then lay down and pulled the cotton blanket up to her neck.

Ignore her, he told himself. She has dismissed you completely.

With the glass held tightly in his slightly unsteady hand, Miguel opened the French doors and walked out onto the balcony overlooking the courtyard. The breeze was cooler than usual, a hint of rain in the air. A million and one thoughts raced through his mind, swirling about, tormenting him, driving him mad. He threw the glass over the balcony. Whiskey flew in every direction, some splattering on his naked chest. The glass hit the rocks below and shattered into pieces.

Miguel clutched the wrought-iron railing, then closed his eyes and prayed. He asked for guidance, for the ability to choose the correct path. And he begged for an hour or two of relief. If only he could stop thinking, stop worrying, stop caring so damn much.

He felt her presence behind him before he heard her soft footsteps or smelled the faint, lingering scent of her perfume. Why could she not leave him alone? Did she not know that her presence alone was driving him mad?

Her small hand touched his back. He tensed, every muscle in his body going stiff. As stiff as his sex.

"Miguel?"

He turned and faced her, but before she could say or do anything, he grabbed her, yanked her into his arms and kissed her. His mouth took hers with a hungry passion, the taste of her far sweeter than he had imagined. She neither fought him nor cooperated, but let him ravage her mouth as he ran his hands over her lush body. Then just as he ended the kiss and started to lift his head, she moaned softly and her mouth responded, kissing him back. Eager and greedy. Wild with need.

Chapter 9

J.J.'s bones dissolved into liquid and her body heated to the boiling point as she and Miguel shared a kiss to end all kisses. Fourth of July fireworks. Hurricane waves crashing against the shore. The thunder of her own heartbeat deafened her as electrical shock waves heated her blood. She couldn't get close enough to him, couldn't meld her body to his as tightly as she longed to do. Only the intimate joining of lovemaking could come close to uniting them in the way she needed to be part of him.

She had been in love once…or thought she had been. And she'd had great sex…or thought she had. But nothing J.J. had ever experienced came anywhere close to what she was feeling now. She had never known what real, honest-to-goodness yearning was until this very moment. Yearning so powerful that it obliterated everything else, reducing her to a purely emotional creature.

As she kept kissing him, tasting him, devouring him as he was her, she rubbed her hands over his shoulders and back, longing for the feel of his naked flesh beneath her fingertips. Rational thought was slipping away fast. If she didn't hang on, didn't force herself immediately to think about what she was doing, she would be lost.

But I want him, an inner voice pleaded. I want him more than I've ever wanted anything or anyone.

She couldn't give herself to him. She could not surrender to the weakness overwhelming her. This wasn't love. This was lust. Primitive animal magnetism, drawing two young, healthy primates together.

All right, so this was nothing more than uncontrollable passion. What was wrong with that? Just because she'd never had sex with a man she didn't care for deeply, why couldn't this be the first time?

J.J. pulled away, ending the ravaging kiss, but Miguel moaned and sought her mouth again, his hands cupping her hips and holding her mound against his erection. Her damp femininity throbbed. Wanting. Needing.

"No, please," she spoke the words against his demanding mouth. "We can't. I can't."

He kissed her again before easing his lips to her jaw and then down her neck, ending up by burrowing his head against her shoulder. When the tip of his tongue flicked repeatedly against her collarbone, she sighed.

"No, Miguel, this isn't fair."

Either not hearing her or completely ignoring her protest, he lowered his head to her left breast. Her entire body tensed with anticipation. His mouth covered the areola through the satin material of her pajama top and sucked until her nipple tightened into a pebble-hard point. While he suckled her greedily, she cupped the back of his head and held him in place at her breast. Spirals of desire spread out from her breasts and connected with the core of her body.

As the last coherent thought floated through her mind—put

a stop to this now while you still can—Miguel dropped to his knees in front of her and kissed a damp path from her breast, over her midriff and across her navel. He paused, slid her pajama bottoms down a couple of inches, stuck his tongue into her navel and laved the small, deep indentation.

J.J. unraveled completely when his big hands grasped her hips and eased her pajamas farther down her hips.

Oh, mercy, mercy. She wanted this. Oh, how she wanted it. But she couldn't let him do it. Could she?

"Miguel?" his name was nothing more than a pleading whisper.

"Yes, *querida?*" His hands paused in their task.

"We can't do this. You know we can't. We met only yesterday. We're strangers. This is all wrong. You know it is." There, she had been sensible and called a halt to this madness.

He nuzzled her mound through the thin satin barrier. "If it's so wrong, why does it feel so right?"

"Because we're acting and reacting from an adrenaline rush," she told him, as she caressed the back of his head. "Danger, fear, intense emotions all combined to heighten our senses. Wanting sex to diffuse tension is the most natural thing in the world."

"I agree." He kissed her mound. She trembled. "The sex would be good. It would be very good for both of us."

"I don't doubt that for a minute, but—"

He made his way up her body, inch by inch, his hot breath searing her through the satin and his big hands working their way up and over her buttocks. When he rose to his full height, he looked down at her, his golden eyes smoldering.

"You are not a virgin?" he asked.

"No, but that doesn't mean—"

"You have been with other men, why not with me?"

"I don't love you. I don't even know you."

He cradled her buttocks with his palms and pressed her firmly against his pulsating sex. "What better way to become acquainted than to make love? I promise that you will not be disappointed. I have been told I am an excellent lover."

"Ah—! What a macho, male, he-man thing to say." His words had been like a bucket of cold water dumped on her head. She shoved against his chest until he released her. "Just when I was beginning to like you, you have to go and be a….a…a man!"

Miguel chuckled. "*Sí, señorita,* I am indeed a man. A man who very much wants to make love to you."

"You want sex," she told him, avoiding eye contact. "Any woman would do."

Frowning, his gaze narrowed as he glared at her. "You do not truly believe that, do you? If sex with any woman was all I wanted, there are dozens of women I could have. I could pick up the telephone and make a call and any one of them would come to me now, in the middle of the night. But I do not want any of those women. I want you."

J.J. stiffened her spine. She believed him. About the dozens of willing women and about him wanting only her. "I'm your bodyguard. My job is to guard you and protect you, to keep you alive during the election campaign. Having sex with you would be unprofessional."

"What are you so afraid of, Jennifer?" Although he no longer touched her, he caressed her with his seductive gaze.

She swallowed, then looked up at him. "The truth?"

"Yes, the truth."

"I'm afraid that I'll become fond of you, that I'll care for you, and I'll get my heart broken."

"*Querida.*" He held his hand out, as if he intended to touch her.

She moved backward, just out of his reach. "I do not have casual, meaningless affairs. The only relationship you and I have now or will ever have is a farce. I'm your pretend fiancée. And that's all."

He dropped his hand to his side. His defeated expression told her that she had finally gotten through to him. "You should go in to bed now," he told her. "I will stay out here for a while longer."

"Will you be all right?" That's it, Jennifer Joy, fawn over the man. Didn't you just tell him that you weren't in love with him, that you didn't care for him except as a client?

He turned his back to her and looked down at the dark garden below, illuminated only by the moonlight. "I will be fine. Go to bed."

Reluctantly, wondering if she was a fool for rejecting a man she so desperately wanted, J.J. went back into the bedroom. She looked down at the chaise and then over to the huge king-size bed. Images of Miguel and her sharing that bed, the two of them naked, thrashing about, making love, flashed through her mind. She groaned as she lay down and pulled the cotton blanket up over her.

How long would Miguel stay outside? Would she still be awake when he went to bed? She closed her eyes and tried to think of anything other than the tall, dark, handsome man standing alone on the balcony. But despite her best efforts to erase all thoughts of him, he filled her mind. And her own traitorous body reminded her of the pleasure his mouth and hands had given her.

Miguel had made certain that he was showered, shaved and dressed before J.J. awoke. He had been exceptionally quiet, trying to not disturb her. He knew she had spent restless hours tossing and turning on the chaise lounge, just as he had in the massive king-size bed. He had finally fallen asleep sometime shortly before dawn and rested for a couple of hours. When he'd left his bedroom suite, J.J. had been awake, but she'd been pretending to be asleep. He understood that she was as reluctant as he to discuss what had transpired between them in the early hours of this morning.

He would leave things as they were. For now. In the clear light of day, he could think more clearly, more rationally. Having a love affair with his American bodyguard might give him immense physical pleasure, but at what price, not only to him, but to her? Was his life not already complicated enough without adding an ill-fated romance to the mix?

When he entered the dining room, Ramona, who was busy overseeing the dishes being brought into the room by the kitchen help, spoke to him.

"Good morning, Señor Ramirez." He could tell that she wanted to ask him something, possibly question him about the dinner party last night.

"Have you heard about what happened at Anton Casimiro's party?" Miguel asked. "About some of his guests having food poisoning?"

"Yes, *señor.* It is in the newspaper, on the radio and on the television. It is a miracle that you, too, were not taken ill." She crossed herself. "We must thank the blessed virgin."

"Yes, we must." Although he hadn't eaten a bite since yesterday's luncheon at the country club, he wasn't sure he could down a full breakfast, so to start with, he poured himself a cup of strong coffee. He knew it would be strong because that was the way he preferred his coffee and Ramona made sure things were done the way he wanted them done. "Has Señor Shea come down this morning?"

"Yes, he was down earlier, but went out. Carlos offered to drive him, but he took a taxi."

Miguel nodded. "Hmm... Yes, Dom is a very independent fellow."

"Will the *señorita* be joining you for breakfast?"

"No, she is still resting. Perhaps you would be kind enough to prepare a tray for her and I will take it up to her later."

"Yes, of course."

Only moments after Ramona disappeared into the kitchen, Miguel heard footsteps in the hallway. When he glanced up, he saw Dom Shea and Will Pierce.

"We came in the back way," Dom said, in English. "No one saw us except the servants. I told them that Will was an old buddy of mine from the States."

"Please, sit. Both of you. Have you had breakfast?" Miguel asked as he placed the cup and saucer on the table and pulled out his chair.

"Just coffee for me," Will said.

Dom poured two cups, added a dollop of cream to his and brought both cups to the table. After handing Will the cup of black coffee, Dom sat down and took a sip from his cup. "J.J. still in bed?"

"Yes, she was still resting when I came down a few minutes ago."

"I guess we should wait for her before Will gives you the results from the lab tests."

"I would prefer to know now," Miguel said.

Dom shrugged. "Sure thing. I'll relay the info to J.J. and you can fill in your people."

"My people?"

"Lopez and Aznar. I assume you plan to share the information with them."

"Yes, of course."

After Will joined them at the table, Miguel and Dom turned to him.

"The cocktail sauce was doctored with a non-lethal amount of dimethatate." Will took a sip of coffee. "If ingested in large doses, it's lethal. There was just enough mixed into the cocktail sauce to cause vomiting and diarrhea in anyone who ate a few teaspoons of the sauce."

"Apparently the goal was not to kill anyone," Dom said.

"And nothing was found in any of the other food?" Miguel asked.

"No, only in the cocktail sauce served with the boiled shrimp," Will said.

"Then whoever poisoned the sauce knew that I would not eat

any because it is a well-known fact that I have an aversion to shrimp." Miguel's worst fear concerning last night's near-tragedy had just been confirmed. "I was not the target. At least not the target of the poisoning."

"Just how many people know you won't eat shrimp?" Dom asked.

Miguel shrugged. "My family. My closest friends. A few colleagues. Enough people that it would be impossible to track down a traitor, if that is what you are thinking."

"Hm… Actually what I'm thinking is that you got hit with three warning messages in one day." Dom shook his head. "They wanted to make their point as quickly as possible, didn't they?"

"We have to assume that yesterday's three events were staged to get your attention and that they were just the prelude to bigger and more deadly incidents."

Will focused directly on Miguel. "You cannot allow them to frighten you into withdrawing from the presidential race."

"Spoken like a man who does not love my family and friends and loyal supporters as I do. You would be willing to shed innocent blood in order to see me become president." Miguel glowered at Pierce.

"Are you saying that they've already won?" Pierce asked. "A blown tire, a few harmless snakes at a luncheon and a couple of dozen people sick with what everyone assumes was food poisoning and you're ready to throw in the towel? I thought you were made of strong stuff, Ramirez. I had no idea you'd tuck tail and run at the first sign of trouble."

Before Miguel could form a reply in his mind, let alone utter a rebuttal, a feminine voice defended him. "Miguel Ramirez is not the kind of man to run from a fight," J.J. said as she entered the dining room. "But neither is he a man who is willing to risk the lives of others, to run roughshod over his people for his own selfish reasons."

"Well, what lit a fire in your belly, Agent Blair?" Will scrutinized J.J. closely as she walked over to the buffet table and poured herself a cup of coffee.

"You have no right to speak to Miguel the way you did," J.J. told the CIA agent. "This is his country and the people whose lives are at risk are his people. And it his decision and his alone whether to withdraw from the presidential race."

A moment of complete, stunned silence followed J.J.'s declaration. In that moment, Miguel sensed a deep emotional bond with Jennifer Blair, something unlike anything he had ever experienced with another person. After knowing him less than forty-eight hours, she understood who he was and what he felt.

In his peripheral vision, Miguel caught a questioning glance that Dom shot J.J., as if he were silently asking her what had brought about her staunch defense of a man neither of them really knew. But that was where Domingo Shea was wrong. He might not know Miguel, but J.J. did. He did not understand how it was possible for someone who had met him only the night before last to see inside his heart and mind so easily.

"Sorry." Pierce's one-word apology broke the awkward silence. "I'm used to dealing with jerks who respond better when they're on the defensive. But if you decide to continue with your candidacy, you will have our full backing and if necessary we can bring in more Dundee agents."

"To do what?" Dom asked. "It would take a small army to protect everyone who supports Ramirez."

"I was thinking more in terms of protecting those closest to him. His family and best friends," Pierce said.

"Before we start making plans on Miguel's behalf, perhaps we should find out what he intends to do." J.J. looked at Miguel, a softness in her gaze that told him she remembered those sweet, passionate moments early this morning.

"I will speak with Emilio and Dolores, with Roberto and Juan and Aunt Josephina, as well as the servants, especially Ramona and Carlos, who have been with me for many years." Miguel would not continue his candidacy unless those dearest to him were willing to risk their lives for the Nationalist cause.

"If they tell you that they do not want you to give in to threats, even threats against them, then you won't quit, is that right?" Pierce asked.

Miguel thought about Dolores, a very pregnant Dolores. How could he ask her to risk not only her life, but the life of her unborn child?

J.J. reached out and laid her hand over Miguel's where it rested on the table. "You should send Dolores away from Nava, perhaps even out of the country, until after the election. The Dundee agency can provide her with a personal bodyguard."

Miguel turned his hand over and clasped J.J.'s small, delicate hand in his. It was as if she had read his mind, as if she knew his thoughts. She understood that his first concern was for his cousin, who was like a sister to him.

"You do realize that since everyone in Mocorito believes you to be my fiancée, you, too, could be in grave danger? Perhaps in more danger than Dolores."

"That may be true, but I am also a professional, a highly trained bodyguard," J.J. told him. "I know how to take care of myself, as well as others."

Only when Dom Shea cleared his throat did Miguel realize that he and J.J. had been sitting there holding hands, staring into each other's eyes and speaking to each other as if they were alone.

J.J. eased her hand from his grasp a couple of seconds before Ramona walked into the dining room carrying a silver tray. She took one look at J.J. and paused, then came straight to her, set the tray in front of her and removed the linen cloth covering the food.

"Señor Ramirez asked me to prepare a breakfast tray for you, *señorita*," Ramona told her. "He intended to bring it upstairs to you himself." The housekeeper smiled warmly at J.J.

"Thank you, Ramona," J.J. said in Spanish. "Miguel is very thoughtful, is he not?"

"Oh, yes, *señorita,* he is the most thoughtful man I know." Ramona blushed. "He will be a good husband."

Yes, he will. Had that been only an instant thought or a heartfelt knowledge? J.J. asked herself. Here she was once again buying into the fiancée fantasy, something she had to stop doing.

"Ramona, will you ask all the servants to come into my study in half an hour?" Miguel asked the housekeeper. "I need to discuss something with all of you."

"Do you want Carlos, too? And Pedro, the gardener?"

"Yes, everyone. Please."

Ramona scurried to do his bidding.

Miguel shoved back his chair and stood. "If you will excuse me, I wish to move forward with my plan to speak to the servants and my family and close friends. I intend to do that this morning. I am going to telephone Roberto and Emilio and Juan right now."

"You haven't eaten anything since lunch yesterday," J.J. reminded him. "Can't the calls wait until you've had breakfast?"

Will rose from his seat. "I should be going. I'll be in touch soon." He looked at Dom. "Contact me when a decision has been made and we'll proceed from there."

Dom stood. "Let me walk you out."

Once Dom and Will left the dining room, Miguel turned to J.J. "I will eat if you will eat. Then we will go into my den and I will telephone my family and friends. I cannot make this decision alone, as you so wisely pointed out to me last night."

"I will not be sent away!" Dolores Lopez planted her hands on her hips and glared back and forth from her husband to her cousin.

"*Querida,* you must go," Emilio told her. "Miguel cannot continue in his bid for the presidency unless you cooperate with us. He will do nothing to endanger your life and the life of our child." Emilio tenderly patted his wife's protruding belly.

"I agree," Roberto added. "Once Padilla's people realize their scare tactics are not working, they could very easily target those of us closest to Miguel."

"If that is true, then how can I leave you behind, Emilio?" She looked pleadingly at her husband. "And you Miguel?"

"You will do what you know you must," J.J. said, hoping she could persuade Dolores to do the sensible thing.

"Are you leaving, also, Jennifer?" Dolores asked. "No, you are not. You are staying with your man, not deserting him when he needs you."

"But I am not pregnant," J.J. said. "By staying, I am not risking the life of my child."

Dolores frowned, but she did not continue to argue. She sat there, on the sofa in the living room, and thought for several minutes before replying. "I will leave Nava, but I do not want to leave Mocorito. Send me, with the bodyguard you wish to hire, to Buenaventura. And no one except Emilio will know exactly where in Buenaventura I am. Will that be acceptable?"

A collective sigh of relief reverberated throughout the room.

By early afternoon the decision had been made that Miguel would not withdraw from the presidential race. And plans had been made to send Dolores to the northern seacoast village of Buenaventura with a Dundee bodyguard. J.J. wondered if, when Sawyer McNamara had told Lucie Evans he was sending her to Mocorito to guard Miguel's cousin, she had pointed out to him that she spoke only "tourist" Spanish. If she had, knowing Sawyer, he'd probably sent along a Learn Spanish Overnight CD and companion workbook on the flight with her from Atlanta to Caracas.

Chuckling softly to herself, J.J. didn't hear the door to the bedroom suite open. When she sensed someone in the room with her, she whirled around, prepared to defend herself. Then she saw Miguel and immediately relaxed.

"You were so deep in thought that you did not hear me, did you?" he asked.

"You caught me falling down on the job."

"What an odd expression. You Americans say the strangest things."

"Yes, I suppose we do."

"What did you find so amusing in your thoughts?"

J.J. smiled. "Just thinking about Lucie Evans, the agent my boss is sending to guard Dolores."

"There is something amusing about Señorita Evans?"

"No, not really. It's just that she and our boss, Sawyer Mc-Namara, have this ongoing feud and have had for as long as I've worked at the Dundee Agency. They cannot be in the same room together for more than two minutes without arguing."

"They have never been lovers?" Miguel asked.

"No. At least not as far as anyone knows. They were both FBI agents before they came to work for Dundee. We figure something must have happened between them way back when."

"Way back when?"

"Back when they worked for the Bureau. Two people don't dislike each other that much without a reason."

"You disliked me before you even met me, did you not?" Miguel walked toward her and looked down at the chaise lounge where she sat. Without even asking her, he sat down beside her.

She sucked in a deep breath, wishing there was room on the chaise for her to scoot away from him, so that his arm wouldn't brush up against hers.

"I drew some conclusions from the information I was given about you," she admitted.

"Was the information accurate?"

"Yes, it seems to have been."

"And were your conclusions also accurate?"

"Partially."

"Only partially? What have you discovered that tells you you misjudged me?"

"Fishing for compliments?"

He threw up his hands expressively. "Another silly Americanism."

"You *are* the old-fashioned, macho type. But I don't believe you separate women into only two categories—lady or whore."

"You forget there are also the nuns," he said.

She smiled. "Yes, of course. I'd forgotten about the nuns."

"What else?" he asked, as eagerly as a child.

"You genuinely care about people. Not just your family and friends, but everyone in Mocorito. The things you say come from your heart. They're not just rhetoric, not just campaign psychobabble."

"Psychobabble?"

"Another Americanism," she told him.

"Ah."

"You didn't like me when Dom and I first arrived. Were you wrong about me?"

"Partially."

She laughed.

"You are every bit the strong, independent woman I believed you to be, but you are not a man-hater. There is a softer, very feminine side to you." He lifted his hand to her face and cupped her chin between his thumb and forefinger. "For the right man, you would make the perfect wife."

J.J.'s heartbeat accelerated. Not again. Don't overreact to a simple compliment. He wasn't implying that he is Mr. Right.

"Do you enjoy the ballet?" Miguel asked.

"Huh?" Slightly startled when he changed the subject so quickly, she shook her head.

"Juan and Aunt Josephina have asked us to join them tonight at the ballet and for dinner afterward. I accepted on our behalf. That meets with your approval?"

"As your fiancée, yes, that meets with my approval," J.J. said. "However, as your bodyguard, I have to tell you that from now on, do not make any plans without checking with me first."

The corners of Miguel's sensuous mouth lifted in a hint of a smile. "That man—your future husband—he will have his hands filled keeping you in line."

J.J. laughed. "He will have his hands *full* keeping me in line," she corrected him.

His gaze traveled over her intimately, pausing on her breasts. "Yes, he will have his hands full."

An undeniable current of awareness passed between them, the sexual tension vibrating like a live wire.

J.J. jumped up off the chaise. "I need to find something appropriate to wear to the ballet."

"An evening gown," Miguel told her. "And be sure to wear the diamond necklace and earrings."

"I have only two evening gowns," J.J. said. "One is purple and one is teal. Would you like to choose which one I should wear?"

"Wear the purple one."

"Are you sure? Don't you want to see the gowns?"

"Teal is a dark bluish green, yes?"

"Yes."

"It is not the color for you. Wear the purple one. It will complement your beautiful violet eyes and flawless skin." When she just stood there smiling at him like an idiot, he said, "I should give you some privacy while you bathe and prepare for this evening."

When he headed toward the door, she called, "Miguel?"

"Yes?"

"Who else knows—other than Juan and his aunt—that we will be attending the ballet tonight?"

"Who else? Emilio, Roberto, Ramona and of course, Carlos. Why do you ask?" He shook his head. "No, do not think it. Not one of them would betray me. They are loyal to me and to the Nationalist Party."

"Then nothing bad should happen tonight, should it? Your enemies don't know where you will be this evening, therefore they can hardly plan a strike of some kind against you."

"I will not live my life in fear. And I will not distrust people who have always been loyal to me."

Miguel did not sound entirely certain in his convictions.

Chapter 10

Miguel had tried his best for many years to appreciate the ballet, but tonight was no different from the other times he had pretended to enjoy himself. Perhaps his lack of appreciation for both ballet and opera came from having been reared as a peasant, growing up with native music and dance, both vibrantly alive to him in a way that the more refined arts were not. He preferred a good soccer game or a bullfight or the racetrack in Colima, events he had attended as a boy with his grandfather, cousins and neighbors. He liked guitar music and songs sung in Spanish, with gusto and heart.

Just from looking at Jennifer, he could not tell if she was as bored as he and if she, too, wished they were somewhere else. Preferably alone together. Her placid expression gave away nothing, but she seemed to be totally absorbed in the performance.

With Juan and Aunt Josephina, there was no doubt. Both loved the ballet and the opera and often invited Miguel to go with them. Usually he came up with a good excuse to decline, but occasionally he accepted out of love for them. He enjoyed their company, although more so at other functions. And dinner tonight would more than make up for the time he felt was wasted at the ballet. Both Juan and his aunt were delightful dinner companions and always chose excellent restaurants. One of their favorites—where they would dine tonight—was Maria Bonita, where the colorful atmosphere and live music was almost more delectable than the delicious, authentic Mocoritian food.

If he could endure a few more minutes of this torture, they could escape to Miguel's waiting limousine and go directly to Maria Bonita. Good wine, good food and good friends. And a beautiful woman at his side. What more could a man ask for and not be considered selfish and ungrateful?

He glanced at his fiancée. No, not his fiancée, only the woman masquerading as his fiancée. Why was it, he wondered, that it was so easy to think of Jennifer as his betrothed? It was not as if she were perfectly suited for the job of First Lady or a perfect match for him. Indeed they were too much alike, both forceful and aggressive. And passionate about the things that mattered to them. He had always pictured himself married to a gentle, demure woman who looked to him for guidance in everything, from her choice in clothes to the way in which they would rear their children. Although capable of playing the part, Jennifer was not that woman.

His gaze traveled over her appreciatively. Her beauty took his breath away. Tonight she out-dazzled every woman there. The bodice of her purple silk gown crisscrossed over her breasts and hugged her tiny waist, then flowed downward, caressing her hips and swaying at her ankles as she walked. The diamonds he had given her sparkled at her ears and neck, their beauty mere accents to hers.

He reached over and grasped her hand resting in her lap. She entwined her fingers with his, but didn't look his way. Leaning toward her, he brought his mouth to her ear and whispered, "I hate the ballet."

She smiled, then moved her head, inadvertently brushing her cheek against his lips. A jolt of sexual energy shot through him. Perhaps she had intended to arouse him? The little tease. She would flirt with him in a place where he could do little about it. But later…ah, yes, later.

They held hands until the end of the performance, then she pulled free and applauded along with the rest of the audience. Miguel clapped half-heartedly and smiled when the house lights came up and Aunt Josephina, who sat to his right, patted him on the arm and asked how he'd enjoyed the performance.

"Very much," he lied. "As always."

Her broad grin told him that on some occasions, it was not a sin to lie. Especially when the lie spared a kind old woman's feelings.

As the foursome made their way out of the Nava Civic Center, Miguel spoke to numerous people, but did his best to avoid being waylaid by anyone who would demand more than a moment of his time. This evening was not about politics; it was about relaxation and camaraderie with friends.

Once outside, while they waited for their limousine—only one in a long line of limos—Jennifer pulled the purple shawl that matched her gown up and around her shoulders.

"Are you cold?" Miguel put his arm around her shoulders and brought her up against him.

"No, not really. But the wind is a bit chilly."

"We should not have to wait long. I believe our car is fourth in line."

"Do you really hate the ballet?" she asked in a hushed whisper as she leaned her head closer.

He glanced over at Aunt Josephina, who was chattering away with the couple behind them. And although Juan appeared to be listening to the conversation, Miguel knew his friend's mind had wandered off somewhere. He'd seen that look in Juan's eyes before and it usually meant he was thinking of a woman.

"Yes," Miguel admitted. "I fear that I have very plebeian tastes in entertainment. I prefer soccer games and bullfights and horse races. And watching movies. I especially like the old American gangster movies with Edward G. Robinson and James Cagney."

"I'm not surprised that you like sports, even something as bloody as a bullfight, but I never pegged you for an old-movie buff. I used to watch those old gangster movies with my dad when I was a little girl."

The smile vanished from her face, replaced by a wistful, bittersweet expression. Why did thinking of her father make her sad? he wondered. "Your father is still alive, is he not?"

Her smile returned, but it was a sarcastic smirk. "Oh, yes, General Rudd Blair is very much alive and quite well. His life couldn't be better. He recently remarried, for the second time since his divorce from my mother. And to a woman only five years older than I am. Or at least that's what I hear. But what makes his life truly worth living is the fact that my eighteen-year-old half-brother has just graduated from military school and even though I don't know for sure, my bet is that he's already been accepted at West Point."

"You do not have a close relationship with your father now?"

"Close? No, not for years and years." Probably without even realizing it, she changed from Spanish to English when she said, "Well, actually, we were probably never close, except in my mind."

"Was this rift between the two of you your choice or his?" Miguel asked, in English, then thought perhaps he should not probe deeper into a subject that might be painful for her.

"I'd say it was mutual. He never did have much use for me because I was just a girl. But I wised up. I finally realized that no matter what I did—even joining the army straight out of college—I would never be the one thing he wanted most."

Miguel kept silent, having no need to ask what her father had wanted most. What a foolish man this General Rudd Blair must be to not appreciate having a daughter such as Jennifer.

"He had a son and that's all he ever wanted. As far as he was concerned, my mother and I were simply mistakes in his past."

"*Idiota!*"

"Yes, you're right, he is an idiot." Jennifer laughed, the sound genuine.

Miguel loved her laughter. He would very much like to fill her life with such joy that she would laugh often and live well. She needed the right man to show her what a priceless treasure she was, a man capable of loving his daughters as much as his sons and taking as much pride in them, also.

"Is that your car, Miguel?" Aunt Josephina asked.

"Yes, I believe it is," he replied. "Are we all ready for a fabulous meal at Maria Bonita?"

"You will simply adore Maria Bonita," Juan told Jennifer. "It is one of my favorite restaurants, perhaps my very favorite."

Carlos pulled the limo to the curb, hopped out and opened the back door. After everyone else was safely inside and out of earshot, Miguel pulled Carlos aside and asked, "You did not leave the car unattended, did you? Not even for a few minutes?"

"No, Señor Ramirez, I have stayed with the car every moment."

"When we arrive at Maria Bonita, I will stay with the car while you take a break, if you would like."

"Thank you. All I require is a few moments, sir."

"You understand why I—"

"Yes, yes. Someone could tamper with the car—the engine, the gas tank or even place a bomb. I understand and I stay vigilant at all times."

The wharfs along the coast of Colima were dotted with numerous bars. Seedy, dangerous hellholes from the looks of them. What better place to meet an agent working undercover without anyone recognizing either of you or giving a damn who you were. The minute Dom entered Pepe's, loud music and even louder customer clatter engulfed him. As he moved deeper into this filthy den of iniquity, searching for Vic Noble, the stench of body odor and the haze of cigarette and cigar smoke assailed him. After searching for several minutes, he spotted Vic at a back corner table, a scantily clad *señorita* standing at his side, rubbing his shoulder and giving him a glimpse of her ample breasts as she leaned over him.

"Mind if I join you?" Dom asked in English.

Vic shoved the bosomy woman aside and gestured to the wooden chair across the table from him. The dismissed lady grumbled loudly in Spanish, most of her words a combination of curses, as she walked away to seek other prey.

Dom sat. He eyed the half-filled shot glass in front of Vic. "Tequila?"

"Want one?"

"Nope."

"Pierce is at the bar now, getting a bottle for the three of us."

"Will Pierce is sitting in on this meeting?"

Vic nodded. "Our government is going to want to know what I found out."

"And what would that be?"

"Wait for Pierce," Vic said. "But I'll tell you right now that once the big boys in D.C. hear about this, they will move heaven and earth to get Ramirez elected."

Pierce made his way through a bevy of client-seeking prostitutes and a couple of staggering drunks, barely managing to keep hold of the bottle of tequila and the two shot glasses he held.

When he reached their table, he slammed the bottle and glasses down, then yanked out a chair beside Vic, turned it backward and straddled the seat with his long legs. "Lovely place you chose for our meeting."

"Thanks," Vic said. "I thought the two of you would appreciate the decor and the atmosphere."

"So, what's this important information you've unearthed?" Dom asked.

Pierce removed the screw-on cap from the cheap tequila and

poured the liquor into the two empty shot glasses, then added enough to Vic's glass to fill it.

Vic leaned over the table and said in a low voice. "If the current president is reelected, he and his people have big plans for Mocorito."

"What sort of big plans?" Pierce asked.

"The kind that involves taking over the military and local law-enforcement agencies nationwide."

"That sounds like the current el presidente has plans for a dictatorship instead of a democracy." Dom rested his elbows on the table as he cupped his fingers together.

"Bingo. Give the man a cigar." Vic turned to Pierce. "Padilla has some rich and powerful supporters, but most of them aren't aware of his plans to return the country to a dictatorship. One of his most loyal followers, a man who is using his money and influence to help Padilla, is Diego Fernandez, Ramirez's half-brother."

"That's not a surprise," Pierce said.

"Fernandez is being kept in the dark about the president's plans for the future. He's being easily manipulated because his hatred for Ramirez has blinded him to the truth."

"Are you defending Fernandez?" Dom asked.

"Nope. Not me. Just stating facts. If Fernandez could be convinced that he's being played for a fool, then he might turn against Padilla."

"And just who is going to convince him?" Pierce scanned the bar, especially the tables nearest them.

"I'd say nobody here speaks enough English to understand anything we've said," Vic told them. "Besides, the music is so damn loud, I can barely hear myself think."

"What if we could place this information in the hands of Fernandez's sister, Seina?" Dom suggested. "If we were one hundred percent sure we can trust Dr. Esteban, he could be given the information and we could ask him to feed it to his lady love."

"Do we trust Esteban without reservations?" Vic looked at Pierce.

"Probably not. I'm not sure it would be wise to trust Esteban or Lopez or Aznar. We are almost certain that one of those three could be a traitor."

"Almost certain? Could be?" Vic's brow furrowed. "I haven't dug up any dirt on Esteban, at least so far. His only sin seems to be having clandestine meetings with Seina Fernandez."

"Then you think we should trust him with the information and ask him to pass it along to Señorita Fernandez?" Pierce glowered at Vic.

"I think Dom should talk it over with Ramirez," Vic said, "and if he says do it, then we do it."

"Ramirez is too close to Esteban to be able to—"

Dom interrupted Pierce in mid sentence. "It's Ramirez's frigging country, not yours or mine. I think he has more right than you do to make decisions that will affect not only him personally, but his fellow countrymen."

Vic coughed, barely suppressing a grin.

"Yeah, you're right," Pierce said. "Sometimes I just need to be reminded that I'm not always right."

The tension between Pierce and Dom subsided. The three men lifted their shot glasses and each took a hefty swig of the tequila.

Maria Bonita reminded J.J. of an upscale Mocoritian home, lavished with handmade tiles and what appeared to be miles of decorative wrought-iron. A mariachi band played traditional music and a dance floor was available. Not only did the members of the band dress in native costumes, but so did the waiters and waitresses. J.J. decided within minutes after their arrival that the food at this restaurant could not possibly surpass the incredible ambience.

Apparently Miguel was well-known here because the staff kowtowed to him as if he were already the president. Other customers waylaid him as their party passed by, everyone wanting to speak to him, shake his hand, kiss his cheek and wish him well. And as his fiancée, the attention spread to her.

Overwhelmed by the enthusiastic adoration showered on them, J.J. didn't realize that the maître d' was escorting them through the building, which was, in fact, an eighteenth-century hacienda, and out onto an enclosed patio. Their table for four was one of six tables placed around a central fountain.

"This place is unbelievable," J.J. said in English.

"What did she say?" Aunt Josephina asked as she was seated.

"Oh, forgive me," J.J. apologized in Spanish. "I was so impressed with this place that I reverted to my native tongue."

"It is perfectly understandable, my dear Jennifer." Aunt Josephina patted J.J.'s hand. "Maria Bonita has that effect on almost everyone the first time they come here."

No sooner had Miguel and Juan taken their seats than a small, bearded man wearing what J.J. thought were the clothes of a cook—or in this case, a chef—came to their table and suddenly burst into song. Totally surprised by the man's actions, J.J. gasped. Then, as she listened to him sing the romantic Latin ballad with such tenderness, she smiled at Miguel when he took her hand into his, showing her the appropriate affection a man would show his fiancée in a public place. No more. No less. After the little man sang two more ballads, he bowed, turned around and walked away.

"Who was that?" J.J. asked.

"That is Rolando," Miguel told her. "He is one of the chefs here at Maria Bonita, but he once had aspirations of being a singer. Since he is half owner of the restaurant, he performs for the customers."

"Especially customers he is fond of, as he is Miguel," Aunt Josephina said.

For a brief period of time, J.J. almost forgot why she was here in Mocorito and that she was not really Miguel's beloved fian-

cée. The wine was sheer perfection, the dinner conversation en-
tertaining and the food was to die for. She ordered the *boquinete
Dulce Vita*, which consisted of white snapper stuffed with shrimp
and mushrooms and baked in a golden puff pastry. Sighing after
finishing almost every bite, she shook her head when Miguel suggested dessert.

"But you must try the coconut ice cream," Juan said. "They
top it with Kahlua." Laughing, he winked at her.

She had decided earlier that she liked Aunt Josephina very
much and just this very second she decided she liked Juan, too,
because she thought he was a genuinely nice person. Even though
in her line of work, it paid to be suspicious of everyone, she wondered if she couldn't mark Dr. Juan Esteban off her list of possible traitors.

"I would love to try the coconut ice cream," J.J. said, "but I
honestly don't think I can eat another bite."

"I will order the dessert." Miguel smiled at her. "And we will
share it."

Flutters rippled through her stomach and trickled along her
nerve endings. She longed to share more than dessert with Miguel.

"And we must order coffee, too." Aunt Josephina glanced at
the waiter, but like a well-brought-up lady of her day, she did not
place the order.

Miguel ordered three servings of the coconut ice cream with
Kahlua, and freshly brewed coffee for four.

As they waited for dessert and chatted pleasantly, Juan suddenly went silent and turned quite pale. J.J. followed his line of
vision to where the maître d' was seating a party of three on the
far side of the patio. From the strong family resemblance the two
women and one man shared, she assumed they were a mother,
her son and her daughter. The mother was tall and thin, with a
regal air about her that proclaimed she found most people far inferior to her. The son was also tall and quite handsome, with wavy
black hair and a thin mustache, reminiscent of old Latin movie

stars. The daughter was a few inches shorter than the mother and far prettier, with a round, soft face and bright black eyes.

Without realizing she had spoken aloud, J.J. asked, "Who are they?"

Juan did not answer, but Miguel turned his head so that he could catch a glimpse of whoever Juan was staring at so intensely. Miguel's face turned ashen.

"That is my father's widow," Miguel said. "And his legitimate son and daughter."

She heard and understood the bitterness in Miguel's voice. Even though she was her father's legitimate child, she felt every bit as much a bastard as Miguel did. She knew what it was like to be the unwanted, the cast-aside, the unloved.

"Perhaps we should leave," Juan said.

"No!" Miguel shook his head. "If they are offended by my presence, let them leave."

When J.J. reached out to grasp Miguel's hand, he snatched it away, withdrawing from her. Oh, God, how terrible this is for him, how raw his emotions must be. If only he would accept her comfort.

"The *señora* is showing her age," Aunt Josephina said. "She looks terrible. Not that Carlotta was ever a beautiful woman. Ah, but your mother, Miguel, she was beautiful." Josephina reached out and patted J.J.'s hand. "Luz Ramirez was as beautiful as you are, dear girl."

Miguel looked at Juan's aunt and smiled. "I forget that you knew my mother, that she and my grandmother worked in your home."

"They have seen us," Juan said. "Diego is glaring at us and his mother is—"

"Dance with me." J.J. scooted back her chair, stood and held her hand out to Miguel.

He stared at her with a questioning look in his golden eyes. Then without uttering a word, he stood, took her hand and led her from the patio, into the hacienda and onto the dance floor.

Apparently the band was taking a break because the music came from a single musician, a pianist who was playing a soft and romantic tune. Miguel took J.J. into his arms and they joined the other five couples on the dance floor.

"You are very good at reading me, *querida*." Miguel rubbed his cheek against hers as he held her close, but not too close. After all, they were in public. "You seem to know what I need before I do."

"Then you did need rescuing, didn't you? Juan and his aunt were making much too much over the arrival of the Fernandez family when you would have preferred ignoring them, as they have done you your whole life."

Miguel slowed, bringing them almost to a standstill, and gazed into her eyes. "How is it that you know me so well?"

"I honestly don't understand it myself," she admitted. "It's odd, but I feel as if I've known you forever."

"It is not odd at all, my sweet Jennifer. I feel the same. As if perhaps in some other life you and I were soul mates."

Yes, that was it. Soul mates. Never in a million years would she have thought she'd use that term to describe her relationship with any man, least of all a Latin lover who was "all man," to the nth degree.

Perhaps we are soul mates in this lifetime, too, she wanted to say, but didn't. Eternal soul mates fated to be together.

Seina excused herself to go to the ladies' room, hoping that Juan would follow her discreetly so they could have a few precious moments together. Stolen moments. She waited outside in the corridor that led to both the ladies' room and the men's room, feeling certain that Juan would show up at any moment. She waited and waited. Five minutes. Ten minutes. Had he not seen her leave her table? Did he not know that she expected him to come to her?

Finally giving up, she started to return to the patio. Then there he was, coming toward her. The joy of her heart. The love of her life.

She rushed to him. He stopped several feet from her. Then she, too, paused.

"I wish I could touch you," she said.

"Seina, please. What if someone were to overhear you?"

"You were at the Civic Center tonight, weren't you?" she asked. "I thought I caught a glimpse of you."

"I was not aware that your family was attending the ballet tonight."

"They did not see Miguel at the ballet. And if they had known he was dining here at Maria Bonita, they would have made reservations elsewhere."

"Your mother and brother hate Miguel and because he is my good friend, they probably hate me, too. That is if they even know who I am."

"Yes, you are right." Oh, my darling Juan, you have no idea how much my brother hates Miguel or to what lengths he is willing to go to prevent him from being elected president of Mocorito.

"You should go back to your table," Juan told her.

"We must find a way to be together again. Soon. I will make an appointment—"

"No." He shook his head. "I cannot allow things to continue. It is unfair to both of us."

In her peripheral vision, Seina caught a glimpse of her mother coming down the corridor. Oh, merciful God, her mother must not catch her with Juan. "Go to the men's room now. My mother is directly behind us."

Juan did as she had told him to do only seconds before her mother approached her. "Is everything all right? You have been gone such a long time, I was beginning to worry."

"Everything is fine, Mother." Seina managed a weak smile. "I am sorry if I worried you. I was on my way back to the table."

"We are no longer on the patio," Carlotta said. "Once I saw *that man* sitting across from us with his friends, I lost my appetite. To think that they allow his kind in a respectable place like this." She made a sound of utter disgust.

"Are we going home?" Seina asked.

"No, certainly not. Diego asked the maître d' to move us to a table inside, and, knowing who we are, he requested that another party exchange tables with us."

So like her mother and brother not to consider the inconvenience of their request for the waiters or for the other guests. "Then we are staying?"

"Of course we are staying. You do not think for one minute that I would allow the likes of Miguel Ramirez to force me to leave one of my favorite restaurants, do you?"

"No, Mother."

Taking Seina's arm and leading her down the corridor, Carlotta asked, "You were not speaking to that man, were you?"

"What man?"

"That Dr. Esteban. I saw him, you know. I thought there for a moment that he had paused to speak to you. He and his aunt have aligned themselves with the Nationalists, despite the fact that at one time Josephina Santiago was considered a lady of some standing in Nava."

"I have heard that Dr. Esteban is a brilliant physician and a good man."

Carlotta stopped and stared speculatively at Seina. "You heard this at the hospital, no doubt, when you have visited your doctor there."

"Yes."

"If he ever tries to make your acquaintance, you are to make sure he understands that you know of his association with Miguel Ramirez and that your family highly disapproves of that despicable man."

"Yes, Mother."

As Carlotta led Seina through the restaurant toward their table, they came face to face with Juan, his aunt, Miguel and his American fiancée. Apparently, they were leaving Maria Bonita.

Carlotta froze to the spot.

"Good evening, *señora* and *señorita*." Miguel looked Carlotta square in the eyes.

She lifted her head, huffed indignantly and marched away.

"Good evening, Señor Ramirez," Seina said. "Please excuse my mother's rudeness, but…"

"We understand," Juan said, then ushered his party hurriedly through the restaurant.

What a perfectly horrible moment, J.J. thought, as they made their escape. Perhaps it was understandable that Cesar Fernandez's widow had hated Luz Ramirez and her illegitimate son, but it was hardly fair to blame Miguel for the sins of his parents.

The night air seemed cooler than when they had arrived, so when Miguel lifted her shawl up and around her shoulders, she smiled and thanked him.

"I don't understand why Carlos isn't bringing the car," Miguel said. "Surely he must see us from where he is parked."

"Perhaps he has fallen asleep," Aunt Josephina suggested.

"Why don't we just walk across the street instead of waiting for him," J.J. said.

"I believe we shall have to," Miguel told her. "Apparently he is not aware that we are ready to leave."

When they approached the limousine, an ominous feeling hit J.J. immediately. "Wait!"

The other three paused on the sidewalk and stared at her.

"What is wrong?" Miguel asked.

"I'm not sure. Why don't y'all wait here and let me check things out?"

Miguel glowered at her. "Certainly not! If you believe something is not quite right, then I shall go—"

"We'll go together!" Dammit, she kept forgetting that she

wasn't supposed to identify herself as Miguel's bodyguard. Her taking charge would be seen as highly inappropriate.

"Very well."

"What is it?" Aunt Josephina asked. "What is wrong?"

"You two stay here," Miguel said to Juan and his aunt.

"Oh my. Shouldn't Jennifer stay here with me and Juan go with—"

Leaving Aunt Josephina still talking, Miguel and J.J. rushed over to the limo and inspected it from hood to trunk. She saw nothing unusual, nothing out of place. Not at first. The only illumination on this dark night came from two streetlights on either end of the block. On closer inspection, J.J. noticed what she thought might be drops of blood on the pavement outside the driver's door.

"Unless you want them to see me draw my gun, then get behind me," J.J. said as she opened her purse and removed the Beretta.

Placing his body directly behind J.J.'s, Miguel blocked her from the others. Holding the handgun in one hand, she reached out with the other and opened the limousine door. Her pulse raced. The moment the door came open, Carlos fell out, head first, his barely recognizable face covered with blood.

Chapter 11

J.J. and Miguel spent over three hours at the police station, explaining several times the details of their evening before, during and after their discovery of Carlos's body. Juan and his aunt gave their statements, then were allowed to leave. The old woman had been nearly hysterical at the scene, but had calmed to a dazed stupor by the time she signed her statement and kissed J.J. on both cheeks before allowing her nephew to escort her outside to their waiting taxi.

When the police had questioned J.J. about the Beretta 950 Jetfire automatic she had in her purse, Miguel answered for her.

"The gun is mine," he'd said. "It is registered to me. As you well know, my life has been threatened, so we go nowhere without a weapon. The small pistol was easily concealed in my fiancée's purse."

Since Carlos had not been shot, there was really no reason for the police to question them any further about a registered weapon. So, by the time Roberto arrived to chauffeur them home,

Lieutenant Garcia had already thanked them for their cooperation and had given Miguel his condolences before asking if Miguel preferred to inform Carlos's family of his death himself.

"Yes, I will go tonight and tell his family. He has two children who live with his parents here in Nava."

"Very well, Señor Ramirez. Please tell them that we will notify them after the autopsy as to when they may claim the body."

"Please, notify me also." Miguel closed his eyes. J.J. understood the pain was almost more than he could bear. "I will handle the funeral arrangements for the family."

"Yes, of course, Señor Ramirez."

A light rain fell softly against the sidewalk and street when they left the police station. Roberto snapped open a large umbrella and held it over them as they walked to his car. Miguel opened the front passenger door of the Mercedes and helped J.J. inside, then slid in beside her. Roberto got behind the wheel and once everyone had their seatbelts fastened, he started the engine and backed out of the parking space.

For what seemed like hours, but was probably less than five minutes, they sat there in the front seat in silence.

Roberto focused on the road ahead of them and when the rain grew heavier, he turned on the windshield wipers. Miguel kept his arm draped around J.J.'s shoulders and she gladly rested her head against him, thankful for the warm strength of his large body. She could only imagine how Miguel felt, knowing that he blamed himself for Carlos's brutal murder. Miguel's chauffeur had not been shot or stabbed, not given a quick death. No, the poor man had been beaten unmercifully—probably with tire irons, the police had surmised. His skull had been crushed, his nose and cheekbones broken, as well as both arms and both legs.

"You will have to give me directions," Roberto said, breaking the mournful silence. "I do not know where—"

"Carlos came from my old neighborhood," Miguel said. "The Aguilar barrio. Take the turnoff on Carillo Avenue, go four blocks and take a right onto Santa Fe. Carlos's parents live in a second-floor apartment at 107 Santa Fe."

"When we get there, if you would rather, I can go in and speak to Carlos's father," Roberto said.

"No, I will speak to Carlos's parents. He was my chauffeur and faithful friend for many years and he was killed because of me. His parents have a right to know this."

J.J. gasped. "You can't say that to his parents. No, Miguel. You mustn't."

"No, not tonight. Tonight, I will tell them only that he is dead, that he was murdered. That alone will be more than they can deal with right now."

She clutched his hand in hers and held it fiercely. "I'll go with you to speak to his parents."

"That will not be necessary."

"I'll go with you."

He didn't reply, just squeezed her hand and tightened his hold around her shoulders.

During the past forty-eight hours, her latest Dundee assignment had transformed from what she had thought would be nothing more than bodyguard duty—protecting a South American political candidate—to an imminent love affair with both a man and his country. Miguel's devotion to and love for his family, friends and employees was contagious. Sitting there snuggled against him, her hand in his, she felt what he felt, experienced every emotion as if it were happening inside her. The strong bond between her and Miguel could not be explained, not in terms that anyone could understand. She didn't even understand it herself.

Two hours later, at three in the morning, Roberto dropped them off at Miguel's home. He offered to come in and stay, but Miguel had dismissed him, telling him to get some rest because the days ahead would be difficult for all of them.

When they reached the front door, it sprang wide open and

there in the foyer stood Ramona and Dom. Ramona's eyes were red and swollen and even now they glistened with fresh tears. Dom looked J.J. over and then glanced at Miguel.

"We need to talk," Dom said in English.

"Can it wait until morning?" J.J. asked. "Miguel is exhausted. We have just come from Carlos's parents' home."

"Señor Ramirez, our poor Carlos," Ramona said in Spanish.

Miguel opened his arms and hugged Ramona as she wept on his shoulder.

Dom pulled J.J. aside. "I met up with Vic and Will Pierce tonight over in Colima. Vic has unearthed some pretty nasty info and the sooner Miguel knows, the better."

"Unless there is something he can do about it right now, I don't want you burdening him with anything else. He's fast reaching the breaking point. You know he blames himself for Carlos's murder."

"I feel for the guy." When J.J. gave him a cynical look, he said, "I mean it. He's being put in a challenging situation to which there are no easy solutions. And what I have to tell him will only complicate matters more."

"What is it? Tell me and if I think he needs to know, I'll tell him."

Dom shook his head. "Sorry, but I'm telling Ramirez tonight."

"No."

"Yes, J.J., I am. He needs to know."

"What do I need to know?" Miguel asked.

J.J. jerked around at the sound of his voice and glanced behind him, searching for the housekeeper. "Where is Ramona?"

"I sent her to bed." He grabbed J.J.'s arm. "Why are you two arguing?" Keeping a tight hold on her arm, Miguel glared at Dom. "Tell me now what it is that you think I need to know."

"It can wait until later," J.J. said. "After you've had some rest."

"We have another Dundee agent here in Mocorito," Dom said and even though J.J. shot him with a condemning glare, he continued. "He's a former CIA operative, with connections here in your country. He has found out something you need to know before you make any future decisions about whether or not to withdraw from the current presidential race."

"After what happened to Carlos tonight, I have no choice but to reconsider my candidacy," Miguel said.

"The decisions you make in the next few days will also decide the future of Mocorito." Dom huffed loudly. "I hate to lay this on you after what just happened to Carlos, but I don't want you making any decisions without having all the facts."

"Just say whatever it is you have to say." Miguel kept his gaze focused on Dom as he eased his hand down J.J.'s arm and clasped her hand in his.

She knew as surely as she knew her own name that Miguel was holding on to her not only for her support, but to draw strength from her. Helpmates. Soul mates.

"Upon his reelection, Hector Padilla and his goon squad plan to take over the military and every law-enforcement agency in Mocorito," Dom said. "The Federalists plan to turn your country back into a dictatorship, even if it means civil war."

J.J. caught her shocked gasp seconds before it escaped her mouth. *Please, dear God, no!* First she sensed Miguel's horror and then she saw it on his face.

"And your half-brother, Diego Fernandez, is helping Padilla," Dom added. "But he has no idea what they are planning. They're using his hatred for you to gain his support, especially his financial support."

"You were right," Miguel said. "I needed to know this and I needed to know it now. Padilla has declared war on me and is willing to kill those who are close to me.

"And now I learn that if I withdraw from the presidential race in order to ensure that others won't die because of me, the Federalists will try to return Mocorito to a dictatorship and possibly throw the country into civil war, where thousands may die."

"You're in what we Americans call a no-win situation." Dom bit down on his bottom lip as he hazarded a glance at J.J.

"Later today, I will have a meeting with Emilio and Roberto and the leaders of the Nationalist Party." Miguel closed his eyes and groaned. "This is not a decision I can make alone."

"I realize I can't tell you what to do, but I'm going to give you some advice," Dom said. When Miguel simply stared at him, he continued. "It's almost a certainty that you have a traitor in your camp, someone who knows every move you make and is in on every decision. I don't think you can afford to trust anyone. Not Dr. Esteban. Not Roberto Aznar." Dom hesitated. "Not even Emilio Lopez."

Miguel glowered at Dom, his golden-brown eyes filled with anger. "You are telling me that I should not trust my closest friends, men who are like brothers to me? You want me to make a life-and-death decision for my country…for my people, without the advice and input of the three men I trust most in this world?"

"One of those men does not deserve your trust," Dom told him.

J.J. tugged on Miguel's arm. "You need rest. We can discuss this more later, after you've had a few hours of sleep."

Miguel nodded. And without saying a word he allowed her to lead him up the stairs and straight to his bedroom suite. After kicking off her heels and tossing her shawl into the nearest chair, she helped him out of his tuxedo jacket and then loosened and removed his tie. When she started to unbutton his shirt, he grabbed her hands and brought them to his lips. After kissing her knuckles, he whispered against her folded hands. "What am I going to do?"

"You are going to rest," she told him as she pulled her hands free and undid the top three buttons on his pleated-front shirt, then she removed his gold cuff links and laid them on the coffee table.

"How can I rest, knowing what I know?"

She turned him around as easily as if he'd been a child and herded him into his bedroom, not bothering to turn out the lights in the sitting room or turn them on in the bedroom. She led him over to his bed, shoved him down on the edge, then knelt at his feet and removed his shoes and socks. Reaching behind him, she yanked the coverlet, blanket and sheet down enough to reveal the big feather pillows.

"Lie down. Right now."

When she walked away, he called after her, "Where are you going?"

"I'll be right back. I just want to get out of this dress."

He scooted up in the bed and laid his head on one of the pillows, then closed his eyes. "After you do that, would you…would you lie down with me?"

"Yes." She had given the answer no thought. There was no need. Miguel was not asking her for sex, not propositioning her. She understood what he wanted, what he needed.

Once in the bathroom, she undressed hurriedly, removing everything, down to her silk panties, then she grabbed her robe from the wall hook where she'd left it, put it on and rushed back into the bedroom. Miguel lay there in the dark, not even a glimmer of moonlight to illuminate his face, only the faint glow from the lights still burning in the sitting room. At first she thought— hoped—he had fallen asleep. But when she neared the bed, he opened his eyes. Eyes like those of a jungle cat.

"I usually sleep well on nights when it rains," he said. "I enjoy the sound of raindrops hitting the roof, pouring down onto the earth."

J.J. went around to the other side of the bed and lay down alongside Miguel, a good three feet separating their bodies.

He turned and held out his hand across the smooth cotton sheet. Without a moment's hesitation, she closed the space between them and when she did, he pulled her into his arms and held her as if she was his lifeline, as if without her, he would perish.

His lips pressed against her forehead. Tender, sweet kisses. She wrapped one arm around him and cuddled as close as humanly possible.

"I have been placed in an unbearable position." His warm breathed fanned the curls she had pushed behind her ear. "No matter what I do, my decision will cost the lives of innocent people."

She kissed his cheek. "Hush, *querido,* hush. This problem cannot be solved right now."

"I fear it cannot be solved at all."

She lay there in his arms for quite some time, neither of them speaking, only listening to the rain and to each other's slow, steady breathing.

Suddenly Miguel sat straight up in bed, his body taut, his hands balled into fists. She sat up beside him.

"Miguel?"

"I am such a fool. I truly believed that I could offer Mocorito a future of prosperity, with equal rights for all citizens. I have been so full of myself, so certain that I and I alone was destined to lead my people into the twenty-first century."

His body trembled. Just a slight tremor, but visible even in the semidark. Oh, God, the pain inside him is ripping him apart.

J.J. wrapped her arms around him. "Don't do this to yourself. Please. Miguel. *Querido.*"

He fell into her arms and rested his head against her breasts. It was then that she felt the dampness of his tears as they moistened her chest where her robe had fallen open.

As she held him, she caressed his head and rubbed his back. Stroking him. Comforting him.

Loving him.

Seina was awakened by the ringing telephone. When she flipped on her bedside lamp and glanced at the clock, she saw that it was nearly five-thirty. Who would be calling this early in the morning? She rose from her bed and put on her robe, then slipped out of her room and down the hall. When she neared Diego's bedroom, she heard him talking. Without knocking, she opened the door and walked in on him.

He sat on the edge of his bed, his hair mussed, his eyes bleary.

"Why was I not notified before now? What? I don't care what she told you, she is like a member of my family, my sister's best friend."

"What is it?" Seina rushed to Diego. "Has something happened to Gala?"

He held up a his hand, issuing a halt gesture. Seina stopped cold.

"Señorita Hernandez's mother is dead and her father is remarried and lives in Buenaventura. I will notify him that she has been in an accident. And my sister and I will be at the hospital this morning."

"What happened?" Seina pleaded for more information.

"Spare no expense on her behalf," Diego said. "Our family will, naturally, pay for everything." He replaced the receiver and turned to Seina, holding his hand out to her.

She grabbed his hand and sat down on the bed beside him. "Tell me."

"Seina was in an automobile accident the night before last and was taken to St. Augustine's. She had no identification on her, no driver's license, no car registration. That foolish, foolish woman. When she recovered consciousness, she refused to talk to anyone, but one of the nurses managed to pry your name from her."

"I'm going to dress now and go straight to the hospital." Seina jumped up.

"Wait and I will go with you."

She glared at her brother. "Why? You do not care for Gala. If you did, you would not treat her as you do."

"What are you talking about? Of course I care for Gala."

"Liar."

Diego stared at her, a look of utter shock on his face.

"I know," Seina said.

"You know what?"

"I know that you forced her to take poison to Anton Casimiro's party so that someone could use it to make Miguel Ramirez's friends and political supporters sick. I know that you are helping President Padilla to undermine Miguel's bid for the presidency by using whatever unscrupulous means you believe necessary."

"How do you know—"

"I overheard you talking to Gala. I know she left our home drunk and frightened. Because of you."

Diego grabbed Seina by the shoulders. "You have to believe me when I say that I did not wish any harm to come to her."

"That is the problem—I do not believe you." She jerked loose from his tenacious hold. "Who are you? I do not know you. You are not the brother I have known and loved all my life. You have allowed your hatred for our brother—yes, our brother, our father's other son—to turn you into a monster. The old Diego helped Gala when she was in trouble. He kept her out of prison and paid for her stay in a rehabilitation center. He might have been a bit cocky and self-absorbed, but he had a good heart."

"Seina, I…I…"

She glared at him.

"I do not know what to say."

"Tell me it is not too late to save your soul."

He hung his head. In shame? She prayed with all her heart that her brother was still capable of feeling shame.

"I am going to take a shower, then dress and drive to St. Augustine's," she told him. "And I am quite certain that Seina will not want to see you. I am not even sure she will want to see me."

J.J. awoke slowly, languidly, her body warm, her limbs relaxed. She felt something touch her neck. Gentle strokes of a fingertip. Her eyelids fluttered.

"Mmm…mmm…" she opened her eyes and looked at Miguel

who lay beside her, staring at her as he ran his index finger down her throat, stopping just short of delving between her breasts.

She smiled at him. "What time is it?"

"Almost six."

She nodded. "How long have you been awake?"

"About fifteen minutes. I have been lying here looking at you."

Her smiled widened. "Have you?"

"I went to sleep in your arms, didn't I?"

"Yes."

He knew that she knew he had cried in her arms before he had fallen asleep. There was no need to mention it, to discuss it. It was a fact only the two of them shared. Now and forever.

"Thank you, Jennifer."

She reached out and cradled his cheek with the palm of her hand. "I want to do everything that I can to help you. These next few days will not be easy for you. You can depend on me to—"

He pulled away from her, sat up and then turned his back on her as he settled on the edge of the bed and slumped his shoulders.

"Miguel?"

"I want you to go back to America."

"What?"

"I want you to take the first flight out of Nava today."

She tossed back the covers and crawled over behind him, then wrapped her arms around him and laid her head on his back. "Don't talk foolishness," she said in English. "I won't leave you. Not now when you need me more than ever. I thought…I mean…after last night."

He shot up off the bed. She caught herself before falling flat on her face.

With his back to her, he said, "Instead of sleeping, I should have made love to you. You were so willing to do anything to make me feel better. Poor Miguel. He is falling apart. Let me comfort him. Let me show him how strong I am."

She got out of bed, but didn't go to him, just stared at his back. "I know what you're trying to do and it's not going to work."

"I am trying to tell you that I don't want you here, that I don't need you, that I want you to go away. You are only a woman and women have no purpose except—"

"Nice try, but it didn't work." She walked across the room and paused behind him. "There's no point in your trying to think of more ways to insult me or hurt my feelings. I'm not buying your mean macho act. You're afraid that if I stay here, I'll be in more danger than you are. You're concerned that the people who killed Carlos might come after me."

She placed her hand in the center of his back. His muscles tensed.

"Miguel, I'm not leaving you."

He turned and looked deeply into her eyes. "If only you were carrying my child as Dolores is carrying Emilio's child, you would go away, as she did, to protect the baby."

Tears sprang into J.J.'s eyes. "Dammit, you've made me cry."

He grabbed her and held her so tightly she could barely breathe and when she lifted her face to him, he lowered his head and kissed her. After he had thoroughly ravaged her mouth and they were both breathless, he ended the kiss and pressed his forehead against hers.

"What am I going to do with you?"

"You're going to let me stay here in Nava with you and help you through the days and nights ahead."

"Yes, *querida,* God forgive me, but that is exactly what I am going to do."

Chapter 12

J.J. clung to Miguel, knowing there was nowhere else on earth she would rather be than right here, with him, in his arms. But the logical part of her brain kept trying to get through to her, warning her that she was setting herself up for a fall. She and Miguel were caught up in a fantasy. A dangerous fantasy that could cost them dearly on a personal level when reality finally slapped them in the face with the hard, cold facts. No matter how sexually attracted they were to each other, no matter how strongly they felt the soul-deep connection that made no sense to either of them, the truth of the matter was that they had known each other for less than seventy-two hours. A bodyguard assignment that should have remained impersonal had altered drastically, metamorphosing into a grand passion.

But this isn't real, that nagging inner voice told her. You are not Miguel Ramirez's fiancée. You two are not in love with each other. And you have no future together.

As if he felt her uncertainty, Miguel eased his tenacious hold on her and lifted his head from where his cheek had been pressed against hers. For a split second she thought about holding on to him, clinging to him with every ounce of her strength, but instead she met his questioning gaze head-on.

"I very much want to make love to you," he said, his voice husky with emotion.

"I know. It's what I want, too…"

"But?"

"But if we make love, I'm very much afraid that I'll fall madly in love with you. And I cannot allow that to happen."

"Jennifer…" He closed his eyes for a moment.

"Please, help me to be strong. I cannot fight you and myself at the same time."

He ran his hands down her arms, then released her. She shivered uncontrollably for half a second, then took a deep breath and stepped backward, putting a couple of inches between their heated bodies.

He studied her intently, silently, as if he were trying to read her mind. Or look into her heart. "At another time, in another place…"

She offered him a fragile smile. "Yes, I know."

"I want you to be safe," he told her. "You should leave Mocorito as soon as possible. As my fiancée—even my fake fiancée—you could become a target. I could not bear it if anything happened to you."

"And if I leave and you are killed because I wasn't here to protect you, how do you think I will feel? I'm a highly trained professional who was assigned the job of protecting you. I understand your reasons for wanting me to leave, but—"

"No arguments." Shaking his head, he groaned. "Domingo Shea can take over as my personal bodyguard. I believe the time for pretense is over. I can no longer allow my ego to dictate my actions."

"I agree that you shouldn't hide the fact that you have skilled professionals protecting you. If you announce that I am not your fiancée, but your bodyguard—"

"I don't think that it would matter, not at this point," he told her. "It is obvious to everyone that we have feelings for each other. You will not be safe here in Mocorito. There is every chance that they will target you, just as they might target Emilio or Juan or the others closest to me.

"I will make no announcements about you or Dom. You will leave Mocorito for your own safety and for my peace of mind. And when Dom takes over and it becomes apparent that he is guarding me, I will say that yes, my cousin is now my personal bodyguard, that it is what he does for a living back home in Miami."

"You're going to downplay the fact. And you're going to keep up the pretense, at least in part."

"Yes. There will be time enough to admit the entire truth, later, after… After you are safely back in the United States and after the election is over."

"I don't want to leave you." She gazed at him pleadingly. "But you are the boss. If you choose to send me away…"

He caressed her cheek tenderly. "If circumstances were different…"

She sighed heavily. "I won't leave today, but I will go, if that's what you want. We can discuss the details later. Your first concern today is to make a decision about your candidacy. And you must make that decision without sharing the damning information about Hector Padilla with your closest advisors."

"Do you believe, as Dom does, that one of them is a traitor?"

"Yes, I do. We know you have a traitor among your closest friends, someone who is privy to all your secrets, all your decisions. Who else could it be if it is not Roberto or Emilio or perhaps Juan?"

"You spent the evening with Juan and Aunt Josephina. Do you honestly think Juan is capable of betrayal? He is a kind, gentle man who has dedicated his life to helping others."

"I know. I like Juan very much. And I adore his aunt. My gut instincts tell me that Juan is just what he appears to be and he would die before he would betray you."

"And yet you still think I should not share the information about Padilla's diabolical plot with Juan?"

"Oh, Miguel…I think the wisest course of action is to tell no one."

Seina Fernandez had packed a suitcase and taken it with her when she left home. Her plan was first to visit Gala in the hospital and promise her that Diego would never threaten her again; then she would go to Juan and tell him that she was cutting all ties to her family, that she wanted to be with him, to marry him and spend the rest of her life as his wife. In all honesty, she was scared to death and uncertain. When Diego and their mother discovered what she had done, they would be furious. And they would do all within their power to bring her back into the family fold. But she could not return to that house. Not ever again. Her mother would force her to marry a man she did not love, caring nothing for her happiness. And Diego had become a criminal, a man so filled with hatred that he could not see that the vile emotion was destroying him.

Seina hesitated before knocking on Gala's hospital-room door. She would not blame her friend if she did not want to see her. After all, she had overheard Gala's conversation with Diego two nights ago and she had done nothing to intervene at the time. In a way, she was as much to blame for Gala's automobile accident as Diego was. If only she had not cowered in the dark, afraid to make her presence known.

"Yes?" Gala said.

Seina opened the door and peeked in, gasping when she saw Gala's badly bruised face and her arm, apparently broken, in a sling. "May I come in?"

"Seina? Oh, God, Seina, I could have killed myself and the

driver of the other car. I am such a worthless piece of trash. How can you want to be my friend?"

Seina walked into the room, closed the door behind her and marched straight to Gala's side. Seeing the tears streaming down Gala's cheeks, Seina retrieved a tissue from the box on the bedside table, then reached down and wiped away her friend's tears.

"Everything will be all right." Seina grasped Gala's hand. "I know what has been going on with you and Diego. I overheard the two of you talking the other night. I—I confronted him this morning and I warned him that I will not tolerate him using you in such a shameful fashion."

Gala's eyes widened in shock. "You know? You heard? Oh, God! Oh, God…I am so sorry…"

Seina wrapped her arms carefully around her friend and stroked her head gently. "I am the one who is sorry. I am sorry that I have been so weak and foolishly naive. If I had acted sooner, I could have spared you this pain."

With her good arm clinging to Seina, Gala asked, "What has given you the courage to defy Diego? I have never seen you like this—so determined, so independent."

"It is time I grew up, is it not? I can no longer blame my mother and my brother for not allowing me to be the person I want to be or to live the life I want. From now on, no one makes my decisions for me."

"Diego will never allow you—"

"Diego cannot hurt you again. Nor will he interfere in my plans."

"You—you're going to blackmail him with what you heard us talking about the other night, aren't you?"

"I hope that will not be necessary," Seina said. "I pray that my brother will see the error of his ways before it is too late for him."

When J.J. and Miguel went downstairs, Roberto and Emilio were waiting for them in Miguel's study. The moment they saw J.J., they asked to speak to him privately.

"I have no secrets from Jennifer," Miguel said.

Roberto and Emilio exchanged anxious looks.

"Have you forgotten that she is an employee, an American bodyguard forced on you by her government?" Emilio asked, his gaze raking contemptuously over J.J.

"Never speak about Jennifer in such a way ever again," Miguel warned his friend.

"See, I told you that he had become besotted with her!" Roberto spat out the sentence, then threw his arms up in disgust.

"Carlos was murdered. Everyone in my employ, every friend, every supporter could well be in mortal danger." Miguel glared back and forth from one man to the other. "And your greatest concern this morning is my personal relationship with Jennifer?"

"I beg your forgiveness," Roberto said. "But Emilio and I…we believe that this woman has too much influence over you, that you are listening to her instead of to us. We are your closest friends, your staunchest supporters, but it seems that you trust a woman you barely know more than you do us."

"Has she bewitched you with her talented lovemaking?" Emilio asked. "Has she castrated the great Miguel Cesar Ramirez?"

Miguel's face flushed and his eyes glistened with barely suppressed anger as he clenched his jaw and knotted his hands into fists. She could almost hear him mentally counting to ten. Didn't Emilio realize that he had waved a red flag in front of a raging bull?

"How dare you!"

Both Roberto and Emilio took several steps backward, closer to the door.

J.J. knew that now was not the time for her to say or do anything.

"Leave me!" Miguel roared in a voice that brooked no opposition.

Like frightened mice scurrying from a menacing cat, both men practically ran from the room. Miguel clenched and unclenched his fisted hands as he walked to the windows overlooking the front of the house. J.J. remained silent and unmoving. He stood by the windows for several minutes, then turned around and focused on her.

"If you wish, I will make them apologize to you."

"Oh, Miguel, don't worry about what they said. It doesn't matter."

"It matters to me. You are—" He halted for a moment, as if considering his words carefully. "You are important to me. While you are living in my house, you are under my protection."

The corners of her mouth lifted as she shook her head. "Remember I am supposed to be your protector."

"You are, *querida*, you are."

Juan had seriously considered having Carmen tell Seina that he could not see her today, that she should leave his office and never return. But he did not have the strength to turn her away. Despite what he kept telling her—that they should stop seeing each other—he lived for the stolen moments they shared. Just a glimpse of her, a word or two spoken between them, would sustain him for days.

How could he have allowed himself to fall in love with a patient? And not just any patient, but with a woman who was betrothed to another man, a woman who was a member of the wealthy and powerful Fernandez family?

The moment he opened the door to his private office, Seina jumped up from her chair and rushed into his arms, giving him no time to prepare himself. He wrapped his arms around her and held her trembling body.

"Juan, my dearest, darling Juan."

"What has happened?" he asked. "What is wrong? You are shivering."

"I have left home," she told him. "I packed a bag and left. No matter what you say, I will not go back."

"I don't understand. How could you—"

She placed her hand over his mouth. "If you do not want me,

if you cannot take me in, then I will make other arrangements. If necessary, I will stay with Gala when she gets out of the hospital."

Juan grabbed Seina by the shoulders and shook her gently. "Stop jabbering nonsense and tell me what is going on."

She jerked away from him, stomped her foot and shook her fists at him. "Humph! Have you not been listening to me? I have left my mother's house and I have no intention of ever returning."

"You are giving up everything to be with me?" He stared at her, an incredulous feeling overwhelming him. "I cannot allow you to do that."

"You do not understand, Juan." She planted her hands on her hips. "It is not your decision to make. It is mine. I refuse to live in the house of a woman who would force me to marry a man I do not love and with a brother who has become a stranger to me."

"Seina…*querida*…what has come over you? You do not sound like yourself."

"Good. I do not wish to sound like a frightened little girl any longer. I want to sound like a woman who knows her mind and has come to claim her man."

"Claim her…do you mean me?"

She marched over to him, grabbed his face between her palms and kissed him passionately. When he lost his breath completely, she released him and smiled. "I want you to make love to me, Juan Esteban. And I want you to marry me. I leave it up to you which you want to do first."

He stared at her, his eyes bulging, his mouth agape.

"But while you are thinking it over and deciding, I want you to take me to see Miguel. Right this minute. I have much to tell him. I must warn him about Diego."

Emilio approached Miguel while he was alone in the courtyard. Miguel had needed time alone to think, without any distractions. He knew what must be done, the only real choice he had, had ever had. If he could survive the upcoming days and weeks until he was elected president, he would then face his guilt and anguish. Others might die, as Carlos had died, their lives, as his, sacrificed for the greater good. And a part of Miguel would never completely forgive himself, but it was a burden that he must bear to save his country.

"Miguel, may I speak to you?" Emilio asked.

Keeping his back turned to his oldest and dearest friend, Miguel replied, "If you have news of Dolores, then I wish to hear it. Otherwise…"

"I am deeply sorry," Emilio said. "Forgive me for the things I said to you, the disrespectful way I spoke about Señorita Blair. I spoke without thinking."

"I accept your apology only if you will go to Jennifer and apologize to her, also."

"I have already spoken with her and begged her forgiveness."

Miguel turned and faced his friend. "I want no derision in my camp, no squabbles among my people. I need you, Emilio, to support me, to be loyal to me, to—"

"Miguel, you must know that I would die for you, for the cause we both have fought for all our lives. I want to rid Mocorito of men like Hector Padilla once and for all."

There should be no doubts in Miguel's mind, no uncertainty over the issue of trust. He would stake his life on this man's loyalty. But could he stake the future of the nation on his belief in Emilio?

"Has Roberto left?" Miguel asked.

"Yes, he stormed out of here very angry. But he will be back. You know what a temper he has. Once he has cooled off, he will return and apologize."

"Yes, of course he will. We are all hot-headed Latins, are we not?" Miguel reached over and draped his arm around Miguel's shoulders. "We huff and shout and snort and puff out our manly chests in a show of strength. But Emilio, in the end, there can be only one leader, one man who must make the hard decisions and live with the choices he makes."

Emilio nodded. "Yes, you are right. And we all know that you, Miguel, are that man. That leader."

Ramona rushed out onto the patio, wiping her hands off on her white apron as she approached. "Señor Ramirez, you have guests."

"Guests?" Miguel asked.

"Yes. Dr. Esteban is here and he has brought a lady with him."

"What lady?" Emilio questioned.

"A very pretty young lady. He introduced her to Señorita Blair and they are sitting in the front parlor now, talking and waiting for you."

"Damn it, woman, who did Juan bring with him?" Emilio glowered at Ramona.

"Señorita Seina Fernandez."

Diego had two-dozen roses delivered to Gala Hernandez's hospital room and signed the card simply, Carlotta, Seina and Diego. His sister had been right about him caring little what happened to Gala. In truth, he did not care. But he also did not wish her harm, did not want her to die. Yes, he had seen her as only a tool, to use for whatever purposes that suited him. But it was not as if she was a respectable young lady, as if she was truly worthy of the friendship Seina bestowed upon her.

As he drove along the boulevard leading to the presidential palace in the heart of Nava, he struggled with his conscience. A conscience that he had conveniently misplaced for quite some time.

Was Seina right about him? Had he become a monster?

No! He had not. He was only a man willing to bend the rules, to manipulate others, to use some unscrupulous methods to achieve the results he desired. Was he really so different from most men? His wealth and power gave him the means by which to exert influence over the politics in his country. His backing and the backing of other wealthy men such as he could practically ensure a candidate's success. But in recent years, since Miguel Ramirez had become the people's champion, the once weak Nationalist Party had tripled in size and now threatened the Federalist Party in a way his father's generation could never have imagined.

What would dear papá think about his bastard son running for president? He would not have been able to back him publicly, but would he, in secret, have cheered Miguel on, even taken pride in his victory, if he won the election?

But he will not win this election. Surely Ramirez must see that it is in the best interests of his people to withdraw his candidacy. Now that Ramirez's chauffeur had been killed.

Diego shuddered at the thought of how the man had died. The newspaper had reported that he'd been beaten to death.

Have you sunk so low that you now condone murder? he asked himself.

Scare tactics were one thing, but murdering people was not something with which he wanted to be involved. When two people had been killed during the assassination attempt on Ramirez—an assassination attempt not designed to kill, only to frighten—Hector Padilla had sworn to Diego that the deaths of the two other men had been accidental. Now he wondered if Hector had lied to him.

The guards at the palace knew Diego on sight and always opened the gates for him and spoke to him with respect. Today was no different, although Hector was not expecting him. He parked his car in the usual place, reserved for special visitors. As he did on most visits, he entered the palace through a side door to which he'd been given a key by President Padilla himself.

Once inside the palace, facing the narrow corridor that led, the long way around, to the president's office, Diego removed his sunglasses and slipped them into the inside pocket of his sports coat. He ran into several lowly staff members, who either spoke or nodded. No one thought there was anything unusual about him being here today since he was a frequent visitor.

When he neared the rear entrance to Hector's private office, which was kept locked and to which only Hector had a key, Diego paused as he saw the president open the door, search right and left, and then quickly usher three men into his office. What were General Blanco and Secretary of Defense, Arlo Gonzalez, doing going into Hector's office, along with the grandson of former dictator, Felipe Menendez?

Slinking into a corner behind a large pillar, Diego hid from their view. Felipe Menendez's wife and children had been exiled from Mocorito after the dictator's execution many years ago. But ten years later, after they swore their allegiance to the new democracy, Menendez's son and daughter had been allowed to return. Felipe III, the old reprobate's only grandson, a wealthy playboy with whom Diego had attended private school, was an arrogant hothead, known for his radical political views.

It was a well-known fact that Felipe Menendez III supported a small band of extremists who wanted the government returned to the old dictatorship.

Why would Hector give such a man a private audience? Why meet with him at all? But an even better question would be, why had Hector included Menendez in what appeared to be a secret meeting with the country's two most powerful Federalists?

Chapter 13

Miguel had assured Emilio that Juan and Seina had come here today on a personal matter, not anything that would concern him. Since Miguel actually had no idea why Juan had brought his half-sister to his home, he had lied to Emilio, who had excused himself saying he had business to attend to at campaign headquarters. But it had been obvious that his feelings were hurt because he had not been invited to stay. Miguel wondered if the rift his own distrust had created between them could ever be mended completely. What if, when the traitor's identity was discovered, it turned out not to be Emilio, as Miguel felt certain would happen? Could his oldest and dearest friend ever understand why he had shut him out? And would Dolores ever forgive him?

When Miguel entered the living room, Juan rose to his feet, a nervous look in his eyes. "Seina has left her mother's home. She will not be returning."

Miguel simply nodded, puzzled by Seina Fernandez's unexpected appearance in his home and not understanding exactly what either he or Juan had to do with the fact that she had run away from home. It was not as if she were a child. She was a woman of twenty-four.

"Seina and Juan are in love," J.J. explained. "Seina's mother intended to force her to marry another man."

Miguel's eyes grew wide with utter surprise as he looked quizzically at Juan. "You and Seina? When did this happen? You have never mentioned the fact that you even knew her and now you come to me and tell me that the two of you are in love and she has run away from home."

There had been a time when his friends had not kept secrets from him. Nor he from them.

"Six months ago I was ill." Seina's gaze pinpointed Miguel. "Juan took over several cases for my regular doctor when he had a personal emergency and that is how Juan and I met."

Miguel glowered at Juan. "She was your patient?"

"Don't be angry with Juan," Seina said. "He tried to tell me that many young women get crushes on their doctors, but I knew it was more than a crush. I knew I was in love with him, so I have been pursuing him…secretly…for months now."

"Mother of God!" Miguel muttered under his breath. There would be no good time to hear this news, but why now, when all hell had broken loose and he was facing a crisis of conscience?

"I have invited your sister to stay here with us," J.J. said.

"You what?" Miguel snapped around and glowered at her. "How could you—"

"I declined the offer," Seina said. "It was most gracious of your fiancée, Miguel, but I will be staying with Juan's aunt until we are married."

"Married?" Miguel rubbed his forehead. "Do you think for one minute that your brother will allow you to marry Juan?"

"I am of age. I have a legal right to marry whomever I please." Seina stared defiantly at Miguel. "And I am not worried about Diego interfering."

"You're not? May I ask why not?"

"Miguel, Seina has something to tell you about Diego," Juan said. "And you must listen and not lose your temper."

J.J. stood up beside Miguel and placed her hand on his arm, whether to caution him to remain calm or to assure him of her support, he wasn't sure. Perhaps both.

Juan sat down on the sofa beside Seina and put his arm around her shoulders. "Tell him."

Seina nodded. "I have only recently learned that Diego blackmailed my friend Gala Hernandez and forced her to do something she did not want to do."

"Gala Hernandez?" Miguel mulled over the name. An image of the woman's body flashed through his mind, then her face.

"She was the woman at the country club who flirted with you," J.J. told him. "And then she showed up again at Anton Casimiro's dinner party. I can't believe you could have forgotten the beautiful woman who flirted outrageously with you."

"Diego made her do it," Seina said. "He encouraged her to try to start an affair with Miguel so that he could use her to gain inside information about him."

"I remember Gala." Miguel smiled. "But she failed in her attempts to distract me from Jennifer, so Diego's plan failed."

"That's not all," Juan said.

"Diego made her carry a vial of some kind of poison to the party at Señor Casimiro's," Seina told them.

"So she is the one who poisoned the cocktail sauce?" Somehow this news did not surprise Miguel in the least. He had distrusted Señorita Hernandez almost from the moment they met. And the fact that his half-brother had provided her with the poison that had made more than a dozen people ill did not shock Miguel, either.

"Gala did not put the poison in the food herself. She simply smuggled in the poison. Someone else took it from her purse and mixed it with the food."

"Who?" Miguel demanded.

"I do not know. I swear." Seina wrung her hands together.

Miguel nodded as he digested this information. This meant that among Anton's guests that night there had been another Nationalist supporter. A spy? An undercover agent? A traitor? "I am not surprised that your brother would do anything to stop me from being elected president. He has made it no secret that he supports Hector Padilla with his money and influence. But unless you have some kind of proof that Diego was behind the poisoning, then the police can do nothing."

"The police!" Seina gasped. "No, please, give Diego a chance to…to…" she struggled for the right word. "If you had known Diego before…before he learned that we had an illegitimate half-brother and before he came under President Padilla's influence, you would know he was not a bad man, not a man capable of harming others."

"But now he is involved with murderers, with people willing to kill countless innocent people to—" Only when J.J. squeezed his arm, did Miguel realize he had been on the verge of sharing secret information. Hector Padilla's plot to return Mocorito to a dictatorship was not something Miguel could share with anyone else. That type of news could easily tip the scales and send the country into civil unrest, which was something he wanted to avoid at all costs. If he could be elected president, then he would put a stop to Padilla's plans.

"I cannot believe Diego had any part in the attempt on your life," Seina said.

"Two men died that day and only last night my chauffeur was brutally beaten to death," Miguel told her. "If Diego is taking orders from Hector Padilla, then he may well be an accessory to murder."

Seina hung her head and wept. Juan frowned at Miguel.

J.J. pulled Miguel aside, out into the foyer. "Do you really want to take your anger out on Seina? She did a very brave thing today. She defied her mother and her brother. She is, in essence, giving up the only life she has ever known for the man she loves. And she is reaching out to you, her brother. She wants your help. She needs you. Are you going to turn your back on her?"

"This is the worst possible time for something like this to have happened. I have the fate of my country in my hands and I must—"

She took his hands in hers, turned them palms up and said, "You must do what is right. Offer her your support."

Miguel closed his eyes and nodded. When he reopened them, J.J. was smiling at him.

"You knew when you asked her to stay, she would decline the offer, didn't you?" he asked. "You simply wanted to show my sister that she is welcome in my home. Such diplomacy, *querida*. And such kindness."

"We should handle this problem, now, then move on to the next one," J.J. said.

"Yes, yes. One problem at a time."

Together, hand-in-hand, they returned to the living room.

"Seina, you and Juan have my blessings and my complete support. Mine and Jennifer's," Miguel told his sister. "It would be my honor for you to stay here in my home and be under my protection, if things were different. But at this time, the lives of those closest to me are in danger from my enemies. I fear you would not be safe here."

Seina's eyes filled with fresh tears, but these were tears of joy. A warm smile spread across her damp face. "I will stay with Juan's aunt Josephina, but I am very grateful that you would—" her voice cracked with emotion.

"We should go now." Juan urged Seina to stand. "I will take you to my aunt's and then I must return to the hospital."

"Of course." Seina offered Miguel and J.J. a grateful smile.

"Juan, I would like a moment with you before you leave," Miguel said, then glanced at J.J. "Jennifer, perhaps you will show my sister the garden."

"Yes, of course." J.J. motioned to Seina. "If you'll come with me, we'll leave the gentlemen to discuss business."

As soon as the ladies were out of earshot, Miguel closed the pocket doors and turned to Juan. "I have decided to ask Mario Lamas to allot me fifteen minutes of airtime this evening in order for me to speak to the people of Mocorito on national television." Miguel reached out and clasped Juan's shoulder. "I want the people to know that I will not—that I cannot!—withdraw from the presidential race. No matter what."

"I had thought perhaps, after Carlos was murdered… But no, no, you are right, Miguel." Juan grabbed Miguel's hand and held it tightly. "If the Federalists are capable of poisoning people, of murder, of attempted assassination, then who is to say what else they are capable of doing. You are a brave man, my friend, to risk everything for this country of ours that you love so much. And you are very fortunate to have found a woman such as Jennifer, who is willing to stand by you and help you fight for what you believe in."

J.J. lifted the black lace shawl over her head as she entered St. Ignacio's Cathedral with Miguel that afternoon. They entered the church alone, after driving here in Miguel's antique Aston-Martin. Dom Shea had followed them in a rental car and he was now parked across the street, guarding the front entrance to the building. The centuries-old cathedral, with its stained-glass windows, statues of numerous saints, the Blessed Virgin and Jesus Christ and the fretwork rising from the walls to form arches across the three-story ceiling, resembled the interiors of numerous age-old churches across Mexico and South America. The utter silence within added to the atmosphere of deep spirituality that prevailed within these holy walls.

J.J. sat with Miguel as he prayed. She admired his deep faith in a higher power. It was to his credit that though he was a modern man, as he thought of himself, self-sufficient and powerful, he still believed in the miracle of prayer.

Facing a terrible dilemma, he had made a gut-wrenching decision. How did a man such as Miguel—an honorable man who loved his country and wanted the best for his people—live with the knowledge that he held the fate of millions in his hands?

As the moments passed, one quickly after the other, J.J. felt an overwhelming need to share in this moment with Miguel, to make some requests of her own.

Help him. Please help him. He is not asking anything for himself. Only for his people. Protect him and protect them from the evil threatening this nation. And let me do what is right, whatever will help Miguel the most.

After they'd spent nearly an hour in the cathedral, they walked outside, hand-in-hand, into the warm sunlight of an autumn afternoon in Nava. On the surface, this city, like the entire country, was an island paradise. But men's greed for power and wealth had once chained this country in bondage. Set free only in the latter half of the twentieth century, Mocorito now faced a return to slavery under an uncaring taskmaster.

Miguel Cesar Ramirez stood alone, his country's savior.

"This evening I will make an announcement on television to the people of my country," Miguel said as they walked toward his car.

J.J. knew without asking what he planned to tell the citizens of Mocorito.

"I want you there with me tonight."

"I'll be right at your side."

"And tomorrow morning, I want you to leave Mocorito."

"No, Miguel. I want—"

He opened the car door for her and when she whirled around to face him, he looked her right in the eyes and said, "If you truly wish to help me, you will go back to America."

She searched his face, studying his expression. Knowing what was in his heart, she realized she had only one real choice. "All right. I'll make arrangements to fly to Caracas in the morning and then on to the United States."

He helped her into the Aston-Martin, then rounded the hood and got in on the other side. "I will telephone Roberto and Emilio and ask them to meet us at campaign headquarters. I have already told Juan what I plan to do and I must tell the others."

"They will support your decision."

"Will they? Even not knowing the real threat that Hector Padilla poses to Mocorito?"

"Yes, even not knowing that if Padilla is reelected he plans to replace democracy with a dictatorship, they will support your decision not to back down, not to allow the Federalists to intimidate you."

Miguel started the car and eased out into the street. "We have only a few hours this afternoon and then tonight to be together." Increasing speed, Miguel zigzagged the little sports car through afternoon traffic, Dom just barely keeping up with them as he followed in the rental car.

J.J. didn't respond. She understood what he meant and knew, in that moment, that no matter what happened tomorrow, next week or next year, this afternoon and tonight she would be, in every sense of the word, Miguel Ramirez's woman.

As Diego drove through the gates, disregarding the guards who waved at him as he left the palace grounds, he could think of nothing except what he had overheard as he had hidden in the room behind Hector Padilla's office.

A plot to overthrow the democratic government and replace it with a dictatorship within weeks of Hector's reelection!

He had been played for a fool! Used as a tool to further a cause he did not believe in and would never willingly have supported. Hector had even mentioned him by name when he spoke to the other men, laughing about how easily Diego could be manipulated.

Diego Fernandez's hatred for his half-brother has blinded him to everything else, Hector had said. *His stupidity has worked greatly to my advantage.*

What was he going to do? He had broken the law, had taken part in criminal activities on behalf of the Federalist Party, had even blackmailed his sister's best friend. He could hardly go to the police, could he?

You can go to Ramirez, an inner voice told him. Go to him and tell him what Hector has planned.

The thought of joining forces with his father's bastard son sickened Diego. He hated Miguel Ramirez as much as he hated admitting he had been wrong. But it was that very hatred that had made him so easily manipulated by that son of a bitch Padilla.

He had to do something to stop Hector and his ungodly band of supporters. And he had to do something soon.

Think about what can be done. Consider all your options. There must be a way that you can do what must be done without destroying your own life.

In three hours they would go to the television station for Miguel to give his address to the nation. Everything had been done to prepare for those fifteen minutes when candidate Ramirez would tell the people of Mocorito that no power on earth could make him withdraw from the presidential race. J.J. had read his speech and wept, knowing what this decision had cost him on a purely personal level. If his life, his future alone was at stake, he would have walked away with many regrets. But understanding fully the enormous impact on the nation if he protected only those closest to him, he had done the only thing he could have done. He had chosen to save Mocorito.

Due to impending rain showers, possibly even a tropical storm brewing off the coast, the humidity had risen gradually during the day, and now dampness hung in the air like an invisible mist. J.J. removed her suit and hung it in the closet, then took off her shoes. Perspiration dotted her forehead and trickled between her breasts. On their ride home from campaign headquarters, with the top down on Miguel's car, J.J. had gotten hot and only now, after ten minutes in the air-conditioned coolness of the house, had she begun to cool off. A little.

But in another sense she was still hot. Burning hot. There was a fire of passion blazing inside her. She and Miguel had a few precious hours to be together this afternoon and then again tonight. Tomorrow morning, she would take a ten o'clock flight from Mocorito to Caracas, and there board the Dundee jet for a flight home. Dom and Vic would remain in Mocorito, Dom as Miguel's bodyguard and Vic continuing to work undercover in conjunction with Will Pierce and the CIA.

"Jennifer?" Miguel called to her from the bedroom.

She walked out of the huge closet/dressing-room area, then halted in the doorway when she saw Miguel standing by the French doors overlooking the courtyard.

He had stripped off his shoes, socks and white shirt, and wore only his black dress slacks. His shoulders were broad, his back wide, his skin a polished bronze shimmering with perspiration in the shadowy light of the overcast afternoon.

Why was it that she felt her entire life—all thirty years—had been bringing her to this point in time, to this one cloudy, gray day in a country half a world away from home, with a man she had known only a few days?

"It is going to rain. Soon." Keeping his back to her, he spoke quietly, a hushed tone to his deep voice. "The wind is blowing very hard now."

Oh, Miguel, Miguel.

She walked across the room. Slowly. Her heart beating fast, her pulse racing. Everything feminine within her vibrated with a hunger she had never known, with a need to love and be loved in the most basic way a man and a woman can exchange that primitive emotion.

Why doesn't he turn around and hold out his arms to me? Why isn't he telling me how much he wants me?

When she came up behind him, she thought surely he would

urn and embrace her. She stood there for several strained moments. Then unable to bear another moment without his touch, she went to him, pressed herself against his back and reached her arms around him. His muscles went taut.

"Make love with me, Miguel," she whispered as she laid her head on the back of his shoulder.

He sucked in a deep breath, then released it as he turned and took her into his arms. He held her there, close to him, embracing her, one big hand resting across her spine, the other cupping her hip. His mouth raked across her temple and came to rest against her ear.

"You will not regret giving yourself to me, *querida?*" he asked, as if his life depended on her answer.

"Oh, Miguel. No. Never."

He grasped her shoulders and forced her to face him. With his fingers biting into her flesh, he said, "This will change nothing. You will leave Nava in the morning. You understand, yes?"

"Yes, I understand." She would leave tomorrow morning. She would get on the plane to Caracas, but she would leave behind her heart. And if he honestly thought that their becoming lovers would change nothing, then he was seriously mistaken. It would change everything.

The tension in his grasp lessened gradually as he lowered his head and brought their lips together. His arms encompassed her again, a forceful yet gentle embrace that claimed her as surely as if he had branded her. She had never before wanted to belong to a man. Body and soul. But she longed to belong to Miguel, in every possible way. And she wanted him to be hers and hers alone. His devouring kiss told her how much he wanted her, how hungry he was for her, as she was for him. But there was a gentleness in the kiss and in the way he held her, as if he wanted her to know that he cherished her, that she was precious to him.

"I ache for you," he said as his lips lifted from hers, then quickly made their way down her throat.

She ran her hands over his naked back, raking her fingernails over his hot, damp flesh. "I ache for you, too." She pulled away just enough to gain access to his chest. While he threaded his fingers through her hair, she spread kisses from collarbone to collarbone, then went lower to flick her tongue over first one and then the other of his tiny male nipples.

Miguel arched his back and moaned, deep and low, the sound guttural, like that of an animal.

Spurred on by his arousal bulging just below his waist, J.J. dropped to her knees and unzipped his slacks, then eased them and his black briefs down his hips until his jutting sex popped up in front of her. Powerful and pulsating, he was a temptation she could not resist. J.J. caressed him with her fingers and sighed when he growled his satisfaction. Taking the next step immediately, she ran the tip of her tongue down and back up, then repeated the process, tormenting him with a promise of fulfillment. She played with him, taking him into her mouth as he held her head in place, encouraging her eager lips and tongue to pleasure him.

Lost in the frenzy of giving him what he needed, J.J. became unbearably aroused, her femininity dripping with moisture, her nipples peaked and aching. Unexpectedly, Miguel eased himself from her mouth, then reached down and brought her up off her knees. Breathless and dazed with desire, she stared at him.

Smiling devilishly, he swooped her up into his arms and carried her to his bed. He placed her on her feet, then reached down to grasp the hem of her silk slip. When he maneuvered the slip up her thighs and over her hips, she lifted her arms into the air, assisting him in undressing her. She stood there on wobbly legs, wearing her white lace bra, bikini panties, silk stockings and garter belt. While she stared pleadingly into his dark eyes, begging him silently to end this torture, he touched her in the center of her chest, between her breasts, with the tip of his index finger, pushing her down onto the edge of the bed.

She sat there, tingling from head to toe, her feminine core

clenching and unclenching with anticipation, as he knelt in front of her. First he undid the tabs on her garter belt, one by one, releasing their hold on her silk stockings. Then he lifted her right leg and slowly peeled off the first stocking, his hands gently seductive. After he rolled the first stocking below her knee, he painted a trail of damp kisses across the top of her thigh. She gasped. What a marvelous sensation. As he took the stocking down her calf, over her ankle and off her foot, his lips followed his hands. He lifted her foot and kissed each toe.

"Such a small, delicate foot," he said before placing it on the floor and turning to her other leg.

He repeated the process of removing her stocking from the left leg. By the time he tossed that stocking on the floor atop the other one, J.J. was quivering, every nerve in her body alert.

She held her breath when he looked at her breasts with longing and only after he unhooked her lace bra and brought the straps down her shoulders, did she breathe again. Her naked breasts rose and fell, the nipples tight and hard.

"Beautiful. Very beautiful."

He lifted her breasts in his palms, then covered them and squeezed tenderly. When his fingertips circled her areola, she thought she would die. Then when she whimpered, he gave her what she wanted. He flicked her nipples with his thumbs and that action released a firestorm of pure sensation inside her. She cried out.

"Did I hurt you?" he asked, concern in his golden-brown eyes.

"No, no. Please, please, don't stop."

He tormented her nipples, with his thumb and forefinger. Then while he pinched one aching point, he brought his mouth down over the other and suckled her until she thought she wouldn't be able to bear another minute of such intense pleasure.

Keening, the sound vibrating in her throat, she tossed back her head and thrust her breasts forward. Miguel rose up over her and then turned her in the bed until she lay flat on her back. Looking up at him, she opened her mouth with silent awe.

"You're beautiful, too," she told him. "Very beautiful."

And very large and very aroused.

Smiling at her compliment, he hooked his fingers inside her panties and pulled them down over her hips. When he stopped and nuzzled her mound with his mouth, her hips lifted of their own volition. As soon as he threw her panties on the floor, he joined her on the bed.

They gazed into each other's eyes, the tension between them electric. His eyes still on hers, he mounted her, delving deep with the first lunge, taking her completely, filling her to the hilt. For half a second she felt stretched beyond her limits, but her body soon adjusted to accommodate him and then she simply felt complete.

And so the dance began, Miguel setting the rhythm. Deep, slow thrusts that made her body sing. She couldn't get close enough, couldn't touch him enough, kiss him enough, say his name enough. He was on her, around her, inside her and yet she wanted more of him. She wanted her flesh and bones to melt into his.

He whispered dark, erotic words and phrases, moaning his desire and his intentions against her breasts. Suddenly he increased the tempo. Fast, hard jabs. J.J. shuddered, her core tightened, preparing for release.

She clung to him, encouraging him with every breath, every movement, every moaned sigh. She repeated his name over and over again, like a worshipful chant. Her climax hit her, releasing the spring on her tightly wound sex, allowing her to come apart completely. She cried and gasped and dug her nails into his back.

And then he jackhammered into her, giving her a second orgasm when he came. He roared out his pleasure, the sound rumbling from deep inside him. And then, after the aftershocks had rippled through them, he fell to one side and stared up at the ceiling, his breathing hard and fast.

She lay beside him. Sated. Spent. Deliriously happy. And totally, irrevocably in love.

Chapter 14

Dom sat with J.J., off camera, in a small, crowded room, as they waited for the moment the on-air commercial would conclude and the cameras would turn to Miguel. More nervous than she could remember ever being, J.J. had clasped and unclasped her hands a half-dozen times. She had rubbed her palms up and down her dress slacks until she feared she had thinned the gabardine. And she had glanced at the oval utility clock on the wall every two minutes. When she tapped one foot up and down, Dom reached over and placed his hand on her knee. She stopped immediately.

"You're making me nervous, honey," Dom said. "Calm down. He'll be all right."

Leaning toward Dom, she spoke in English as quietly as possible, hoping not to be overheard. "No, he won't be all right. He's aware that by swearing he will run for president, no matter what, he might be condemning other people like Carlos to death."

With so many supporters around them—everyone from Roberto and Emilio to Juan, Aunt Josephina and Seina—J.J. felt suffocated. And muffled. She couldn't say what she wanted to say to Dom, couldn't vent her frustration and anger at the top of her lungs. If only she could scream. Just once.

Dom took her hand and gave it a good squeeze, then released it. "God forbid anyone should think I'm flirting with my cousin's fiancée."

"Yes, God forbid." Knowing he had hoped to gain a smile from her, J.J. failed him. The best she could do was to stop frowning for a brief moment.

"You've gotten in over your head on this one, haven't you?" Dom said.

She pinned him with a be-quiet glare. "You have no idea," she whispered. Both Roberto and Emilio spoke some English and although both men knew who she really was, she didn't want to share her private feelings with either of them.

Lowering his voice, Dom said, "I never in a million years thought you'd fall for a guy like Ramirez."

J.J.'s mouth curved into a self-deprecating half smile. Thinking what a fool she must seem to Dom, she replied, "I didn't see it coming. It caught me totally unaware. Attraction is one thing, but…"

"You're in love with him." Dom looked at her, sympathy in his black eyes.

She didn't respond. She didn't need to.

"It is time." Emilio signaled to the group by fluttering his hands. "Quiet everyone. The future president of Mocorito is about to speak to us."

J.J. said so softly she wasn't sure Dom heard her, "Take care of him when I'm gone."

Dom mouthed the words. "I promise."

Mario Lamas, the Nationalist Party sympathizing owner of Nava's television station faced the in-house and at-home audience. First he cleared his throat. Then in a loud, distinct voice he announced that tonight Miguel Cesar Ramirez would be speaking to the people, speaking to them from his heart. Mario went on to praise Miguel, to recount his humble beginnings and brag about him as a teacher might a favorite student. As Mario's introduction continued, J.J.'s thoughts escaped from this place, from this moment in time, to the most glorious two hours of her life. Two hours spent with Miguel in his bedroom suite, shut off from the rest of the world. For those one hundred and twenty minutes, she had been in heaven. The heaven she and Miguel had created together.

These next fifteen minutes would be pure hell for Miguel and if they were that agonizing to him, then they would be to her. His pain was her pain. But once the deed was done, once he had made his stand, drawn his line in the sand, there would be no turning back. All they could do was wait for Hector Padilla and his Federalist cohorts to make their next move. Her instincts told her that they would strike again and soon. Another murder? The death of someone else near and dear to Miguel? But when would it happen? And to whom?

Hating the helpless feeling of knowing there was nothing she could do to prevent another tragedy, J.J. stood and paced around the room. As she passed by Aunt Josephina and Seina, the two women flanking Juan, she offered them a weak smile, doing her best to reassure them that all was well. What a damn lie!

This small room at the studio was filled with people who loved, admired and respected Miguel. Having realized upon their arrival tonight what a perfect time this would be to kill those closest to Miguel in one fell swoop, she and Dom had thoroughly searched this room and then Dom had excused himself and gone over every inch of the television station.

"Mind if I take a couple of your security guards with me to check things out?" Dom had asked Mario. "I just want to make sure my cousin is safe tonight for the broadcast."

Mario had not only given Dom his permission, he'd sent four security guards with him and given them orders to follow Señor Shea's every command.

"Best I can tell, this whole place is clean," Dom had told her.
"If the bad guys are planning something, I don't think they're
going to blow this place sky-high. At least not tonight."

"They must know what Miguel plans to say tonight. Whoever
the traitor in Miguel's camp is, he or she must already have
shared the information with Padilla."

"You said he—or she. Do you think the traitor could be female?"

"I don't know. If it is, we can rule out Dolores, of course. So
that leaves only Ramona and Aunt Josephina and both of them
seem devoted to Miguel."

The moment Miguel appeared on screen, everyone congre-
gated in the small room at the station broke out in applause. J.J.
clapped the longest and the loudest, a part of her wanting to
whistle and stomp her feet and shout, "Viva Ramirez! Viva el
presidente."

God, what love could do to a woman!

From the very second Miguel spoke his first word, J.J. kept
her gaze focused on the television screen mounted on the wall.
He looked so handsome. He had chosen his suit, she his shirt and
tie. Clasping her hands in her lap to prevent them from trembling
nervously, she recalled buttoning his pale blue shirt and wrapping the gray, navy and white striped tie around his neck, then
tying it. He had kept kissing her while she knotted his tie and
she had laughed as she struggled to keep her mind on the job at
hand. What she had truly wanted, just as he had, was to go back
to bed and make love again.

Tonight, she told herself. Tonight when this is over, when we
go home, when we are alone in his bedroom suite. They would
make love all night long.

And in the morning she would leave. Tonight might well be
the last time she would see Miguel, the last time they would be
together. Neither of them knew what the future would hold.

Diego sat in front of the television in the wood-paneled study
of his father's home. Even though his mother now owned this fine

house, which would one day be his, he would always think of it as his father's home. Reminders of Cesar Fernandez were in every room. Diego's mother had altered nothing since her husband's death. His favorite pipes remained on the desk in this room and the smell of his tobacco still permeated the upholstery and drapes. The liquor cabinet contained his preferred liquors and every article of clothing he had owned remained in the closets and chests upstairs. An oil painting of Cesar in his youth hung over the fireplace here in the den and another of him, in his prime, hung over the mantel in the front parlor. And Diego's mother kept her wedding photograph of a smiling young couple in a silver frame on her bedside table.

As Diego downed another swig of his father's aged brandy, he wondered how a man who had been loved so devotedly by a woman such as Carlotta could have lowered himself to sleep with the likes of Luz Ramirez, a gutter whore from the Aguilar barrio.

Looking at Ramirez on the television screen, Diego saw his father's fine features. The nose, the mouth, the bone structure identical to their father's. Yes, damn it—their father. Miguel looked far more like Cesar than either Diego or Seina. Diego had been told by many people that he was a cross between his parents. And who had not heard numerous times that Seina was the image of her grandmother Fernandez, for whom she had been named.

"I have come to you tonight to pledge my life to you, the people of Mocorito," Miguel Ramirez said.

Diego lifted his glass and saluted him.

The man had the eyes of a jungle cat. Yellow-brown. Cunning. Dangerous.

When Diego had arrived home today, his mother had met him at the door, ranting and raving about Seina having packed a bag and left home. He had done his best to soothe his mother and assure her that, in time, Seina would come to her senses and return home. He knew better. His sister would never return home. And it was all his fault. His evil deeds had run her off.

"Everyone in Mocorito is aware that my chauffeur was murdered, but what you do not know is that threats have been made against others, against those closest to me," Miguel said. "I have no proof against anyone. We do not know who killed Carlos or who might perpetrate other crimes against my family, my friends and my supporters.

"But I say to you—and to them—if their purpose is to force me to withdraw my candidacy, then they have failed. I will continue campaigning, continue seeking your vote. No matter what happens, I promise I will give you, the good people of Mocorito, the choice between two candidates. Between Hector Padilla and Miguel Cesar Ramirez!"

"And I'm going to vote for you, you bastard," Diego saluted Miguel a second time with his now nearly empty glass of brandy. "If you live to election day."

Hector Padilla seethed as he listened to Miguel Ramirez address the people of Mocorito. Damn fool, Hector thought. Or was the man a heartless bastard? Yes, that was how they should play this. The man was willing to let innocent people die, murdered by some unknown madman intent on keeping Ramirez from becoming president. Of course he would do nothing himself, say nothing. But his publicity people could spin an ugly little tale and share it with the newspapers, as well as broadcast it from person to person, like juicy gossip.

He had ordered the chauffeur's death, had even specified that he wanted it to be particularly bloody. But three deaths had obviously not been enough to convince Ramirez that he should do the right thing. Perhaps another death would be necessary. A fourth death, even closer to home.

Such a pity that Miguel had feelings for his pretty little American bodyguard. It would be doubly tragic when she was struck down. The country would mourn for Miguel and he would be devastated. Then, if he insisted on continuing his candidacy, the people would know him for the heartless bastard he was. How could he put his own ambition above the lives of others?

There would be some within his circle, fellow Federalists, who would protest another killing, the ones who had cried over the deaths of the first three people. But they were weak men who could not be told the truth. Men like Diego Fernandez.

A brilliant idea formed in Hector's mind. He snapped his fingers, then laughed. But of course. He would send an expert marksman and tell him to aim at Ramirez and when his little bodyguard got in the way, to shoot her.

Diego could not complain if the target had been Ramirez. He hated his half-brother and probably longed to see him dead. He knew what he would say to Diego.

Too bad that the phony fiancée had gotten in the way.

Diego was gullible enough to buy that explanation. And Ramirez would be destroyed, knowing she had given her life to save him.

The moment Miguel entered the small room at the studio, his friends surrounded him, patting him on the back, congratulating him on a fine speech, telling him how brave and fearless he was. Did they not understand that because they were here, supporting him, loving him, cheering him on, that they were in danger, that their very lives were at stake?

Trying his best to act appreciatively as he made his way through the well-wishers, Miguel sought the one person who understood him, the one person who knew what tonight's speech had cost him. Where was she?

And then he saw her, coming through the crowd, coming straight to him. Their gazes met and locked. He moved away from Roberto, who had been shaking his hand, and met Jennifer in the middle of the room. Surrounded by his supporters, Miguel reached out and pulled Jennifer into his arms. She

hugged him fiercely and laid her head on his chest. A resounding cheer rose from the group. Jennifer lifted her head and
looked around them, then gazed up at him and smiled. Tears
filled her beautiful violet-blue eyes and cascaded down her al-
abaster cheeks.

All he wanted now was to take this woman home, to go upstairs to his room with her and close out the whole world for the
rest of the night.

As if she had read his thoughts, she stood on tiptoe and whispered in his ear. "We can't leave yet. All the workers from campaign headquarters are outside in the parking lot, along with a large
group of your supporters. You'll have to put in an appearance."

"You, *querida,* are a very understanding fiancée."

She clasped his hand. "I'm ready to face the crowd when
you are."

Dom came up on the other side of Miguel as they approached
the front entrance of the television studio. Although it was unlikely he would be targeted, judging by recent events, his bodyguards would be stupid to take any chances with his life.

If only each person in his entourage had their own personal
bodyguard. If only he could ensure their safety. Tonight. Tomorrow. And in the days ahead.

He could not provide everyone who supported him, who
worked tirelessly for his cause, a personal bodyguard, but he
could see that Emilio, Roberto, Juan and Aunt Josephina had protection. And even his sister, Seina, now that she had publicly
claimed him. They were the people most likely to become tar-
gets. Later tonight, he would speak with J.J. and Dom about making arrangements to call in more agents.

With his senses at full alert, Miguel exited the studio, and with
his arm around Jennifer and Dom practically attached to his
other side, he marched across the street.

Followed by the group who had come from inside the studio,
Miguel made his way to the parking lot where an enormous

crowd waited. The moment they saw him, they cheered and began rushing toward him.

Dom Shea cursed under his breath.

Jennifer clutched Miguel's arm to halt him. "This is bad," she said. "If they overrun us, there will be no way we can protect you."

Yanking away from her, thinking fast on his feet and yet not considering all the risks, Miguel crawled up into the bed of a parked pickup truck and lifted his arms in a gesture that requested his supporters to cease and desist. Within seconds, Jennifer and Dom had joined him in the truck bed, followed shortly by Emilio and Roberto.

"You're an easy target up here," Jennifer told him. "You can't stay here."

"Only for a few minutes. Just until I speak to these people and give them a few minutes of my time. That's all they want."

He motioned for the cheers and shouts to stop, but it took a good three or four minutes before anyone could hear him over the noise. Finally, he managed to make himself heard. He said a few words of thanks and asked for their continued support. Then, when J.J. and Dom escorted him down from the truck bed, the applause started anew. He wrapped his arm around Jennifer's shoulders and together they headed straight for Dom's rental car. Several people followed them, mostly his closest friends. He shook hands with Emilio and Roberto again, then hugged Aunt Josephina and held out his hand to Seina and when she placed her hand in his, he lifted it to his lips and kissed it.

"Thank you for being here tonight," he said.

"You're welcome, Miguel."

He then shook hands with Juan. "I will depend on you to take good care of my little sister."

"I vow to you that her happiness means more to me than anything else."

Miguel turned around and, with his arm still draped across J.J.'s shoulders, they walked toward Dom's car. Suddenly, before

Miguel had any idea what was happening, Dom barreled into him, knocking both him and J.J. to the ground. J.J. rose up quickly and threw her body over Miguel's.

Reaching out, he grabbed her shoulders and began rolling her over to his side. He would not allow her to die for him. He would not!

The sound of a rifle shot was almost muffled by frightened screams as people ran in every direction.

J.J. gasped. Once.

With his weapon drawn and his gaze scanning the area, Dom hovered over them. "Are either of you hit?"

"I am fine," Miguel replied, then looked over at J.J.

When she stared at him, her face chalk-white, he saw the pain in her eyes.

"Jennifer? J.J.?" he cried her name as he ran his hands over her body.

She groaned. He withdrew his hand from her side. His fingers dripped with blood. Jennifer's blood.

Chapter 15

Miguel paced the floor, like a caged tiger, his teeth bared, his claws ready to rip apart the first person who dared to cross him. Dom had tried to help him moments after the shooting, but Miguel had clung to J.J. as if he thought letting go of her would mean her death. Then later, Dom had tried to persuade Miguel to allow the paramedics to take J.J. from him, but to no avail. In the end, Juan Esteban had worked out a compromise that Miguel had agreed to reluctantly—they had allowed him to sit at her side in the ambulance. Dom had driven directly behind them, all the way to St. Augustine's, praying as hard as he'd ever prayed in his life. When he'd been a navy SEAL, he'd seen comrades killed, their heads blown off, their guts hanging out. But he'd never gotten used to the sight of death, the loss of a human life. Since going to work at the Dundee Agency, he had been faced with the injury of a fellow agent a couple of times. Both had survived.

As they waited now for word on J.J.'s condition, he knew what

Miguel was thinking and understood part of what he was feeling. He was thinking how small and delicate J.J. had looked lying there on the street, blood covering her beige jacket. He was thinking that if the bullet had hit a couple of inches over, he would be the one in the operating room right now.

Dom loved J.J. like a little sister. He liked to kid her, enjoyed how she could take a practical joke and the fact that she always understood that his ribald sense of humor held no prejudice or malice. In many ways, he knew J.J. far better than Miguel Ramirez did. At least he'd known her a lot longer. But he wasn't in love with J.J. and he suspected that Miguel was. If he wasn't a man in love, he sure as hell was giving a good imitation of one tonight.

Miguel had been inconsolable and unreachable after they had arrived at the hospital and the attendants had wheeled J.J. directly into an elevator to take her to the operating room. He had bellowed like a wounded bull when they'd told him that he could not go with her. If it had not been for Dr. Esteban finally being able to calm Miguel, the security officers would have taken him into custody.

Juan's aunt had arrived with Seina Fernandez, both of them having ridden to the hospital with Emilio. Roberto had come separately, two campaign staff members with him. The ten-by-twelve waiting room was filled to capacity and to a person, they had each tried to talk to Miguel, to reassure him, to give him hope. He had not responded to anyone, ignoring them as if he were deaf, dumb and blind. Part of the time, he paced the floor, looking neither right nor left, but straight down, as if he found the floor utterly fascinating. The rest of the time he stood and stared out the windows into the dark night. About an hour ago, it had started raining, and just now Dom saw streaks of lightning crackling through the black sky.

They had been waiting for three hours—the longest three hours of Dom's life. When he'd first arrived, he'd stayed outside long enough to call Vic and tell him what had happened. Vic had made him promise to call him once J.J. came out of surgery.

"She'll pull through," Vic had said. "She may look like a fragile china doll, but our little J.J. is as tough as nails."

He'd been acquainted with Vic long enough to realize the guy didn't make friends easily. He was a loner and although everyone at Dundee liked and respected him, no one could say they really knew him. J.J. had come closer than anyone to breaking through that impregnable wall surrounding Vic Noble, probably because she wasn't intimidated by him. God knew most women were. Intimidated and attracted. Vic had that mysterious Clint Eastwood gunslinger thing going for him that kept other men at arm's length and intrigued women.

"If she dies, so help me God..." Vic had left the rest unsaid. But Dom hadn't needed to hear the words to know what Vic meant. If J.J. died, there would be no place on earth for those responsible to hide.

But J.J. was not going to die. Dr. Esteban had told them that the bullet had entered her right side and his guess was that it was lodged in the lower rib cage.

"I don't believe the bullet hit any vital organs," Juan had told Miguel. "But we won't know the extent of the damage until we operate. Much depends upon the type of bullet that was used."

At seventeen minutes past eleven, Dr. Esteban, wearing green surgery scrubs, appeared in the waiting-room doorway. A hushed silence fell over the room. Miguel paused in his relentless pacing, looked at Juan and froze to the spot.

Juan walked toward Miguel and when he was within a couple of feet, he paused and said, "She came through surgery quite well. We removed the bullet. There was no injury to any vital organs. She is resting comfortably in recovery and we will move her to intensive care shortly."

"She will live?" Miguel asked.

"Yes," Juan replied. "Barring any complications, she should

recover fully in a few weeks and she should be able to travel in four or five days."

"I want to see her," Miguel said.

"She won't know you are there. She hasn't come out from under the anesthesia yet and when she does, we will keep her heavily sedated for the next eight to twelve hours."

"She will know I am there," Miguel said.

"It is highly irregular," Juan told him. "Family is usually permitted only brief visits with a patient in the intensive care."

"Make arrangements for me to stay with her."

Juan sighed heavily, then nodded before patting Miguel on the shoulder. "Stay here. I will send someone for you very soon."

When Dr. Esteban left without saying a word to anyone else, and apparently no one was brave enough to face Miguel, Dom made the first move. He walked over to Miguel and paused at his side where he still stood in the middle of the room.

"When she comes to, don't start babbling a lot of nonsense about this being your fault," Dom said in English. "That's not what she'll want to hear."

Miguel didn't reply.

Dom lowered his voice. "The way she'll see it is that she was doing her job. Her first instinct was to protect you."

"Yes, I know." Still Miguel did not look at Dom

"When you're thinking a little more rationally, we'll talk. Until then keep one thing in mind—you might not have been the target."

Miguel snapped his head around and glared at Dom.

When J.J. awoke, groggy and confused, she glanced around the room and realized she was in the hospital. Then she saw Miguel, sitting at her bedside, his head bowed, his eyes closed. Was he sleeping?

What happened? her dazed mind asked. Then slowly, bit by bit, she recalled the events of last evening. The crowds. The cheers. Miguel and she walking toward Dom's rental car. Dom knocking them off their feet. Her instincts taking over as she sought to shield Miguel with her own body.

Had that happened only this past evening? Just how long had she been in the hospital? She opened her mouth and tried to speak, but she couldn't manage to make a sound other than a gurgling gasp.

Miguel's eyelids flew open instantly and he came up out of his chair and hovered over her. "Jennifer? *Querida?*"

She tried to smile at him, but she wasn't sure whether she did or not. Then she tried to lift her hand, but couldn't do it. What was wrong with her? Why was she so weak?

Miguel grasped her hand tenderly and lifted it to hold over his heart. "Don't try to talk. Just rest, *querida.*"

She moaned, wanting desperately to communicate with him.

"Are you in pain?" he asked, his voice edged with near panic.

She managed to shake her head. She was uncomfortable, but not really in pain. I must be drugged, she thought. Doped up on some heavy-duty pain killers.

She tried to speak again and this time managed to say one word. "Miguel."

"Yes, I'm here." He kissed her hand, then placed it down by her side and leaned over to kiss her forehead.

"What happened?" she asked.

"Do you not remember?"

"Some." Then she recalled the searing pain hitting her in the side. "Was I shot?"

"Yes, you…you were shot."

"Am I going to be all right?"

He nodded. Tears pooled in his eyes.

"Is everyone else all right? You? Dom?"

"No one else was harmed. Only you." Frowning as if he were in immeasurable pain, Miguel momentarily closed his eyes.

"I guess I can't leave Mocorito now, can I?"

Caressing her face and looking at her with concern, he said,

"You should never have come here in the first place. If I had known… I would die before I would put your life in danger."

"I know that." She felt herself fading, as if this brief conversation had sapped all her strength

"We have talked too much already," Miguel said. "You must rest. No more talk."

"Stay with me."

"I won't leave you. I promise.

She sighed, then closed her eyes. "I love you."

The last thing she heard before she fell asleep was Miguel saying in an anguished voice, *"Querida…querida."*

Miguel spent forty-eight hours in the hospital, sleeping very little, eating only when Ramona came with food from home and threatened him with bodily harm if he did not eat. When Jennifer began staying awake for long periods of time, after that first night and day, she'd told him to go home and shower and shave, but he had refused. Then this morning, when a stranger arrived at the hospital and Dom Shea had brought the man in to see J.J., she had told Dom to take Miguel home.

"This is Geoff Monday," Dom had introduced the burly Brit, a rugged blond with bulging muscles and a friendly grin. "He will stay here and guard J.J. while you and I go back to your house."

Miguel had not wanted to leave, but J.J. had insisted, so, to please her, he acquiesced, promising to return in a few hours.

No sooner had he and Dom exited the hospital than a horde of reporters swarmed down on them. Behind the reporters, countless people carrying signs and shouting for justice crammed the parking lot and the street.

"What's going on?" Miguel asked.

"It started yesterday," Dom said. "These are your people, Ramirez. The citizens of Nava, up in arms over the second attempt on your life. They blame the Federalists and some have out-and-out accused President Padilla of plotting your death."

"Why did no one tell me what was happening? We cannot have rioting in the streets."

"Emilio and Roberto wanted to tell you, but I warned them that you had enough to deal with and that you'd find out soon enough. Besides, I don't think there's much you can do about it. You can hardly tell these people that they're wrong, that their president is innocent."

"I am surprised that Padilla hasn't sent out army troops to suppress the protests." Miguel stood on the sidewalk, Dom at his side, while the hospital security just barely managed to keep the reporters at bay.

"So far, these protests have been peaceful," Dom said. "But I doubt they'll stay that way. I think you'll have to make a statement to the press right now. If nothing else tell them your fiancée is recovering nicely, that the police have not caught the shooter and you will have more to say later today."

"Yes, you are right about what I must do, what I must say. And later, when I have had time to think, I must come up with a way to defuse this ticking time bomb."

Miguel then spoke to the reporters, making the brief statement that Dom had outlined for him.

"Okay, now that you've temporarily taken care of that problem, let's get out of here," Dom told him.

"How do we do that?"

As if on cue, the roar of a big black Hummer alerted the crowd to get out of the way or be plowed down in the monster vehicle's path.

"What—?" The one questioning word was all Miguel said before Dom grabbed his arm and, shoving through the reporters, raced with him to the Hummer.

Once safe inside, Dom said, "Vic Noble sent some of his friends to pick us up."

J.J. awoke later that afternoon, feeling more human than she'd felt since the shooting. She figured Juan Esteban had lowered the dosage of her pain medication, which had helped her not only to stay awake, but also to be at least partially alert. She hated that woozy, drugged feeling, that sense of not being fully in control of her mind or body.

Geoff Monday had been in and out of her room all day. Every time a nurse came in for whatever reason, they had asked him to step outside. She had been bathed, fed, prodded and poked. Although she knew the nurses checked her vital signs only at regular intervals, she felt as if they were doing it every hour on the hour. How on earth did anyone get any rest while they were in the hospital?

When a pair of nurses shooed Geoff out, he smiled, shrugged and left willingly. But when they wheeled her hospital bed out into the hall, he stopped them immediately. They explained in rapid Spanish that they were taking J.J. down for some X-rays.

"My Spanish is a little rusty," Geoff admitted as he kept his big, meaty hand planted on the foot of J.J.'s bed, effectively blocking the path. "Did they say something about some X-rays?"

"They're taking me downstairs for some X-rays," J.J. told him. "I'm not sure why, but I suppose it's simply hospital procedure. Apparently, Juan Esteban issued the order."

"I'll ride down in the elevator with you," Geoff said.

"I'll tell them that my friend will be going with us." She then turned to the two nurses and spoke to them in Spanish.

They both nodded and smiled, so Geoff moved out of the way and followed them to the service elevator. With one nurse at the head of her bed and the other at the foot, they maneuvered the bed into the elevator, then one of the nurses hopped out of the elevator in front of Geoff while the other one hit the down button.

"What's going on?" J.J. demanded half a second before the nurse covered her face with a foul-smelling rag.

Dom received a frantic call on his cell phone from Geoff Monday, who referred to himself by every conceivable name in the book for allowing J.J. to be snapped up right under his nose. Almost simultaneously, Miguel's cell phone rang.

"Answer it!" Dom shouted. "J.J.'s been kidnapped.

Chapter 16

Miguel's heart stopped for a moment, a part of him dying on the spot. That brief hesitation gained him another shout from Domingo Shea.

"Answer the goddamn phone."

With robotic movements, Miguel removed his cell phone from his belt clip, flipped it open and placed it to his ear. "Yes, this is Miguel Ramirez."

"Are you missing a wounded fiancée?" the obviously disguised voice asked.

"Where is she? What have you done with her?"

Dom clamped his hand down on Miguel's shoulder and gave him a look that told him not to panic, to stay calm.

Laughter. He heard the person on the other end of the phone laughing. When he found this person, he would rip out his heart.

"She is well. For now," the voice said. "Whether she lives or dies depends on you."

"What do you want?" Miguel asked, his heartbeat thundering in his ears.

"We want you to make another appearance on television. Call your friend Mario Lamas and arrange for another national broadcast."

"I can do that," Miguel said. "What am I supposed to announce?" He knew, but he had to hear the words said aloud, the demand made.

"If you wish to save Señorita Blair's life, you will withdraw from the presidential race. Make up any reason you choose to tell the citizens of Mocorito. If you do not do as we request, your American fiancée—" the man chuckled "—will die and her blood will be on your hands."

"I understand."

"You have until five o'clock today to speak to the people of Mocorito."

"And if I do as you request, you will release Jennifer unharmed?"

"Yes, of course."

The line went suddenly dead. Miguel gripped the phone with white-knuckled rage. He turned to Dom Shea. "They say they will kill her, if I don't—" He looked at his cell phone. "I have to call Mario Lamas and make arrangements for a few moments of air time."

"Tell me what the hell he said to you."

Miguel shook his head. "It does not matter. I know what I must do."

Dom grabbed Miguel's shoulders and shook him. The two men faced off, like two warriors preparing for hand-to-hand combat. "Don't try to handle this alone. Don't go all power-hungry on me. For God's sake, it's J.J.'s life that's at stake here."

Bristling, every muscle in his body taut, Miguel said," Do you think I do not know what is at stake?"

"Yeah, sure you do. Just fill me in," Dom told him. "You're not going to play God where J.J. is concerned. You're not making any decisions on your own. Do you understand?"

"They will kill her if I do not withdraw from the presidential race. There, I've said it. Does that change anything? No, it does not." He shrugged off Dom's hold and lifted his cell phone. "I must contact Mario and—"

Dom grabbed Miguel's wrist, effectively stopping him from making the call. "Hold on."

"I have only until five o'clock." Miguel glanced at his wrist-watch. "It is now two-thirty."

"What proof did they give you that they have J.J.?"

"She is missing, is she not? Was she not kidnapped from the hospital, despite one of your Dundee agents being there to protect her?"

"There's no reason for you to go off half-cocked. You need to slow down and think. What assurance did they give that, if they actually have J.J., they will release her unharmed when you publicly announce your withdrawal from the race?"

An overpowering sense of total deflation hit Miguel, as if all the wind had been knocked out of him. "They gave me no proof that they have her and I have only one man's word that she will be released unharmed if I do as they say."

Dom squeezed Miguel's wrist, then released him. "Call Mario and ask for air time at four-fifty. Tell him to make some public service announcements, starting immediately, that Miguel Ramirez will again speak to the people of Mocorito. At four-fifty this afternoon. That will buy us some time."

"What can we do in two hours and fifteen minutes?"

"We can turn this city upside down and right side out and if we're lucky we'll find her. If not, then you'll go on TV."

J.J. came to in a darkened room, the smell of fish and seawater strong. If she had to venture a guess as to where her kidnappers had taken her, she'd say it was somewhere near the waterfront. And since she seriously doubted that they were keeping her in any of the luxurious condos and cottages with ocean views in Nava, that probably meant she was in Colima. Like Ebano, Colima was little more than a suburb of Nava, but much less upscale than Ebano.

J.J.'s side ached something awful, the pain bearable, but for how long? She'd been kept on painkillers for days now, but she didn't know how long it had been since her last injection because she had no idea what time it was. Dim light came through the row of small, high windows near the top of the twenty-foot wall. That meant it wasn't nighttime yet.

When she tried to move, she realized her wrists were tied to the wooden arm rests on either side of the chair in which she sat. And her ankles were bound together.

While she was still trying to get her bearings and figure out what, if anything, she could do, a door on the far side of the room swung open, ushering in a bit more light which outlined the tall, menacing figure standing in the doorway.

"Good afternoon, Señorita Blair," the familiar voice said to her in Spanish.

When he walked into the room and came closer, close enough for her to see his face, she looked him right in the eye and said, "So it is you who are the traitor."

Diego went to the palace when Hector summoned him, and he sat there with the president and the secretary of state while Hector explained to Diego that some loyal Federalists had whisked Señorita Blair from her hospital room.

"She is being held now—quite safe you understand—in Colima, at the old abandoned Cristobal canning plant on the waterfront." Hector had smirked, thinking he was placating Diego by sharing every tidbit of information with him. "Since the assassination attempt several evenings ago went awry, our supporters were forced to improvise."

"If Ramirez withdraws his candidacy, you will free Señorita Blair?" Diego asked, doing his best to not appear at all concerned.

"Certainly. Of course."

Diego knew the man was lying to him. Lying now as he had been doing for the past year. He had flattered Diego, praised him and used his hatred for his half-brother to bring out the very worst in him. The dark, demonic side that lived deep inside every man.

"I know you have been concerned, my friend, about recent events." Hector Padilla looked remorseful, as if he truly regretted the horrible things that had been happening. "I, more than any-one, long for peace. But often the price of peace is the lives of in-nocent people. You understand, Diego, a man of your intelli-gence."

Diego nodded. "Yes, I understand, el presidente."

"Good. Good. Now that this is settled, come, join us for a late lunch. And tonight come back to the palace. I believe we will have much to celebrate then."

"Regrettably I must decline the offer of lunch. My mother is greatly concerned about my young sister who has left home. It is a family crisis and I must do what I can to help my poor mother and bring my sister back to her family."

"Yes, yes, of course." Hector rose from his chair and patted Diego on the back as he walked him to the door. "Be sure to watch television this afternoon at four-fifty. That bastard brother of yours will once again address the nation. But this time he will be saying what we want to hear."

At four-fifteen, just as Miguel and Dom entered Mario La-mas's office at the television station, Dom's cell phone rang.

"I cannot believe this has happened," Mario said. "There must be another way to handle this. You cannot withdraw from the presidential race."

Dom stepped outside into the hallway to answer his cell phone. Miguel prayed that the call was news about Jennifer.

Geoff Monday had joined Vic Noble, who had in turn called in Will Pierce and every contact either man had in Mocorito had been assigned the job of finding out where J.J. Blair had been taken. So far, not one lead had panned out. Time was running out. In thirty minutes, he would have to make the most difficult speech of his life. He had truly believed that he would always put Mocorito first, above everything and everyone. Had he not been willing to risk the lives of his family and friends in order to save his beloved country? How was it that now he planned to forsake every pledge he had made to his people in order to possibly save one woman?

Jennifer.

Dom came back into the office, a look of disappointment on his face. He glanced at Miguel and shook his head.

"If I refuse to do as the kidnappers asked, they will kill Jennifer," Miguel said to Mario.

"You are being asked to choose between the woman you love and the country—the people—that you love." Mario shook his head. "No man should be asked to make such a choice."

"You know what J.J. would tell you to do, don't you?" Dom said in English, knowing Mario would not understand him.

Dom Shea's words fell on deaf ears.

"And I wish I had the strength to do what she would want," Miguel said. "But I do not. I cannot let them kill her."

"Damn it, man, don't you know that no matter what you do, they're going to kill her."

No! He could not bear to hear the truth. And he knew, in his heart, that what Dom had been trying to tell him for the past couple of hours was the truth. No matter what he did, unless they could find J.J. soon, she would die.

If she were not already dead.

And if she could make the decision for him, she would tell him not to give in to threats, to tell her kidnappers to go to hell. She would expect him to stay in the presidential race and win.

Suddenly Miguel's cell phone rang. All three of them stared at the phone clipped to his belt. With a slightly unsteady hand, Miguel removed the phone, flipped it open and took a deep breath.

"This is Miguel Ramirez."

Silence.

"Who is this?"

Silence.

"Is someone there?"

"This is Diego Fernandez."

Miguel swallowed hard. "What do you want?"

"I realize you have no reason to believe me, no reason to trust me. If I were in your shoes, I would not trust you."

"What are you talking about?"

"I know where Señorita Blair is being held."

Miguel's heart stopped. "Why have you called? To torment me? I am here at the television station right now, preparing to announce my withdrawal from the presidential race at approximately four-fifty. What more can Hector Padilla ask of me?"

"To hell with Padilla," Diego said. "I am asking you not to withdraw from the race. And I am telling you that if you come now, you can save the American woman. I can tell you where she is."

"Why should I believe you?" Miguel's pulse raced, his heartbeat accelerated alarmingly. "Why would you want to help me?"

Mario's eyes widened inquiringly. Dom Shea came over and mouthed, "Who is it?" as he narrowed his gaze and frowned at Miguel.

"When you are elected president, I want a full pardon for any crimes I may have committed, in ignorance, on behalf of President Padilla," Diego said."

"If I swear to give you what you ask for—"

"I am only a few yards away from where she is being held," Diego told him. "Give me your solemn vow that you will pardon me unconditionally and I will tell you where she is."

"I swear to you, Diego Fernandez, that when I, Miguel Cesar Ramirez, am elected president of Mocorito, I will pardon you for any and all crimes."

"Come to Colima," Diego said. "They are holding her at the old Cristobal canning plant on the waterfront."

The line went dead. Miguel closed his cell phone, then faced Dom as his mind went into overdrive trying to figure out what had just happened.

"She's in Colima," Miguel said.

"What the hell was that all about?" Dom asked. "You were swearing some kind of oath to your half-brother?"

"Mario, go on television at four-fifty and tell the people that Miguel Ramirez will speak to them shortly, that his car has been held up by the thousands of supporters who are lining the streets and blocking traffic."

"Yes, Miguel." With a stunned look in his eyes, Mario nodded.

Miguel headed for the door, calling out to Dom without slowing down. "Let's go. I know where they're holding J.J."

Following behind Miguel as he ran down the corridor, Dom called out, "How do you know that Diego Fernandez isn't sending you off on a wild goose chase?"

"Why would he try to stop me from publicly withdrawing from the presidential race?"

"Hell if I know."

Dom kept pace with Miguel as he shoved open the front door and pushed his way through the horde of supporters who descended upon them.

Once they finally made it to Dom's rental car, Miguel held out his hand. "Give me the keys. I will drive. I know where we are going."

Dom tossed Miguel the keys, then rounded the trunk and got in on the passenger side. Miguel revved the motor, backed the car out of the parking slot and nearly ran over several people blocking the street.

"Call Vic Noble and Will Pierce," Miguel said. "Tell them to meet us in Colima as soon as possible."

Dom started dialing his cell phone immediately. "Exactly where in Colima do you want them to meet us?"

"On the waterfront. At the old Cristobal canning plant."

Chapter 17

When he was a child, Miguel had come to Colima often with his grandfather and they had sat for hours fishing off the pier. Sometimes his grandfather's old friends would drop by and bring a bottle of tequila or some domestic beer and the men would reminisce about when they were young. Without fail, a man named Joaquin would recall one of his amorous moments with this or that young lady and Miguel's grandfather would have to remind him that there was a child listening.

Joaquin would always rub Miguel's head, mussing his hair, and say, "Someday this one will be quite the man with the ladies."

"Miguel will have more important things to do with his life than charm the ladies," his grandfather had said.

The others would laugh and ask what could possibly be more important.

The memory filled Miguel's mind as he parked the rental car in the middle of the desolate street in Colima.

Dom glanced over at him and asked, "Is this it?"

"No, the old canning plant is up at the end of the block." He pointed the direction. "I think it best if we walk the rest of the way. I have no idea exactly where Diego is waiting for us."

"*If* he's waiting for us."

When Miguel got out of the car, Dom followed him.

Glancing over his shoulder as he headed up the street, Miguel replied, "You think we could be walking into a trap, don't you?"

"Anything is possible. We need to be prepared." Dom patted his hip where his holster was attached to his belt, then paused, bent down and hiked up his pants leg. There attached to his thigh was a small holster containing a 25-caliber pistol, at most four inches long. He withdrew the automatic and held it out to Miguel.

"Take this and keep it on you," Dom said. "It's loaded. It holds a six-shot magazine and it's a single action."

Miguel paused, turned and took the gun. After looking it over, he pocketed the pistol and continued walking. Since every building within a two-block area was empty, some in crumbled ruins, others dilapidated and on the verge of ruin, it was highly unlikely they would run into anyone. When they neared the end of the deserted street, Miguel paused and scanned the area around him, carefully looking and listening.

"You stay here. I'll go the rest of the way alone," Miguel said. "If Diego is here and he was telling me the truth—"

"There you go again, playing God, issuing orders and thinking you have to do this alone."

"If Diego did set us up, there is no sense in both of us taking a chance, is there? If you hear gunfire, feel free to come to my rescue. Besides, if Diego was being honest with me, then J.J. is in that building and we're probably going to need backup. You should wait here for Will Pierce and the other Dundee agents."

"Nice try," Dom said. "But I'm not buying. We've come this far together, we'll go the rest of the way side by side."

Miguel would have argued, but time was of the essence. "I

Diego is waiting for us, he is probably in the alley between these two buildings."

Alert to every sound, prepared to act on a moment's notice, they crept down the shadowy alleyway between the old canning plant and the three-story brick building beside it. Halfway down the alley, Miguel caught a glimpse of a man's silhouette slinking along the wall, then disappearing into an alcove.

Miguel glanced at Dom, who nodded and drew his 9 mm. They found Diego Fernandez pressed up against a closed door in the alcove. Miguel grabbed his half-brother by the lapels of his tailor-made sports jacket and yanked him out into the alley.

"Where is she?" Miguel demanded.

"In there." Diego nodded toward the canning plant. "I'm not sure exactly where."

"If you're lying to me, I'll kill you," Miguel told him.

"If she's not here, then Hector Padilla lied to me," Diego said, pulling away from Miguel. "He's the one who told me where they are keeping her."

"Why should we believe you?" Dom asked.

"Because I can go in there and take Miguel—or you—straight to her, past any guards. Everyone knows that I am a close friend of el presidente's."

"Yeah, so we've heard," Dom said. "So why change horses in midstream?"

"What?" Diego stared at Dom quizzically.

"He is asking why, if you are such good friends with Hector Padilla, would you help me, a man you profess to hate?"

"I do despise you, Ramirez," Diego admitted. "But President Padilla has proven that he is not my friend. I hate him far more than I do you."

Miguel had to trust his gut instincts because there was no time for second-guessing. And his gut instincts told him that Diego was telling him the truth. He turned to Dom and said, "I will go with Diego. You stay here and wait for the others."

"What others?" Diego asked.

"You did not think we would come here without arranging for backup, did you?" Miguel's gaze clashed with his half-brother's.

"Very wise of you." Diego nodded.

Dom grabbed Miguel's arm. "I don't think you should—"

"I have to be the one," Miguel said. "Put yourself in my place. If she was your woman…"

Dom huffed out an exasperated breath. "Okay. Okay." He let go of Miguel's arm. "You two go in first, but if I hear one gunshot or get a gut feeling things are going down all wrong, I'll be a one-man cavalry to the rescue. And the minute the others show up, we're coming in."

Miguel patted Dom on the shoulder, then turned to Diego and said, "I am ready."

The pain in J.J.'s side had grown progressively worse, but she hoped it was now about as bad as it was going to get. She figured she'd been here a couple of hours or close to it, since coming out of her drugged stupor. The outside light spilling through the high windows had begun to fade, which told her the sun would soon be setting. So far, she had seen only three men. Two goons that she pegged as flunkies and a third man who had ordered the other two outside to act as guard dogs.

"I will keep Señorita Blair company until after the broadcast," he had told the others. "El presidente will telephone me personally when the time comes."

"What broadcast?" she had asked.

He had smiled wickedly, and she wondered why she had never noticed that evil glint in his eyes before now. "Miguel will make an announcement withdrawing from the presidential race at four-fifty this afternoon." He had glanced at his wristwatch. "In approximately three minutes."

"Miguel will never—"

"He will do it to save your life."

"No, he won't," she'd argued. "Miguel knows that I would not want him to sacrifice the future of his country to save me." She had glowered at her captor, the man Miguel had called a friend. "Besides, he knows better than to trust his enemies. He knows I will be murdered regardless of what he does."

"Love is blind, is it not, *señorita?*"

If she had thought talking to this man, reasoning with him, would do any good, she would have talked her head off, but she knew he would show her no mercy. No matter what Miguel did, whether he withdrew from the presidential race or not, his dear and trusted friend, Roberto Aznar, was going to kill her. And she suddenly realized that the son of a bitch would enjoy killing her, would take pleasure in destroying someone who meant so very much to Miguel. How he must hate Miguel. But why?

A loud knock sounded on the closed door.

"Señor?" one of the guards called out. "You have a visitor. Someone sent from el presidente himself. He wishes to see the *señorita.*"

"Perhaps Miguel has already made the announcement," Roberto said as he walked toward the door.

When he opened it, J.J. strained to see who their visitor was. But before she caught a glimpse of the new arrival, Roberto laughed and shook the man's hands.

"Come in, Señor Fernandez, come in."

"President Padilla has sent me to watch the execution," the man said. "He thought perhaps seeing you kill Ramirez's American whore would amuse me."

When Roberto returned to the room, the other man came with him. She recognized him instantly. Diego Fernandez!

"How do you plan to kill her?" Diego asked as he looked her over contemptuously.

"I'm going to slit her lovely little throat." Roberto walked over to the chair in which he'd been sitting, reached down beside it and picked up a long, leather sheath. He removed a knife with a gleaming twelve-inch blade.

"Why do you hate Miguel so much?" The question popped out of J.J.'s mouth before she realized she's spoken.

Roberto glared at her. "Are you speaking to me or to Señor Fernandez?"

"To you, you damn Benedict Arnold. I know why Fernandez hates Miguel."

"Americans have such a strange way of speaking, do they not?" Diego chuckled, then glanced at her.

What was that odd look Diego Fernandez just gave her? Had she imagined it? Or had he actually tried to communicate to her with that peculiar expression?

"You, Diego, hate Miguel because he is your father's bastard son," she said.

"I hate him for that, yes." Diego swooped down on her, his face right up in hers. "And I hate him for believing he, the son of a harlot, has a right to be president of my country." Eye-to-eye, his warm breath on her face, Diego whispered, "Be prepared."

Be prepared for what? For Roberto killing her? No, that wasn't it. He would have shouted his comment from the rooftops if he hadn't wanted her alone to hear it. God, this didn't make any sense. If she didn't know better, she'd swear that Diego Fernandez intended to try to help her.

He rolled his eyes and tilted his head backward ever so slightly as he backed away from her, then turned to Roberto, chuckling in a good-natured, buddy-to-buddy manner.

"I am also curious, Aznar, as to why you hate my bastard half-brother. The whole world believes you are his good friend."

J.J. glanced toward the closed door, wondering if Diego had been trying to signal her to expect someone to come through that door.

Was she losing her mind? Had she become delusional? What made her think that Diego Fernandez would help her, that it was even remotely possible he had brought help?

"I hate Miguel because he is a fool." Roberto placed the knife on the chair. "When we first became friends, I knew he would one day run this country, but what I did not realize was that he actually meant all the things he said, that the promises he made the people were actually vows he took seriously. He wants this country to be a great democracy, with equal rights for all. Even women." He glared at J.J. "He would make all people equal under the law."

"And that is not what you want, is it?" J.J. asked.

"I want money and power. I believed that Miguel was the man who could give me these things, that they were the things he wanted. But I was wrong. I thought as he gained more power, he would realize how foolish his lofty ideas were, but he did not. He was not the man I thought he would become. I now know that only Hector Padilla can give me what I want."

Diego placed his hand on Roberto's shoulder and led him away from J.J. "You did bring a bottle of wine, did you not, my friend, to celebrate later?"

"No, but I can send one of the men to a nearby cantina to pick up a bottle."

He's taking Roberto's attention away from me, J.J. thought, and he is physically moving him as far away from me as possible. Was she right about Diego or was this simply wishful thinking on her part?

Suddenly the outer door burst open. She caught a glimpse of Miguel as he stormed in, Dom Shea and several other men behind him. Roberto whirled around and knocked Diego aside, grabbed the deadly knife off the chair and lunged toward her. As he came down over her, aiming the knife directly at her heart, a single shot rang out. The bullet hit Roberto in the back of his head. Blood suddenly shot everywhere, spraying the floor and the walls and raining down on J.J. She clenched her jaws tightly to keep from screaming. As Roberto's body dropped to the dirt floor, the twelve-inch blade fell from his hand and landed on the ground only seconds before he did.

Miguel rushed to her, dropped on his knees and looked at her, relief in his eyes. Without saying a word, he untied her hands and then her feet.

"How—how did you find me?" she asked as Miguel lifted her into his arms and carried her toward the door.

"Diego Fernandez led us to you," Miguel told her.

She caught a glimpse of Dom Shea, Vic Noble and Will Pierce as Miguel carried her through the door and out onto the wharf. Several other men stood around watching over the two bodies lying at their feet. The two guards who had held her prisoner were also dead.

"Why would Diego help you?" she asked.

"Hush, *querida*," Miguel said. "Stop asking me questions. I was half out of my mind, thinking I might have already lost you. Then I find you alive and I am forced to kill Roberto, a man who had been my friend…a man I thought had been my friend."

Miguel kept walking as he talked, carrying her down a long, shadowy alley, while the others followed. "Roberto was a traitor. He would have murdered you. And the brother who has hated me, who has plotted and worked against me, helped me. I owe him your life.

"I was prepared to go before the people this afternoon to withdraw from the presidential race—for you. To save you because I would rather die myself, would rather see the whole world destroyed than to lose you. What kind of president would be willing to sacrifice a nation to save one woman?"

J.J. winced as pain shot through her side when she lifted her arm and draped it around Miguel's neck. She laid her head on his shoulder and said softly, "You wanted to sacrifice Mocorito to save me, possibly even believed you would do it, but when the moment came, you would have made the right decision. You would have done what you knew I wanted you to do, what I would have expected from the man I admire and respect…and love."

"Damn you, Jennifer." He marched out into the street and straight to Dom's rental car. "I am taking you back to the hospital and I am not leaving your side until you are well enough for me to put you on a plane back to America."

"Whatever you say, Miguel." She closed her eyes and smiled. If he thought he was going to pack her off back to Atlanta, then he had another thought coming. Surely he didn't believe that after she had come this close to death and now knew beyond a shadow of a doubt how he truly felt about her, that she would ever leave him. When she recovered and was released from the hospital, she had no intention of going anywhere, except straight to the presidential palace with Miguel when he won the election.

Chapter 18

True to his word, Miguel had stayed at the hospital day and night for the next seventy-two hours—except for some sort of secret mission that had taken him away for an hour yesterday. Then this morning, Juan Esteban had arranged for a private-duty nurse for J.J. so that she could be sent home. Home to Miguel's house, not home to Atlanta. She suspected that the hospital staff had begged Juan to find a way to remove Miguel from the premises because not only had he guarded J.J. like a hawk, questioning everyone about everything they did, even tasting her food to make sure it wasn't poisoned, but he also told the nurses that he would check J.J.'s vital signs himself.

So, here she was wearing a yellow silk nightgown, lying in the middle of Miguel's king-size bed and propped into a sitting position with six feather pillows. Her gunshot wound was healing nicely and although it would leave an ugly scar, Juan had assured her the scar could be all but erased with plastic surgery. Ramona had been fussing over her like a mother hen, bringing her more food than she could eat in two days, let alone at one meal. Aunt Josephina and Seina had sent Nurse Orlando downstairs and told her to take a long break. They chatted away with J.J. while they arranged the three dozen floral arrangements that had been brought upstairs, placing half in the sitting room and the other half in the bedroom so that J.J. could see and enjoy them from her bed. She was told that another three dozen decorated every room in the house and Miguel had ordered that any others that arrived today be sent to St. Augustine's.

The three women had shooed Miguel downstairs, where "the men" were waiting for him. He had gone, if somewhat reluctantly. J.J. suspected that "the men" consisted of two Dundee agents, one CIA agent and Emilio Lopez. And perhaps even Diego Fernandez. She had tried to bring up Diego's name several times while she'd been in the hospital and every time, Miguel had told her that they would discuss his half-brother later.

"Will you two stop fussing," J.J. said. "Come over and sit and tell me what's going on." She patted the bed.

Aunt Josephina and Seina glanced at each other.

"Perhaps we should go," Seina said. "You need to rest. Miguel cautioned us not to let you overtire yourself."

"You two are not going anywhere. Something is going on and I want to know exactly what it is."

Aunt Josephina smiled guilelessly. "Whatever do you think we could possibly know, my dear Jennifer? We are only women. You do not think the men would share any information with us."

"Cut the bull, Aunt Josephina." J.J. couldn't help laughing when the old woman's mouth fell open. "Come on. Woman-to-woman. Miguel won't tell me anything. He just keeps saying that everything is fine, that I should not worry. And Dom and Vic haven't even been allowed to do more than say hi and bye to me in the past three days."

Seina sighed. Aunt Josephina glanced at the closed door.

"Hector Padilla has been arrested," Seina said, practically

whispering. "Only this morning. He was caught trying to escape from Nava."

"What?" Of all the things she had expected to hear, this wasn't one of them.

"My brother, Diego, went on television with Miguel yesterday and told the people what President Padilla had been doing and that he planned, when he was reelected, to overthrow the government and form a new dictatorship." Seina sat down on the edge of the bed. "As soon as they knew that President Padilla had lost Diego's support and the support of all the other important families in Nava, his own cabinet members turned against him and agreed to testify in court about what they knew."

"Holy sh—" Why hadn't Miguel shared all this incredible news with her? "So this means that Miguel will become president by default, right?"

Aunt Josephina shook her head. "No, no. Our Miguel insists that the Federalist Party choose another candidate. He says it is the only fair thing to do."

J.J. smiled. "Our Miguel would say that wouldn't he? That man has to be the most honorable, most noble man on God's green earth."

"Today I am proud of both my brothers," Seina said, but she had a bittersweet expression on her face. "Diego is not a bad man and in the end, he did what was right."

"He saved my life," J.J. told her. "You know that don't you?"

"Yes, I know, but he—he bargained with Miguel for your life."

"What do you mean?" J.J. asked.

"Miguel does not want her upset," Aunt Josephina said.

"I'm not upset." J.J. reached out for Seina's hand.

Miguel's young half-sister grasped her hand and looked at her pleadingly. "Diego did many bad things for Hector Padilla and he did them because he hated Miguel."

"That's not exactly a surprise to me."

"When Diego learned where you were being held, he used that information to force Miguel to agree to pardon him for all of his crimes once Miguel is elected president."

"Oh, I see. So, Diego won't be punished for anything he did, is that it?"

"Yes, that is correct. Of course, he did not have to agree to testify against President Padilla nor did he have to contact all his friends and associates, many fellow Federalists, and tell them the truth about the president, but he did. And he went on television with Miguel and—"

J.J. squeezed Seina's hand. "It's all right. You don't have to keep defending Diego. He's not exactly my favorite person, but regardless of why he did it, his actions did save my life."

"You are very generous," Seina said, her eyes misty with tears.

"So, what is the meeting downstairs all about and why all the secrecy?"

Seina looked to Aunt Josephina, as if asking for permission to speak. But before the old woman could approve or disapprove, a female voice called out from the sitting room.

"Where is everyone?" Dolores Lopez came waddling into the bedroom, Lucie Evans directly behind her. "So here you all are." Dolores came straight over to the bed, sat on the opposite side from Seina and leaned over enough so that she could wrap her arms around J.J. "You look well for a lady who was shot less than a week ago. How good it is to see you recovering so nicely."

Surprised—no shocked—by Dolores's conciliatory manner, J.J. hugged Miguel's cousin and said, "It's good to see you, too."

Nailing Seina with her sharp gaze, Dolores said, "And you must be Miguel's half-sister. I hear you are going to marry Juan. He is a good man. You are very lucky."

"Yes, I know," Seina said shyly.

"Thank God this nightmare is over and we can return to our normal lives." Dolores waved her hand at Lucie, who rolled her eyes and came over to help Dolores to her feet. "Thank you. I am so fat I cannot get up out of a chair on my own these days."

Lucie looked down at J.J. "How are you…really?"

"I'm fine. Really."

"Perhaps we should all go into the sitting room and leave these old friends alone," Dolores said. "Come, Aunt Josephina. You must tell me about the plans for Juan and Seina's wedding."

As soon as they were alone, Lucie sat on the side of the bed. "Sawyer is sending the Dundee jet to Nava tomorrow to pick us all up. When he called to tell me to bring Señora Lopez home today, he asked me to find out if you'll need for him to send either a doctor or a nurse for you. I told him I'd call him back once I spoke to you."

"I will not require a doctor or a nurse."

"Are you sure?"

"I'm very sure. You see, Lucie, I'm not going back to America with the rest of you."

Lucie widened her eyes. "You're not? Mind telling me why?"

"I'm going to stay in Mocorito with Miguel."

Lucie frowned. "Has he asked you to stay?"

"No, not yet, but he will."

"Oh, honey, he may not. I mean, after all, it's not as if you were his real fiancée. You came here on an assignment and under a tropical moon, with a handsome Latin lover charming your pants off, you could easily have misinterpreted passion for love."

"I didn't misinterpret anything." J.J. studied Lucie's expression. "Spill the beans. What are you not telling me?"

"You don't know that yesterday when Miguel and Diego Fernandez appeared on television together that Miguel confessed that you were not really his fiancée, that you came to Mocorito to work as his bodyguard. He said something to the effect that you had gone above and beyond your duty as his protector."

J.J. couldn't speak, couldn't think. God, she could barely breathe. Finally she managed one word. "Oh."

"Damn, J.J., I'm sorry."

J.J. waved her hand in an it's-all-right gesture. Tears lodged in her throat, threatening to choke her. Why would Miguel have confessed to everyone that their engagement wasn't real if he planned to marry her?

He doesn't plan to marry you, that pesky inner voice told her.

"Men can be such pigs," Lucie said. "They screw you one night and the next morning, they can't remember your name."

"Miguel isn't like that. He's not."

Lucie reached over and hugged J.J. "You're really in love with the guy, aren't you?"

"You have no idea," J.J. said as she laid her head on Lucie's shoulder and cried. Damn it, she didn't cry. Not ever. Crying was for sissies. Well, hell, she was a woman, wasn't she? Couldn't a woman cry and not be seen as weak? Especially a woman with a broken heart.

"I better get downstairs and let the men know they can't make all the decisions without me." Lucie took hold of J.J.'s shoulders and helped her sit back against the pillows. "Dom and Vic and Will Pierce are helping Señor Ramirez and his people tie up all the loose ends. You know, cross all the t's and dot all the i's. When President Padilla and his cohorts go on trial, nobody wants them getting away with anything. Our country wants Padilla and his friends to spend the rest of their lives locked up."

"So that's what the big powwow is all about, huh?"

"That's it."

"Would you tell Aunt Josephina and Seina that I'm taking a nap and I do not wish to be disturbed."

"Sure thing," Lucie said as she headed for the door. "I'll catch you later."

J.J. hadn't realized that she had actually fallen asleep until something woke her. What was that tickling her cheek? It felt like her hair was being blown against her face. She opened her eyes, but the room lay in semidarkness. How long had she been asleep? She rolled over from her uninjured side to her back and looked up into a pair of golden-brown eyes. Miguel! He was lying beside her, propped up on his elbow, gazing down at her and blowing softly against her ear.

"Miguel?"

"Yes, *querida*."

How dare he call her *querida!* "What time is it?"

"It is past seven in the evening. You have missed dinner. I can have Ramona bring up a tray—"

"No, that won't be necessary. I'm not hungry."

"Are you thirsty?" he asked. "Would you like some water or tea or a cola or—"

"No, nothing, thank you." She couldn't bring herself to break eye contact, but damn it, looking at him was tearing her apart inside. "Are Lucie and the others still here?"

"No, they have all gone to their hotel."

"Even Dom?"

"Yes, even Dom."

"Lucie told me that Sawyer McNamara is sending the Dundee jet in the morning to pick everyone up," she said.

"Yes, I know."

"He offered to send along a doctor or a nurse for me."

"That was very kind of him."

J.J. nodded.

"But of course you told Señorita Evans to tell Señor McNamara that you did not require the services of either a doctor or a nurse, did you not?"

"Yes, I did, but—"

"Juan tells me that you should be fully recovered by election day," Miguel said.

And where would she be on election day, the day Miguel became the president of Mocorito? In her apartment in Atlanta? Visiting her mother in Mobile?

"You are very quiet, *querida.* Are you all right?"

"Stop calling me *querida.*"

He looked at her questioningly. "Jennifer…J.J., what is wrong? You seem upset. If someone has said or done anything to upset you, please tell me and I will deal with them."

"Stop pretending with me," J.J. told him. "I know. Do you hear me—I know. Lucie told me."

"Señorita Evans told you what?"

"That when you and Diego made your eventful TV appearance yesterday, you confessed to the people of Mocorito that I am not really your fiancée, that I'm nothing but your bodyguard."

Miguel laughed. Damn him, he laughed.

"Yes, I told the people the truth. There was no longer any reason to keep up the pretense, no reason to continue living a lie."

"Of course not."

"*Querida,* I want—"

J.J. shoved on his chest trying to push him away from her. "Stop calling me *querida.* I'm not your darling. I'm not anything to you."

He grasped her shoulders and held her gently but forcefully. "Jennifer Joy Blair, you are my darling, my *querida.* You are everything to me. How could you not know this? I love you. I love you more than anything, even more than Mocorito."

J.J. didn't know if she was more stunned by Miguel's confession or by her own stupidity. "I am an idiot, aren't I?"

"No, you are the woman I love, the woman I want to be my wife, the mother of my children, the first lady of Mocorito." He reached in his pocket and pulled out her engagement ring. "They had to take off all your jewelry when you were in the hospital. If you would prefer to choose a different ring, I will understand."

She grabbed the ring and put it on the third finger of her left hand. "This ring is perfect. And this time it really is my engagement ring." She threw her arms around his neck and hugged him, then kissed him on both cheeks, on his forehead and finally his mouth. "You confessed the truth to your people because you didn't want to start our marriage with a lie."

"You know me so well."

He kissed her and within minutes passion flared between them. When she accidentally grazed her bandaged side against his belt, she whimpered. Miguel pulled away from her.

"I hurt you. Forgive me. I should go now and—"

She grabbed him by the front of his shirt. "You aren't going anywhere. Take off your clothes and get in bed with me right now."

"Jennifer, you are still recovering from being shot. I will sleep in another bedroom."

"I don't want you sleeping in another bedroom. I want you to sleep here with me and hold me in your arms all night."

"You wish to torture me?"

She laughed. "Well, actually, I want you to make love to me."

"No, *querida,* you are not well enough for lovemaking."

"I'm not strong enough for anything vigorous, but if you do all the work and I just lie here and enjoy it…"

He pressed her gently back against the pillows, then leaned over her, bracing himself with his elbows on either side of her. "You are a wicked, wicked woman tempting me this way."

"For goodness sakes, shut up, and kiss me again, will you?"

He did as she requested. He kissed her. And kissed her again. And soon there was not one inch of body that he had not kissed— except the small, thick square of gauze covering her healing wound, which he circled lovingly with his fingertip.

She lay there, naked and aroused, allowing him to worship her body, to touch and kiss and lick and soothe until she was half out of her mind with desire. He spread her legs and ran his tongue up and down and then back up each inner thigh. He nuzzled her mound, then separated her intimate lips and made love to her with his mouth. When she came, she cried out his name, telling him how much she loved him.

As the aftershocks of her release rippled through her, he

moved up beside her, kissed her lips and eased her gently over onto her good side.

"Yes?" he asked, as he pressed his erection against her buttocks. "I will be very careful not to hurt you."

"Yes," she told him. "Yes, yes, yes."

Yes to his lovemaking, to the sweet joining of their bodies. And yes to the love he offered her and she returned to him with equal passion and devotion. Yes to a future together as man and wife. And yes to all the joys and sorrows, all the triumphs and disappointments, to every moment, every hour, every day, every year they would share for the rest of their lives.

Epilogue

Today the Ramirez family gathered their friends together at the presidential palace for a double celebration. Miguel had just been elected to his third term as el presidente. And he and J.J. had been married for eight years. They had married on election day, in the church in the Aguilar barrio where Miguel had been christened, with only a handful of their loved ones there. Several months later, after the inauguration, J.J.'s mother and stepfather had flown in from Mobile and hosted a lavish reception at the palace.

Dolores waddled toward J.J., a wide smile on her full face. She was expecting her third child, another boy the doctors had told her, which made Emilio exceedingly happy.

"Are you sure you want to do this?" Dolores asked. "Four more years of this insanity. I do not know how you do it, Jennifer. Being Miguel's constant helpmate, serving on a hundred different committees, hosting endless social events and somehow managing to win Mother of the Year awards."

J.J. slipped her arm around Miguel's waist and hugged him to her. "I can do all this because I have such a good husband. He somehow not only manages to run this country, but he finds the time to be a loving, attentive husband and a hands-on father."

Ramona brought the children in to say good-night to their parents. Dolores and Emilio's two strapping boys, young Emilio, the image of his mother, would soon turn eight and four year-old Dario, the little mischief maker, resembled his father. Behind the two Lopez boys came three adorable little girls. Six-year-old Carlotta Josephina Esteban ran straight to her proud papa's arms. The spoiled only child was not only lovely but had a winning personality.

Not allowing their young cousin to outdo them, seven-year-old twins, Luz and Lenore, named for their grandmothers, rushed straight to their father. He gathered them up in his arms and placed one on each hip. They looked a great deal like J.J., both petite and raved-haired, but they had inherited their father's golden eyes. Then last but not least three-year-old Cesar escaped from Ramona and ran to his father, grabbing Miguel around the leg. Curly-haired and chubby, his blue-violet eyes gazed up adoringly at his papa.

"We are richly blessed," Aunt Josephina said. "Three happy marriages, six perfect children—" she eyed Dolores's protruding belly "—soon to be seven. And a democratic nation in which to raise the next generation."

J.J. walked over to Seina's side and put her arm around her sister-in-law, then gave her a hug. She understood the momentary sadness in Seina's eyes, a sadness that soon vanished. Carlotta Fernandez had never forgiven her daughter for marrying Juan and befriending her half-brother. And although she occasionally saw Diego and his wife, their relationship had never quite recovered. So the people gathered here this evening had become Seina's new family, as they had become J.J.'s.

Her father had died last spring. A heart attack at the age of sixty-six. Miguel had gone with her to his funeral to pay her last respects to a man who had never loved or respected her. And he had held her in his arms while she wept that night and many nights afterward. But in the end, the most precious solace he had given her had been the joy of watching him with his own two daughters, whom he not only loved as dearly as he did his son, but of whom he was every bit as proud.

Tears misted J.J.'s eyes as she laughed when Miguel tumbled onto the floor and took all three of their children with him. He tickled them, then hugged them and kissed them good-night before turning them back over to Ramona.

"Your mother and I will come upstairs in a few minutes to tuck each of you in," Miguel promised them and they knew, even at their tender ages that their father never made promises he did not keep.

After Ramona had ushered the band of wild little heathens out of the room, Miguel came over and slipped his arm around J.J.'s waist. "Family and friends, feel free to stay up as late as you wish, continue the party until dawn. But my wife and I are going up to say good-night to our children and then we are turning in for the evening."

He then urged J.J. into movement and led her into the hallway. As soon as they were alone for half a minute, he pulled her into his arms and kissed her.

"And after we say good-night to our children, Señora Ramirez, the president would like to see you alone in his bedroom. I believe he intends to make love to you. Does his request meet with your approval?"

She wrapped her arms around his neck, stood on tiptoe and rubbed herself against him seductively. *"Sí, sí, el presidente. Sí, sí."*

* * * * *

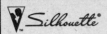

INTIMATE MOMENTS™

presents

A heart-stopping romance by
VICKIE TAYLOR

Her Last Defense
(Silhouette Intimate Moments #1381)

In the wilds of Texas's Sabine National Forest, Dr.
Macy Attois and Texas Ranger Clint Hayes race to
protect the world from a deadly epidemic. But can
they protect their hearts from the intense attraction
they feel for each other?

*Available August 2005
at your favorite retail outlet.*

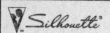

HARLEQUIN®
Next™

Coming this August

Three women, two missions, one silver Jag and a road trip to find
the boys who started it all.

OLD BOYFRIENDS

from *USA TODAY* bestselling author

Rexanne Becnel

If you enjoyed what you just read,
then we've got an offer you can't resist!

Take 2 bestselling
love stories FREE!
Plus get a FREE surprise gift!

Clip this page and mail it to Silhouette Reader Service™

IN U.S.A.
3010 Walden Ave.
P.O. Box 1867
Buffalo, N.Y. 14240-1867

IN CANADA
P.O. Box 609
Fort Erie, Ontario
L2A 5X3

YES! Please send me 2 free Silhouette Intimate Moments® novels and my free surprise gift. After receiving them, if I don't wish to receive anymore, I can return the shipping statement marked cancel. If I don't cancel, I will receive 4 brand-new novels every month, before they're available in stores! In the U.S.A., bill me at the bargain price of $4.24 plus 25¢ shipping and handling per book and applicable sales tax, if any*. In Canada, bill me at the bargain price of $4.99 plus 25¢ shipping and handling per book and applicable taxes**. That's the complete price and a savings of at least 10% off the cover prices—what a great deal! I understand that accepting the 2 free books and gift places me under no obligation ever to buy any books. I can always return a shipment and cancel at any time. Even if I never buy another book from Silhouette, the 2 free books and gift are mine to keep forever.

240 SDN D7ZD
340 SDN D7ZP

Name	(PLEASE PRINT)	
Address	Apt.#	
City	State/Prov.	Zip/Postal Code

Not valid to current Silhouette Intimate Moments® subscribers.

Want to try two free books from another series?
Call 1-800-873-8635 or visit www.morefreebooks.com.

* Terms and prices subject to change without notice. Sales tax applicable in N.Y.
** Canadian residents will be charged applicable provincial taxes and GST.
  All orders subject to approval. Offer limited to one per household.
  ® and ™ are trademarks owned and used by the trademark owner and/or its licensee.

INMOM05   ©2005 Harlequin Enterprises Limited

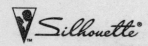
Silhouette®